THE JONAH

THE JONAH

James Herbert

NEW ENGLISH LIBRARY/TIMES MIRROR

First published in Great Britain in 1981 by New English Library Limited

First NEL Paperback Edition October 1981

NEL Books are published by
New English Library Limited,
Barnard's Inn, Holborn,
London EC1N 2JR.

Printed and bound in Great Britain by
Cox & Wyman Ltd, Reading

0 450 05316 4

April, 1950

HER FINGERS curled around the sides of the newspaper and lifted it from the small table's surface where it had been lying flat. One top corner flopped over with the tightness of her grip. Her meatless buttocks stopped their jiggling on the hard wooden chair, the gentle rhythm of Billy Ternent's orchestra failing to stir them now.

One-and-tuppence! One-and-bloody tuppence for a tin of sardines! And the silly buggers were going to do away with the price control on other fish next week! That was it then: Eugene would just have to enjoy his white beans a bit more. It should have made things easier with food rationing being phased out, but lack of money in the pocket did a better job than any ration book. You'd think they'd do more to help war-widows. Soddin Attlee and his Welfare State. What about her bleedin welfare? And Eugene's?

She sighed heavily and let the creased newspaper flop back onto the table.

Vera Braid was a tiny woman and she needed to be to fit into the cupboard that was her office. For some reason the door, which should have provided a barrier between herself and the smells of the ladies' lavatory she was attendant to, had been removed long ago. No one knew why it had been taken, nor who had taken it. Misfortunes of war.

It wasn't the piss and shit that smelled so much, but the gallons of disinfectant she used to disperse the stink. Many a visitor might have preferred the more offensive but less overpowering natural smells; the disinfectant had a way of tearing through the nasal passages and singeing the brain. Those who knew Vera and took time to have a quick brew with her down there claimed even her tea had an antiseptic tang.

Vera tucked a wayward strand of hair back into her green turban and glanced through the net curtain she had fixed across the doorframe; the flimsy material gave her a token privacy but hardly kept unwanted aromas away.

Was the lady still in there? Seemed a long time. She could have slipped out unnoticed. Vera had only been conscious of a black shape flitting past the net curtain several minutes before; she had been too engrossed in reading about Danny Kaye's new film to take much notice. Eugene loved Danny Kaye. Still, he'd have to wait until it came round local; she couldn't afford to take him up West. She'd have loved to have gone up there – some lovely shows on. *Annie Get Your Gun, Castles in the Air* – she thought Jack Buchanan was smashing – *Fallen Angels*. She didn't fancy that one with Vivien Leigh in it, the one she'd heard about. What was it? Oh yes – *A Motorcar Named Desire*. Sounded like a load of rubbish. The last time she'd been up West – and the *only* time – was when Harry had taken her to see the Crazy Gang. Just before they'd shipped him off that was, just before they killed him. Baskits. How was Eugene going to turn out without his dad?

She sighed heavily, then groaned when Billy Ternent went off the air and the Holy Week talk was announced. A church service was to follow, making matters worse! Easter bleedin Saturday and she was stuck down here. Poor Eugene had wanted to see Brumas the bear, but she couldn't take time off for the zoo. She needed the job and people needed to piss, even on Easter Saturday. She'd get him some ice cream tonight to make up for it. At least the Ministry of Food was now going to let them have as much milk as they wanted to make the stuff. It tasted like bloody cardboard, some of it.

Vera flicked over the pages to find the wireless programmes, refusing to become involved in the stories of the tuberculosis scare and the smallpox outbreak in Scotland; she had her own problems. She found the appropriate section and squinted her eyes to read the small print. Not much on until *Variety Bandbox. Have a Go!* after the one o'clock news. *PC 49* later.

6

She switched it off and frowned at the trailing words. What material possessions were they, you silly old sod? A roof over your head? Food for your belly? An evening sitting indoors listening to *In Town Tonight* and Semprini? Vera might not forget God, but He had forgotten her and thousands like her. That sound again . . .

A funny . . . little . . . sound.

Footsteps descending the stone steps made her look up, the sound becoming sharper as high-heels clattered along the tiled floor. A young girl passed by the net curtain and Vera heard the sound of a penny dropping into its slot. A cubicle door opened and closed, an ENGAGED sign clicked on. Vera went back to her newspaper.

Nothing but trouble. Strikes, threats of strikes. Now the clerical workers wanted six-pounds-ten-shillings a week. The Engineering and Shipbuilding Unions wanted an extra pound a week. The dockers were out. Even the bleedin taxi-drivers were out. They've all gone potty! Iodine in the salt had something to do with it. Affecting their bleedin brains no matter what Bevan said.

A door banged shut and high-heels clattered back along the shiny floor. Didn't take her long, Vera thought. What about the other one though, the first one. Where'd she got to? Vera pushed her small frame erect, using the table top for support. One hand tucked itself into the pocket of the green, shortsleeved overalls she wore, while the other pulled the net curtain aside. She poked her head around the doorframe and looked along the twin rows of closed cubicles. A uniform pattern of light bounced off the shiny floor as sunlight shone through small glass squares imbedded in the ceiling. Even so, the white, brick-tiled wall at the far end, spotlessly clean though it was, appeared to be a gloomy dark grey. She thought she heard a sound, but couldn't be sure because of the droning voice coming from the wireless behind her. The voice was reminding anyone bothering to listen that the BOAC Constellation Airliner that had just journeyed from Australia to London in the record time of three days, four hours and fifteen minutes was a sign of mankind's escalation into a new era of world peace, but one in which God's word could soon be forgotten in the demanding search for material possessions, possessions that . . .

Vera's slippered feet shuffled along the damp flooring and she peered at each door she passed, her head turning from left to right, eyes narrowing to read the VACANT signs. Last one, left. Last one, right. Both VACANT. She stopped and listened.

No sound now.

Then there was.

Just.

It was difficult to locate the source, and difficult to tell what the noise was.

Somehow familiar, though.

A tiny choke.

She banged on the door to her left, calling out, asking who was there. There was no reply so she banged on the door to her right. No answer from there, either.

Vera reached into her overalls pocket and pulled out the master key to all the doors. She inserted it into the coin-lock of the door to her right and pushed it open. The cubicle was empty. She turned to the door behind her and went through the same procedure. There was something on the floor inside.

The small sound again, and this time the realisation began to sink in. Vera stared for a few moments at the loose bundle of rags on the wet floor, then slowly moved forward, a hand extended before her. She stopped when the bundle moved.

The snuffling, choking sound made her reach towards the rough material again and she drew back the folds, taking care with the movement, half-afraid, mostly dismayed.

Grief filled her eyes when she uncovered the baby. Its tiny head was damp with blood-flecked slime, and fluid dribbled from its nose and mouth. The eyes were closed tight against the harsh surroundings as though not wanting to see the basement cell in which it had been abandoned. The baby was no more than a few hours old and already its skin was turning deathly blue.

It tried weakly to push away the rags that smothered its frail body. And the thing that lay next to it.

ONE

KELSO'S EYES narrowed as he peered through the windscreen. He made a conscious effort to contain the anxiety he felt well beneath his belt-line but, as always, the leaden weight rose steadily and began pushing against his chest. He swallowed and tried to keep the movement as silent as possible.

'Relax,' a voice said from the back seat of the Granada. 'Dave won't lose it.'

Kelso turned his head to look at the detective inspector. If anything, Cook looked depressed.

'There's so much traffic,' Kelso said pointlessly.

'Always is, this time of morning.' Cook looked through the rain-spattered side window. 'Used to be my beat, this,' he remarked, nodding towards the damp pavements as though remembering them specifically. 'Great training-ground for a raw copper.'

'Up ahead, guv. At the lights,' the driver said, gently easing his foot down on the brake pedal.

Kelso swung round and spotted the dark blue van. 'You think they've picked it up yet?'

Cook shrugged. 'They've got plenty of time before it gets to Woolwich. Anyway, I thought your info was that they'd be waiting on the other side of the river.'

'That's what I was told. It doesn't feel right, though.'

DC Dave Riley glanced at Kelso. 'It makes sense for them to pull it on the other side. It's a bit quieter there. I don't think they'd like getting stuck in a traffic jam.' He released the hand-

9

brake as the lights ahead turned to green.

Cook leaned forward and rested an arm on the back of the passenger seat. 'It doesn't really matter where they try it. We've got cars all along the route. Give the other units a call, tell them our position.'

Kelso reached for the car radio, then scanned the road on either side.

'Just going into East India Dock Road from Commercial Road,' Cook told him. 'Heading for the Tunnel.'

Kelso relayed the information into the mouthpiece and switched off after he had received acknowledgements.

'There's a white transit just behind the wages van, guv,' the driver said, an edge to his voice now.

'Okay, might be nothing. We've a ways to go yet.' Cook sat back and adjusted the Smith and Wesson at his hip. Uncomfortable bastards, guns. For a few moments he studied the young DC, who was leaning forward in his seat, anxiously staring after the security van they were following. Kelso had done well on this one – *if* it came off. How old was he now? Thirty-one, thirty-two. Good undercover man. Worked well on his own. But then he had to. Funny how some were like that.

'I don't know why they don't pay their wages straight into the bloody bank.' DC Riley's fingers did a drum beat on the steering-wheel as the police car drifted to a halt once more, the vehicles ahead stopped by some unseen obstacle. 'It'd save all this trouble. There wouldn't be wages snatched if the governors didn't pay out in cash.'

Cook smiled grimly. 'The working man likes his money in readies at the end of the week. Always has done. Unless they're the socially mobile C2s, that is.'

'The what?'

'Young kids, moving away from their origins. Better educated – or, at least, with more idea of what they want. Getting married, after a mortgage, not wanting to live on Council property like their mums and dads. They're not so frightened of banks any more.'

Riley eased the car into First as the traffic began to roll forward once again. He chuckled. 'Made me laugh when the dockers asked for police protection a few years back. Remember that? They were getting mugged on their way home on Friday nights after being paid. Dockers – mugged!'

Neither of his two companions shared his amusement. Cook regretted that there were few dockers, if any at all, left in this part of East London nowadays. Most of the docks this far upriver had closed down and much of the bustle had left with them. Only snarled-up traffic trying to pass through relieved the grey drabness of the area.

Kelso's eyes were glued to the road ahead. Months of lonely, risky undercover work had preceded this operation. He had never been fully convinced of his own acceptance into the criminal fraternity, but that was no bad thing – it meant he was always on his guard, never lulled into a false sense of security. He had been able to finger small blags on the way, but this was the important one, the job they had been waiting for. They had wanted Eddie Mancello for a long time now, ever since he had walked away from the Ilford bank job. Cook thought he'd had him bang to rights, but two witnesses said they were in Mancello's mini-cab at the time of the robbery and Mancello was the driver. Of course, they were friends of Mancello's – one was even a cousin of sorts. There was no way they could hold him, even though he had been bubbled by a villain who had been unlucky enough to get caught on the same job. Cook wanted him badly, but he wouldn't allow a fit-up. Be patient, Mancello would commit himself. As usual, the detective inspector had been right: Mancello had pushed his luck.

Kelso hadn't been involved with the crew itself, but he'd got to know fringe members. One earwig in particular liked to boast his knowledge of current dodgy activities, implying he was somehow part of them. He wasn't of course, and never would be with a mouth like his. He was just a nose, a bragger, a dopo. One day he'd be found minus his nose and ears, but until then he was useful to certain people. People like Kelso, who had the back-up to check out small items of information, who could set up obos on certain individuals, who could shape fragments into a recognisable pattern. Mancello was a sizeable fragment.

'Coming up to the Blackwall Tunnel turn-off,' the driver announced, keeping the car's speed at a steady pace.

'What's that, Brunswick Road?'

'That's it, guv.'

'McDermott's there. He'll tag along behind.'

11

'The white transit's going on,' Kelso remarked, almost disappointed.

'Your info was right,' Cook told him. 'They'll pull it on the other side.'

'If they pull it at all.' Riley kept his eyes straight ahead, but Kelso knew the comment was aimed at him.

'It'll happen,' he said quietly.

The Granada took the left-hand turn and all three saw the vehicle parked half on the pavement of the downward curving road at the same time.

'Couldn't be more bloody obvious, could they?' Cook did not bother to conceal the irritation in his voice. For a brief moment, his eyes met Detective Sergeant McDermott's, who was in the passenger seat of the police car they were now passing. The DS frowned at the scowl he received.

'I suppose we should be grateful he didn't wave at us,' Cook commented.

The Granada stopped and waited behind other vehicles that were held up by the traffic lights near the entrance to the tunnel. Cars and lorries already on the main southbound road flowed past, angry toots from their horns directed at the lorry that had just pulled away from the kerbside and was elbowing its way into the stream of traffic. They watched the truck crawl past their position on the adjacent stretch of road, drivers behind it even more angry at its slow progress. They saw it speed up as the lights ahead turned to orange and Riley shook his head in disgust when the lorry roared through on red.

'Silly fucker,' he murmured.

Kelso looked back at Cook and saw he was frowning. Over the DI's shoulder, he noticed the car carrying McDermott and two other Flying Squad detectives easing its way into the waiting traffic.

The Granada moved forward as the lights changed in their favour. There were quite a few vehicles between the security van and the police car.

'Don't lose sight of it in the Tunnel, Dave,' Cook instructed. 'There's a few bends down there.'

'It's all right, the van can't turn off anywhere.'

'Just keep it in sight.'

They entered the long tunnel, both of its southbound lanes

crammed to capacity. Kelso knew its sister tunnel would be just as packed, probably even worse, as car commuters struggled to reach destinations on the north side of the Thames. Even at under 40mph, their speed seemed unsafe. Grey walls rose on either side and curved toward the centre, the concrete arch holding back the River Thames above. Just one tiny crack in the structure, Kelso thought, and a million gallons of water would crush their car like an egg shell . . .

'Keep up, Dave!' Cook's voice snapped Kelso back to attention.

'I can't go faster than the bloke in front, guv,' the driver complained.

'Switch lanes then, get over to the right!'

Riley quickly glanced over at the adjacent lane. He shook his head, then stabbed down hard on the accelerator. Kelso pushed both feet against the passenger footwell as the car in front rapidly loomed up. At the last moment, Riley swung the Granada into the next lane. The car whose space it had infringed upon braked sharply and they heard its horn echoing around the tunnel.

'There she is!' Riley shouted and they saw the blue van ahead. The truck they had watched shoot the lights was two cars in front of it.

'Try and get closer, Dave,' Cook said, now leaning forward in his seat. 'I've got a nasty feeling . . . '

As if triggered by the same control, pairs of brake lights appeared in sequence before them as each vehicle screeched to a sliding halt. They heard the crashing of metal against metal as cars smashed into one another. The three policemen braced themselves, but Riley's quick reaction prevented serious impact; his foot had been on the brake pedal as soon as the first set of warning lights had flashed on. The police car rocked backwards and forward, shifting the three men in their seats. Before they had the chance to recover, they were thrown forward by a back-breaking jolt as the car behind crashed into their rear. Kelso's head hit the windscreen and he fell back, momentarily stunned.

Cook had been thrown forward and he stayed in that position, hands gripped over the backrests of the front seats. 'What's happening?' he shouted.

'It's the lorry,' the driver replied, his neck craned forward for a better view. 'It's jack-knifed across the bloody road!'

Their eyes widened as they saw four men jump out from a car which had crashed into the back of the security van. The men's heads were covered by balaclavas.

'The bastard's are pulling it in the Tunnel!' Cook exclaimed.

One door at the back of the jack-knifed lorry swung open and three overalled figures dropped to the roadway. Their faces, too, were hidden by masks. Cook just had time to see that two were carrying snub-nosed objects that could only have been sawn-off shotguns. The third was holding something that looked far more cumbersome.

'Get on the radio,' he ordered Kelso. 'Get some back-up down here! I want the entrance and exit sealed off, too!'

Kelso blinked his eyes, still stunned by the blow he had received. But Cook's words cut through his confusion. He reached for the transmitter and pressed the button. 'All Units, this is Leader One. Request immediate assistance in the Blackwall Tunnel. Robbery in progress.' He waited for acknowledgements, but no sound came from the receiver. Both he and Cook understood the problem at the same time.

The driver stared at Kelso. 'What's wrong? Get through to them!'

'He can't.' There was anger in Cook's voice. 'The fucking tunnel's blocking the transmission! We're on our own!' He reached for the .38 at his hip and Kelso dug into the pocket of his combat jacket for his own gun.

'Sorry, Dave,' Cook said to the driver. 'You'll have to come in on this.'

'Okay, guv.' Police drivers usually kept away from the heavy stuff, but Riley knew he had no choice this time.

Kelso pushed the passenger door open and whirled when a hand grabbed his shoulder. The man whose car had crashed into the back of the Granada staggered backwards when the gun was pushed into his face.

'What's going on?' he asked, his hands held out before him as though to ward off any bullets fired from the Smith and Wesson.

Cook, who had just stepped from the Granada, gave the man a vicious push. 'Get back into your car and stay there!' He joined Kelso, and they quickly took in the scene before them.

A dozen or so cars lay between them and the security van. Drivers were getting out of their vehicles to see what had happened up ahead; they jumped back in just as smartly when they saw two hooded figures approaching, both carrying shotguns. The armed men were reaching into the vehicles and snatching out the keys; they tossed them across the road. One driver who tried to protest was struck with the butt of a shotgun. A metallic whining noise filled the tunnel, spinning off the curved walls and amplified by the acoustics of the confined space. Horns from the held-up line of traffic which stretched back to the tunnel's entrance added to the noise. Cook suddenly knew what the cumbersome object carried by the third man was: they were using a chainsaw to open up the security van, ripping into its armoured side like a tin opener.

'Keep down!' Cook shouted as he ran forward, his body crouched.

Kelso ducked and sprinted over to the inside lane, using the stalled vehicles as cover. He moved swiftly past an Allegro and a woman passenger stared out at him curiously, her eyes widening when she saw the gun he was carrying. Cook was just ahead of him in the opposite lane, Dave Riley following close behind. Kelso raised his head and saw the two gunmen were only a few cars away, one approaching in the centre of the road, the other on the far side. The one in the centre would soon spot Cook and Riley in the channel created by the two rows of vehicles. He hurried forward, hoping to draw level with the two villains before his DI and driver were discovered.

He risked looking over the top of the next car as he ran, and froze when he saw the nearest gunman had stopped and was pointing his weapon down the centre channel.

'Hold it you!' he heard the masked figure call out.

Cook felt naked under the glare of the black twin barrels. He dropped to one knee and raised the .38. 'Police! Put the gun down!'

Instead, the masked man raised the shotgun to his shoulder and pulled back the two trigger hammers.

'Drop it!' Kelso shouted, his arms stretched across the car roof before him, both hands gripping the Smith and Wesson tightly.

The gunman whirled and released one of the triggers. The

shot mangled a broad section of the car's roof, shredding and scarring its shiny surface, but Kelso had dropped down, reacting by instinct as soon as the barrels had been swung his way.

Cook pulled open the passenger door of the car he was kneeling beside, breathing a swift prayer of thanks that it wasn't locked, and used it as cover. The passenger shrank away from him, almost crawling into the lap of the driver by his side.

The sound was deafening as the blast tore into the door, pushing it against the crouching DI, some of the shot passing through to splatter against his clothes. The window above him shattered and fragments of glass showered his head.

Without hesitation he pushed the car door away from him and staggered to his feet, knowing the gunman had used up both shots. He went for the villain, grabbing the barrel of the shotgun and using his own weapon as a club. He relished the jarring sensation as the gun connected with the man's covered scalp. Both men went down onto the road's hard concrete surface.

DC Riley ran forward to help his senior officer and stumbled to a halt when he saw the frightened, staring eyes of the other gunman, who was standing in the gap between two cars which hadn't quite connected in the pile-up. The shotgun in his hand was unsteady, but it was aimed at Riley's chest.

The police driver was not armed, for it had not been his intention to take an active part in the arrests. He saw the hammers on both barrels had been drawn back.

'Kelso, get the bastard!' he screamed.

Kelso, who had been scrambling across the bonnet of the Allegro, stopped halfway. Half-sitting, he raised the Smith and Wesson towards the gunman, reluctant to fire, but knowing he had to. He pulled the trigger.

Nothing happened.

Both barrels of the shotgun exploded and Riley was thrown back, his feet leaving the ground, arms outstretched, body curved inwards as the blast ripped through his stomach. He hit the concrete like a loosely filled sack and lay there, unmoving.

For a brief second, Kelso and the gunman could only stare at the still form. Even Cook had stopped struggling with the semi-conscious villain on the ground. The chain-saw never stopped its whirring.

The masked man holding the smoking weapon quickly looked from the dead policeman to Kelso. Wild panic showed through the holes cut out for his eyes. Kelso slid from the bonnet off the Allegro and ran towards him. The gunman turned to run and Kelso flinched as a shot rang out from behind. The shotgun clattered to the ground as the fleeing criminal cried out and his hands tried to reach the bullet wound next to his spine.

He hit the ground just as Kelso got to him, his body squirming with pain. The noise from the chain-saw stopped abruptly and the hooded figures around the security van were running, ducking beneath the body of the lorry blocking the tunnel, making for the two cars waiting on the other side.

Kelso heard pounding feet behind him and he turned to see McDermott and three other detectives running towards them. McDermott's gun was still aimed at the sprawled villain and Kelso knew it was he who had fired the shot.

'You bastard, Kelso! Why didn't you get him before he shot Riley?' The detective sergeant was panting hard as he kicked away the shotgun. The other policemen pushed their way past, going after the escaping criminals.

'My gun jammed!' Kelso shouted, but McDermott had not stopped to listen. He was helping Cook to his feet.

'What a fuck-up!' McDermott said to the DI.

'Shut up and get after those bastards!'

With one venom-filled look back at Kelso, McDermott took off after the other three detectives.

Cook brushed past Kelso, hardly giving him a glance. He knelt down beside the motionless policeman and touched two fingers beneath his jawline, feeling for the pulse. He shook his head and muttered something under his breath. Then he stood up and stared at Kelso.

'Stay here and keep an eye on those two,' he pointed at the prone gunmen. That was all he said, but Kelso felt the disgust in the words. And he knew the disgust was directed at him.

Kelso could only gaze blankly at the gun he held, as Cook turned his back and walked away.

TWO

It was rare, but only one person occupied the lift as it zoomed up to the fourth floor of Scotland Yard. Kelso leaned back against the rear wall, his head bowed as though studying the light-coloured but grubby sneakers he wore. He drew in deeply on the last inch of cigarette, filling his lungs, then expelling the smoke in a blue haze. The anorak he wore over faded denims was a size too big for him, making his shoulders seem slighter than they actually were. Dark hair, made flat and damp by the steady drizzle outside, hung limply over his forehead; he shivered as droplets of water found their way inside his shirt collar and ran down his back. He ran a hand over his chin, glad that he had taken the time to shave that morning; even so, the skin felt rough and made a scraping noise against his palm. The lift bumped to a gentle halt and he tucked his hands inside the anorak's loose pockets, pushing himself away from the wall with his buttocks.

He almost collided with someone entering the lift, but managed to slide around, barely touching the tall, dark-suited figure. Leonard Seyrig, Operational Chief of CID, six foot three – and still growing, some said – glared down at him.

Kelso nodded without returning the gaze, and squelched his way along the corridor towards his department's office. Seyrig frowned at the trail of wet footmarks and slowly shook his head as the lift doors closed.

The noise hit Kelso even before he opened the office door. Pounding typewriters, ringing telephones and filing cabinets being drawn open and slammed closed were the mechanical sounds that joined with raised voices and general conversation buzz to create the clamour. A few heads turned in Kelso's direction as he walked in, but no acknowledgements were given. He headed for his desk which was tucked away in a corner of the room which was large but seemed ludicrously small because of the office furniture, equipment and manpower crammed into its forty-by-thirty-foot area.

He turned his head when he heard his name called. Detective Sergeant McDermott, a telephone receiver held momentarily against his shoulder, was pointing with his thumb towards the DI's office. 'He wants to see you. Now.' McDermott resumed his telephone conversation.

Kelso completed the journey to his desk, stubbed out the remains of his cigarette and pulled out a greasy bag containing two bacon rolls from his anorak pocket. He tossed the bag onto the desktop and made his way towards Cook's office. Breakfast was cold, anyway.

The DI's room was merely a partitioned wall, half of it glass, in the main office area, only a door giving it some credence. Cook was just re-reading his own report on yesterday's foul-up, wondering whether an added word here and there would make it read more favourably, when he saw the DC in the open doorway.

'Come in,' he said, and continued reading. 'Close it,' he added, his eyes not losing their scanning rhythm. Kelso closed the door and settled himself in the chair opposite his chief. He crossed an ankle over his knees and slumped down in the seat, arms crossed. Then he straightened. Why pretend to be relaxed?

Cook sighed heavily and let the sheaf of papers he was holding fall onto his desk. No additions were going to improve it. His eyes met Kelso's and they sat in silence for several seconds before Cook spoke. 'What happened?'

'Gun jammed,' Kelso replied evenly.

'I know the fucking gun jammed! We've had it checked. I'm talking about the blag. You told us it would go off on the other side.'

Kelso leaned forward, resting his elbows on his knees, his face anxious. 'That's the information I was given, Frank.'

'Who's your grass? What's his name?'

20

'He's not a grass. Just a loose mouth. He doesn't know I'm a cop.'

'You know how this is going to make me look, don't you, boy? A prize pillock.'

Kelso's body stiffened in rising anger.

'The AC's been on at me twice this morning already,' Cook went on. 'One copper dead – and a Squad driver at that – two villains collared, and that's it. The rest clean away.'

'But I gave you names . . .'

'Yes, and we've brought four of them in. The trouble is, no one's saying much.'

'You've got Mancello?'

'We've got him. His brief'll have him out in five minutes when he hears about it.'

'You haven't nicked him?'

'On what charge? He's got an alibi just like the last time. Guess what?' Cook nodded patiently as Kelso raised his eyebrows. 'That's right. In his cab, running a fare. Two witnesses again. We're holding him on sus.'

'What about the villain who did the shooting. He'll talk to save himself.'

'Are you kidding? He's a lifer now. Automatic. No amount of talking's going to help him. In fact it could make life in stir very unpleasant for him if he did.'

'Christ!'

'Yeah, Christ. You're going to have to give us some more names. Like who mentioned the job in the first place.'

'It'll blow my cover.'

'Not necessarily. Anyway, it looks like you'll be on a different beat soon.'

Kelso sat back in the chair. 'You're pulling me out?' He shook his head in disbelief. He had worked for a long time to get himself accepted by certain members of London's criminal fraternity. They generally thought of him as a small-time goby, a fixer, an arranger. Nothing big, just a junior-league go-between, a messenger. If they had ever learned his true identity, his torso, minus arms, legs and head, would have been found floating in the Thames. Unless, of course, they fed it to pigs instead.

Cook's tone changed; he seemed almost resigned. 'Look Jim,

you've done a good job over the past six months or so, but your use on the streets is coming to an end. It's a long time, you know; I think you've stretched your luck to the limit.'

'That's not why you want to pull me out, though, is it?'

Cook took a cigarette from the pack lying open on his desk. He lit it and pushed the pack towards Kelso, who shook his head.

The DI exhaled a heavy stream of smoke. 'I've been going through your file, Jim. It doesn't read too good.'

Kelso shifted uncomfortably.

'Oh, you've done your job well enough,' his senior officer reassured him. 'In fact, your undercover work has been excellent, couldn't be better. But I think you know what I'm talking about.'

'You'd better spell it out.'

'Right. Certain jobs over the past few years have turned nasty when you've been on them.'

'Come on, Frank, you can't blame . . . '

'Hold on, hold on. No one's putting any blame on you. I'm just pointing out certain facts. Four months ago, the blag on the jewellery shop in Hatton Garden. You got us the tip-off, just like yesterday. And the car you were chasing the villains in crashed into a bus stop, killing a civilian.'

'I wasn't driving, for Christ's sake.'

'I didn't say you were. Just listen, will you?'

Kelso reached for the cigarettes on the desk and pushed one into his mouth. He forgot to light it.

'A few months before that, on the warehouse job. We went in after thieves helping themselves to electrical gear, loading up the company's own lorry to get the stuff away in. You were going over the rooftops with a couple of other detectives. Detective Sergeant Allan went through the skylight, broke his back.'

Kelso opened his mouth to protest, but Cook held up a hand. 'I know – not your fault. Course it wasn't, nobody's saying it was.'

Kelso started searching for his matches.

'Then there was the night you were on obo in Notting Hill Gate.'

Kelso stopped searching. 'Ah, come on, Frank . . . '

22

'All you had to do was watch the comings and goings of certain dubious individuals in the house opposite. What happened? The house you and Georgie Fenner were in burnt down. It'd read like a fucking comedy script if it wasn't so serious. Fenner had third degree burns all over his body. He'd have died if you hadn't got him out of there.'

'I still think we were sussed. Somebody started that fire deliberately.'

'If they did, we couldn't find any evidence of arson afterwards. There were kids living in the flats downstairs, Jim. They could have all gone up in smoke.'

Kelso yanked the unlit cigarette from his mouth. 'What's all this leading up to, Frank?'

Cook ignored the insubordination in the DC's tone. 'There are plenty of other incidents I could mention, going right back to when you were on the beat. There's even that business with your girlfriend.'

Kelso avoided the senior officer's gaze. He found his matches and lit the cigarette.

'So what I'm trying to say is this: You've got a reputation, Jim; you're bad news. I've got to regard my men as a team and, frankly, you don't fit in too well. Why the fuck do you think you've been put on undercover work? The men are a bit lairy of you, Jim. As it happens, you work better on your own. You're a loner, you don't conform to organisation.'

'Then why take me off undercover?'

'I didn't say I was.'

Kelso looked puzzled.

'The Drugs Squad are short-handed. You're going over to them.'

'Drugs? What the hell do I know . . .'

'No arguments, son. That's it, you're going over. I've already spoken to their DCS; he'll be glad to take you. Starting from Monday next you're on a new team. Good luck.'

Kelso knew there was nothing he could say; the decision had been made and it was final. He walked to the door and looked back when Cook spoke. 'Give the name of your informant to McDermott, Jim; he'll be no good to you now.'

Kelso went out, closing the door quietly behind him.

Cook slumped back in his chair. He hated to lose a good

man, but he had no choice: the others wouldn't work with him any more. They could be made to, of course, but that would only breed unease, resentment. He liked to keep his team tightly knit, no rifts. The funny thing was that he hadn't really explained it to Kelso, hadn't needed to. They both knew what it was all about.

Nobody wanted to work with a Jonah.

THREE

HE CRUNCHED his way along the shingle beach, hands tucked deep into the pockets of his black reefer jacket. The collar was turned up to protect the back of his neck from the March breeze which carried with it the chill dampness from the North Sea. He enjoyed the feel of shifting pebbles beneath his feet, the stones at first yielding then joining firmly to resist his weight. The sound was that of a distant army.

Dark shapes squatted along the beach to his right; weather-beaten fishermen's huts, deserted now, only the heavy smell of their daily catch clinging to the sea-impregnated boards. There was a quarter moon tonight, and the stars littered the sky like glitter-fun, piercing every inch of darkness to deny its dominance. Kelso was relieved that the dark, swollen clouds which had gathered over the town during the day, threatening to fall the final few feet and crush everything below, had moved on to menace others. He looked up to seek out the aircraft, whose droning noise competed with the harsh lapping of waves on the shoreline. The A-10 was low, its searchlight stabbing through the night, red lights a startling contrast to the silver shimmering pinpoints it seemed to pass through. The aircraft was headed inland, homing towards the NATO base just a few miles away; others had scratched the sky with long vapour trails throughout the day, usually in a formation of two as though the American airmen were afraid to wander through British airspace alone. The moving lights rumbled by, the strange upright tail fins that Kelso had come to recognise invisible in the darkness. Soon it was gone, sinking lower until the houses on the cliff at the back of the small coastal town screened the rest of its descent completely. Kelso shivered, then looked back towards the shoreline.

There were more lights stretching along the beach in either direction, but these were strung out and solitary, lonely beacons of sea-anglers who were content to suffer the night's coldness for the sake of a good catch. Their nocturnal activity had surprised him when he had arrived in Adleton three weeks before, but he was slowly becoming accustomed to the habits of the local fishing community. He almost tripped over a taut steel wire used to winch a fishing boat up onto the beach; other such craft, similarly hauled ashore, lay around the area like stranded whales, slumped and useless without the water that gave them purpose. Kelso made towards the narrow concrete roadway running parallel to the shoreline. He paused by the small sea-wall, and sat for a moment, cupping a hand around the flame he lit for his cigarette. He drew in smoke and flicked the match back onto the shingle. A lifeboat on its concrete mounts, ready and eager to sprint to the sea, loomed over him.

It was a good town, its residents preparing for the early summer rush and grateful to Lowestoft and Great Yarmouth, the two big holiday resorts further up the coast, for taking the main brunt of the holidaymakers. It was quiet – after eight o'clock in the evening, three people walking down the high street constituted a crowd – so quiet that Kelso thought he was wasting his time. There was no drugs pushing here; there were hardly any young people to push drugs on to. The incident of a month before had to be a freak, or maybe someone playing a particularly nasty trick. It didn't merit a lengthy undercover investigation. Three weeks and he'd discovered nothing. He continued walking, the narrow strip of road bordered by closely huddled houses on one side, the sea-wall on the other. Windows glowed with friendly lights, increasing his feeling of being an outsider. Or worse – a snooper.

A middle-aged couple strolled by, arm in arm, their mutual affection spreading a little to include Kelso when they bade him a good evening. He guessed they were from the hotel just ahead, out for sea air and stars before an early bed, perhaps a freshening of their marriage. If they were married. The woman giggled like a schoolgirl when the man whispered something,

26

and Kelso wondered if the joke was on him. Easy to get paranoid when you were on your own. Even easier when things happened that you couldn't explain.

He passed by the hotel, its exterior brilliantly lit by floodlights. The restaurant, open to view through a wall of glass, was almost empty, the diners existing on separate islands, communication between them restricted to occasional side glances, only the waitresses puncturing their reserve. The summer trade would change all that. There were very few lights ahead: the tiny coast-guard tower was in darkness but, just beyond, stood a curious windmill-shaped building, its sails missing, every window lit up. After that, there was only the muddy track leading to another strangly shaped building, a round fortress left over from the Napoleonic wars, this, too, a private residence. The old defensive Martello tower faced water on either side, for a wide river ran parallel to the sea, its estuary several miles further down the coast. The fortress stood on the strip of land that divided sea and river, the river itself widening out into a natural, protected harbour as it turned inland and cut a decisive path through the marshlands towards less yielding territory. High banks on either side strived to contain the waterway, the waterlogged fields behind them giving evidence to their lack of success.

The ground on which he stood had once been an opening into the natural harbour, but centuries of silt had built up to block the entrance, the locals eventually using the land as it became more firm. Now boats that moored inside the inland harbour had to travel down the coastline and enter through the estuary, avoiding the treacherous sandbanks around its mouth, then wind their way back along the calmer waters. A small quay had been built for the two fishing boats that were too large to haul up onto the beach. Kelso could just make out their bulky shapes among the more elegant sailboats and motor launches as they stirred on the gentle waters. He had spoken to one or two of the fishermen over the past few days, careful not to mention the incident that had dismayed the townspeople a month ago, talking only of the nature reserves in the area and the scavengers that awaited their catch. True to their image, the fishermen were brusque but friendly enough, finding some inner amusement at his questions. They were well-used to ornithologists visiting the many bird sanctuaries in the area and, if they found him a little different to other bird men they had met, they gave no indication. It would have been totally out of context to ask them about the constant flow of river traffic, whether they had noticed any unfamiliar boats using the estuary recently, but, given time, he would guide their conversations in that direction. And he had plenty of time, it seemed.

He took one last drag from the cigarette, then crushed the stub with his foot. It was pointless to get angry again, but it was hard to contain the resentment he felt. They couldn't sack him – he was a good cop – but they had put him where they considered he could do the least harm. His reputation, apparently, had followed him into the Drugs Squad; now he was on loan to the undermanned Suffolk Constabulary, attached to the drugs team based in Lowestoft. A perfect solution for his boss in London: send him out to assist the yokels, let them have some of his bad luck. Cook and his counterpart in Drugs had made a deal, probably not unkindly. Cook wanted him away from the Yard for a while, away from the hostility growing around him, giving it a chance to die away; Detective Inspector Wainwright of the Drugs Squad had provided the answer. Kelso wondered how many bottles of booze it had cost Cook.

And yet there might be something to the case he was now on. The coastline, with its vast deserted stretches of shingle, marshlands and natural inlets, was perfect for a certain kind of criminal activity. A more than keen vigilance was kept on the sea port of Harwich by Customs and Excise, but the same observation could hardly be maintained all along the coastline. In the old days, the area, like Devon and Cornwall, had been notorious for smuggling and piracy. Now drugs had become the main, illicit, merchandise because Britain had become a clearinghouse for them since Spain had clamped down. Deals worth millions of pounds were negotiated along the Algarve, a natural trading-post for such transactions, for it was close to the major cannabis production areas of North Africa and the Middle East; from there to Britain, then onwards to countries like Holland, Belgium, Scandinavia and America. The authorities suspected that this part of the coast was being used, but so far had made no major hauls.

The quayside itself was small, more of a jetty, but big enough to allow the two drifters that used it to load up their catch directly on to waiting lorries. Now the fishing boats were silent and brooding, straining against their moorings, waiting for the pre-dawn when they would thrum with life again. Kelso turned away, the cold breeze making him ache for somewhere warmer, the dark emptiness of the night increasing his need for human companionship – the rumble in his stomach for something inside it.

His cover was that of an ornithologist working on a project for a certain London-based conservation society. The paper he was to write (which, he had told locals interested enough to ask, might eventually be turned into an illustrated book) was on the increasing pollution in the waterways of East Anglia and its danger to the many species of wild fowl inhabiting the marshes and woodland sanctuaries. It had seemed a reasonable cover, giving him a good excuse to move freely around the area and talk to people, but although he had gone out of his way to be friendly to the natives, particularly those of his age or younger, he was getting nowhere. As yet, no one had even mentioned the strange happening at the Preece house.

The police had been called to the Preece home just a month ago by neighbours who had become alarmed at the strange screams coming from inside. When the local policeman had arrived – it was early evening – he had been surprised to see the youngest member of the Preece family, a boy of eleven, standing on the windowsill of the upper floor, his arms outstretched as if he were about to dive into the garden below. The constable called to the boy, who informed him that he was about to fly over the town. And he had attempted to do so.

Fortunately, the house was not very tall and the small garden consisted mainly of soft flower beds. The boy only dislocated his shoulder and sprained an ankle.

As the policeman, PC Sherman, knelt over the squirming boy, shrieks from inside the house distracted him. By then, several neighbours had joined him in the garden and, giving orders for someone to call an ambulance, the constable approached the house, two of the neighbours going with him. They had to get in through the back door and they found the boy's mother crouching beneath the kitchen table, her hands covering her eyes as though she were afraid to see. They tried, gently at first, to pull her out, but she resisted with a vigour that frightened all three men. She screamed every time they tried to take her hands away from her face. The policeman left the two men with her and went in search of her husband. He found him in the sitting-room, in an armchair, smiling, staring. The man pointed at the wall and the policeman turned to look; all he could see was a flower-patterned wallpaper. The man nodded enthusiastically, although his movements were slow, dreamlike. The constable tried to speak to him, but only a soft crooning noise came from the man. When PC Sherman noticed the dilated pupils and Preece's apparent serenity, he began to understand what was happening. The boy, the mother, the father, were all in a state of trance. They had been either hypnotised or . . . Or drugged. That was it; they were tripped out. A bad trip for the boy and his mother and, it seemed, a good one for the father.

Shouts from the kitchen sent PC Sherman tearing back down the hallway. One of the neighbours was on the floor, a bewildered look on his face; the other was just disappearing through the open doorway. The woman who had crouched under the table was gone.

The policeman rushed to the back door and was just in time to see Mrs Preece running through the allotments behind the row of houses. He knew a footbridge crossed the narrow waterway that separated the houses on the edge of the town from the open marshlands and guessed the woman was making towards it. She wasn't. She plunged into the stream.

Fortunately, the water was only a few feet deep, but the woman seemed determined to stay beneath the surface. It took the constable and another two neighbours at least five minutes to drag her screaming from the water.

The Preece family were swiftly taken to hospital where the constable's guess was proved correct. The couple and their son were hallucinating and urine analysis showed traces of lysergic acid in their systems. The effects gradually wore off some hours later, suggesting that the intake had not been too great or that the LSD had been diluted in some way. But the mother had suffered a mental breakdown and, although she had been released from hospital two weeks later, her local GP was keeping a close watch on her.

So how had it happened? How had a quiet family who had

lived in the town all their lives without causing any bother, any scandal, any controversy, suddenly become involved with drugs. Particularly with LSD, the more dangerous kind. The husband, who worked in the town's boatyard, was known to enjoy a drink in the evening, but that was the extent of his high living. The rest of his free time was usually spent in his allotment tending his vegetables. The mother was a timid sort of woman who worked part-time in the high street bakery and whose idea of a good night was to watch telly with a hot pot of tea by the fireside grate and a box of Milk Tray on her lap. The son was no problem, inconspicuous at school, helpful to his father in the allotment. After interviewing them all – it had been several days before they could get any sense out of the woman – the CID from Leiston came to the conclusion that it was a freak incident, that there was no way that the Preece family could be taking drugs. It had been a normal Tuesday evening for them: the boy had gone to meet his father from the boatyard, they had returned to the house, had dinner, then settled down to watch television. Within the hour, the boy was running around the room, laughing and shouting that he had no weight, that he was as light as a feather, the mother was hiding in the kitchen screaming that the walls were closing in on her, and the father was watching the dazzling neon lights in the wallpaper. The CID found no pills in the house apart from a box of Anadin. No powders, no syringes. How the Preece family had absorbed lysergic acid into their systems was still a mystery.

The Lowestoft Drugs Squad was called in and they, too, were mystified. They knew of no drugs ring in that area, but believed the incident might uncover one. Unfortunately, their small drugs team was overstretched; they could not spare officers on what could have been a fruitless investigation. Assistance was requested and it was the Yard, itself, who supplied someone, a man who had experience of undercover work, someone who had the knack of getting on well with the more unsavoury elements of society. Kelso, go to the top of the unsavouries class. And take your time with this one, there's no rush. It might be nothing, but dig around; something could turn up. If you're lucky. Grin.

Kelso lit another cigarette.

He wasn't renowned for his good luck.

He turned away from the harbour and walked back towards the town. Water had seeped through his sneakers, making his socks damp, the big toe on his left foot numb. That was always the first one to go. Poor blood circulation. He was conscious of the stiff breeze glancing around the tip of his nose.

Kelso had watched the Preece house for several days, squatting on the embankment on the far side of the marshland which separated the town from the river. The bank rose pyramid-shaped from the water, descending just as sharply to the marsh on the other side. It was manmade and meant to contain the floodwaters when they rushed up the ten-mile estuary from the sea. Several canals crisscrossed the marshland, natural drains for when the river overwhelmed its confines; one such canal bordered the allotments which led up to houses on the town's edge. The Preece woman, poor cow, would have drowned in there if she hadn't been dragged out. Kelso had watched through powerful binoculars, a natural aid to an ornithologist, as Preece had dug his vegetable patch. Preece worked alone, for his son was still in hospital with his dislocated shoulder, and Kelso had seen no suspicious activity. The man usually worked till dusk, stopping occasionally to chat to neighbours. He would leave his tools inside a small hut on the site (Kelso had searched the hut by torchlight one night and had found nothing other than rusting and blunted garden equipment) and then return to the house. And he would stay there. Even his evening drink had been forgotten.

But maybe tonight he would change his mind; he may have regained his thirst by now. It was reason enough – and a good excuse – for Kelso to visit the man's local.

The lights of the town beckoned him back and he left the coastal path, sliding down a concrete incline to the car park which was used by tourists in the busy season, but empty now. It was a convenient short-cut to the high street, but like dropping into a large, black pit. The urgent sound of waves pounding on the shore was muffled by the sea-wall and concrete slope, the breeze skipping over the barrier to swoop down towards the middle of the dark arena. The gravel beneath Kelso's feet had a less satisfying crunch to it, too compact and, unlike the sea-washed beach, too filled with dirt. He cut a diagonal path across the car park, both hands tucked into the pockets of his reefer jacket, cigarette dangling from the corner of his mouth, his shoulders slouched and head bent forward as though studying the ground before him. His footsteps slowed; he came to a halt. He took the cigarette from his mouth and raised his head.

He looked around.

Nothing but black shadows. Lights ahead, stars above; in between – darkness. His nose twitched and he whirled around. No one there, but he could smell that faint, familiar aroma. Familiar because it had come to him before, sometimes in dreams, sometimes when he was awake. An odour that was elusive, yet sometimes strong. He had been a child when the strange smell had first come to him and then it had merely been unpleasant; now he had learned to fear it. It was the smell of vomit. Vomit and blood. And corruption.

He felt himself tremble and his eyes tried to drink in the darkness, to absorb it and see what lay beyond. Was there a shadow darker than the rest? Something moved and his eyes locked on to it. But he was mistaken; he edged closer and there was nothing hiding there, no person, no creature. The smell had gone.

Kelso backed away, the coldness tightening his spine. He turned, but did not run. His footsteps were swift, though.

He left the car park, grateful for the modest glow from the streetlights and glanced back over his shoulder. The car park was empty. But the darkness could have hidden a hundred demons.

FOUR

IT WAS like walking onto the set for a Western. The bar was long, almost stretching the whole length of the one-room public house; black pull-pumps – *genuine* pull-pumps – projected from the bar's rough wood surface, each one denoting a different strength of local brew. The walls were covered in planking which had originally matched the uncarpeted flooring; rough boots had removed any sheen that the floor may have had at one time. The coal-burning stove in the middle of the floor, its pipe ascending to the ceiling, then turning right to run the length of the room and disappear through an outer wall, emphasised the unique cowboy flavour of the small, English pub, although two elements managed to spoil the image to some extent: dozens of chamber-pots hung from the ceiling, an unusual addition to the decor, to say the least, and a fruit-machine stood near the double-door entrance. Even most of the clientele, given the right garb, had the rugged appearance of ranch-hands. And that included the women.

The smoke haze made Kelso blink his eyes for a second or two; he hid the reaction by turning and carefully closing the double-doors behind him. Heads looked in his direction and one or two nodded an acknowledgement. He had tried all four public houses in the town, but had soon realised that this was the one which might provide some useful information, for many of the drinkers here were boat people: local fishermen, or those working in nearby boatyards. Several of the younger members of the community also gathered here, youngsters who might be vulnerable to the temptation of speed or grass; there was little else to provide kicks in the town.

Kelso made his way to the bar and eased his body between the backs of two solid-looking individuals, careful not to jog their drinking arms. The barman was already waiting for his order, having seen him enter. It made a refreshing change from London pubs.

'How'd you get on today, then?' The barman's voice had a pleasing local drawl to it, not unlike the Cornish accent, but softer, less broad.

'Not bad. I kept hearing distant bangs all day, though. It frightens the birds.'

'That'd be the bomb disposal. Your usual, is it?'

Kelso nodded. His 'usual' was the strongest of the local brew; somehow he felt intimidated by the pub's atmosphere and clientele into drinking the ale.

The barman filled the straight pint glass and placed it before Kelso. As he counted out Kelso's change, he said, 'Be years before they're finished there.'

'Can't be many left, can there, after all these years?' He took a deep, grateful swallow of the beer.

'You wouldn't have thought so. But they say there's hundreds of those mines left over after the war. Got covered by silt, you see. It's worse where they've drifted up the estuary. Always finding something there. There's little danger now, though, so you don't have to worry.' He smiled reassuringly, then strolled away to serve someone else.

Kelso took another long drink of beer, feeling his nerves settle a little more. He had been glad to get into the brightness and warmth of the pub after the strange experience in the car park. Maybe not so strange – it hadn't been the first time he'd had such feelings. The dark liquid was satisfying and he could already feel its soothing influence. He casually turned his head, looking for a familiar face.

There were several in the bar whom he knew by sight, a few he had spoken to. It was the man at the fruit-machine who drew his attention, though. Kelso picked up his beer again, sipping it this time, and studied the man's back, waiting for him to turn his head so he could be sure. It looked like one of the young fishermen he had spoken to down by the quayside just a few days ago. He was a cousin or nephew to the man who owned a drifter moored in the natural harbour; fishing was mainly a family business and most boats were worked by members of the same clan.

Kelso watched him thump the machine angrily with the flat of his hand, then place another coin in the slot. The detective swiftly looked around and saw the unattended half-filled beer glass resting on a table on the opposite side of the double-doors. It was a small table and no one else sat at it. Kelso casually walked over and pulled out a low stool that nestled between the table's legs. He lit a cigarette.

Within minutes a figure slumped into the seat opposite and he knew he had guessed right.

'Hello, there,' he said and the young fisherman stared back in surprise. He was somewhere in his mid-twenties, heavyset with thick black curly hair matched by a thick black curly beard. The beard was shorter than his hair, but not much shorter.

'I spoke to you the other day,' Kelso told him, seeing the puzzlement in his eyes. 'Down by the quay. Remember?'

'What. Oh yeah? Bird-watcher or something, aren't you?' He reached for his beer and drained it in three noisy gulps. When he placed the empty glass back on the table, his eyes flicked around the bar. He seemed distracted. Or perhaps nervous.

'Another one?' Kelso asked.

'Eh? Oh, yeah. Lovely.'

Kelso scooped up the glass and went back to the bar, feeling the fisherman's eyes on his back. He returned with both glasses full to the brim.

'I didn't catch your name the other day,' the bearded man said, reaching for the proffered ale.

'Jim Kelly.'

'And you're writing a book or somethin.' The Suffolk accent was even stronger than the barman's.

'That's right. It's to do with the bird sanctuaries in this area.'

'Oh, aye. There's plenty of those.'

Conversation ended momentarily as they both drank, Kelso surreptitiously studying the other man over the rim of his glass. He wiped his lips with the back of his hand. 'I didn't get your name, either,' he said.

'Trewick. Andy.'

'You look as if you've had a heavy day.'

Trewick's voice was sharp. 'What makes you say that?'

Kelso shrugged. 'You look a bit tired, that's all.'

'So would you be if you'd been out on the sea since four this morning.'

'Tired? I'd be dead.'

Trewick grunted something unintelligible.

'Still,' Kelso said, unperturbed, 'there's not much to do around here at night, is there?'

'Oh no?' The bearded man managed a grudging smile. 'There's plenny if you know where to look.'

'I've been here a couple of weeks now, and I haven't seen anything in this town. Apart from the little cinema and the pubs, that is. So where's all the action?'

'Depends on who you know. There's always a party goin on some place.'

'Yeah? Well, I suppose I'll have to get to know a few more people. Still, you can get a bit fed up with drinking every night.'

'There's more'n just drinkin.'

Kelso's senses became instantly keener. 'Like what?'

Trewick grinned, one black-stained tooth spoiling what could otherwise have been a handsome face. 'Like screwin.'

He laughed aloud and Kelso forced himself to join in. 'You can even have too much of that,' he said.

'I can't. Can't get enough.' Once more Trewick laughed aloud, but the sound died quickly when the swing-doors opened. Kelso saw the apprehension in the bearded man's eyes just before it vanished as two giggling girls entered the pub.

'No, in London there's other things you can get into, know what I mean?'

'Ah, fuck London. You think you've got it all down there, but you'd be surprised, boy. There's a lot going on aroun here.'

Kelso felt close to something, but decided not to push his luck. It was always a tricky time, knowing just when to press further or back off. 'Any time you fancy showing me, I'll be around. I've got a lot of work to do yet.'

'Watchin birds. Funny kind of job for a bloke.'

'Yeah, I think that myself sometimes. Beats working for a living, though.' Kelso grinned, but there was no amusement on

Trewick's face. Instead there was a trace of hostility.

Oh shit, Kelso thought, I'm messing this one up.

'What kind of money d'you get for doin that sort of stuff?' Trewick asked.

'Not much. Enough to get by on.'

'About how much?'

Kelso cleared his throat, then sipped his drink. Trewick waited, his eyes not leaving the detective's face.

'Er, about three hundred to begin with, then a percentage of the royalties on the book if it comes out.'

Trewick scoffed and sat back against the wall. 'Three hundred? That wouldn't keep me in baccy papers, boy. I need . . .' Once more his head swung toward the swing-doors as they opened. This time the alarm stayed in his eyes as a figure entered.

Kelso glanced towards the entrance as he raised his glass to his lips. If the man who had entered knew Trewick, he did not show it; he strolled towards the bar, pushing his way through the crowd without looking left or right.

The bearded man's eyes followed him.

'You all right?'

Trewick didn't seem to hear. He slowly reached for his beer and took a long, deep, swallow. Then he looked at Kelso. 'What?'

'I said are you all right? You look a bit pale.'

'Yeah, yeah, I'm all right. Got to get goin, that's all.'

'Another party?'

'No. Got to make an early start tomorrow. Need some kip.'

'Do you want another beer before you go.'

'No. It's my turn anyway. I'll get you one next time.'

He slid out from the bench against the wall, buttoning his anorak as he did so. Without another word to Kelso, he pulled open one of the double-doors and stepped out into the cold night.

Cheers, Kelso said silently, raising his glass in mock salute. He moved around into the seat just vacated and casually looked towards the bar; the man who had seemed to unsettle Trewick was standing alone, drinking what looked like gin or vodka. For an instant, their eyes met, but the man turned his head as though studying the crowd in general. His hair was cut short, resting flatly over his skull and his features had a hardness to them that had nothing to do with an open-air life. He wore a thigh-length leather jacket and as he raised his glass, Kelso noticed the little finger of his right hand was missing.

Kelso wondered if he were being overly suspicious, making too much of the man's arrival. Maybe Trewick really did need his beauty sleep. The man at the bar was making no attempt to hurry his drink and had now turned his back on Kelso. The detective waited to see if he would follow the bearded man.

Ten minutes went by and Kelso decided he had been wrong. The man with the missing finger had ordered himself another drink and had joined in the conversation with a group of men at the bar. The detective stifled a yawn, then drained his glass. He felt tired, the smoke haze inside the pub and the strong ale in his stomach a wearying combination for someone who had spent the day trudging along footpaths and swallowing lungfuls of sharp, sea air. Boredom with his assignment didn't help, either.

He rose from his seat and strolled to the door, glancing at the man at the bar to see if his departure had caused any reaction. The man seemed engrossed in a story being told by one of the group he had joined. Kelso left the pub, coldness leaping at him as though it had been waiting for fresh prey.

Back inside the pub, the man in the leather jacket watched the doors close in the long mirror behind the bar.

Kelso walked down the quiet high street, making for the opposite end of the town where the caravan site was situated. It was a discreet location, for the town council went to great lengths to prevent any eye-sores from spoiling the charm of their seaside resort, much of which was protected by a charter designating it as an Outstanding Conservation area. The site was tucked away behind buildings on the very fringe of the town and was mostly empty of occupants, the holiday season not having yet begun. He had rented the caravan for an indefinite period, telling the site manager, who was rarely there, that it all depended on how long his project took. The caravan, itself, was small but not uncomfortable – he'd had experience of far worse quarters on other operations – and had most of the conveniences to make life bearable. His budget for the investigation did not allow for anything much better and the isolation and self-catering aspect certainly gave him more freedom of movement.

Tomorrow, he knew, he would have to give a report concerning his progress (or lack of it) to HQ in Lowestoft, and his dilemma was whether or not to inform his superiors that the case was a complete waste of time. All reason told him that it was, that there was no organised drugs ring in the area, but he had an uneasy feeling . . . He had come to rely on irrational instincts, for they had been justified in the past, and there was something about this place that disturbed him. Perhaps it was because the town was too quiet, the outlying areas too peaceful. In many ways it was ideal for smuggling of any sort, and the fact that he had found little indication, let alone evidence, of such illegal operations aroused the contrary side of his nature. He was suspicious because he had, as yet, found nothing to be suspicious of. The darkness closed in around him as he left the high streets and entered the narrow lanes of the town. Soon there was not even the friendly glow from windows for company.

He entered the caravan park. There were nearly twenty similar types of trailers in the grounds, only another two occupied as far as he knew. His was to the rear of the site, its back close to a bushy hedge, with open fields beyond the natural boundary. He could hear the waves rolling in onto the shingle and feel the wind cutting across the land between the caravan park and the sea to rattle fiercely against the fragile frames. He reached his temporary home, looking forward to some good, strong coffee and a soft, warm bed. He was too tired to eat. As he searched for the key in his jean's pocket, he thought he heard a movement inside the caravan. It may have been the wind whistling around its structure.

But when he carefully pushed the key into the lock, he discovered the door was already open.

FIVE

THE BEARDED man's pace was brisk, almost a run. He repeatedly glanced over his shoulder. Near the edge of the town now, he should have turned off to his right to reach the small terraced house in which he rented an upstairs room; but someone was waiting for him on the corner just ahead. The dark figure stepped into view when the bearded man was no more than ten yards away.

Trewick stopped dead, his mouth suddenly dry, the ale he had consumed an uncomfortable and shifting weight in his stomach. Hurried footsteps from behind confirmed his fear that he was being followed.

The man in front said nothing as he approached, but Trewick began to move sideways, out into the road. He raised a hand as though it would halt the man's progress, but the gesture had no effect. He saw the one who had been following him now, the one who had been waiting for him outside the pub, waiting for him to be flushed like a pheasant from the undergrowth.

'Wait! Look . . . ' Trewick knew that words would not help him.

'You were warned, Andy.' The man's voice was soft, almost regretful.

Trewick turned away from the two men and ran, almost tripping over the kerb on the other side of the narrow road. He plunged into a small sidestreet, one hand scraping against the brickwork to steady himself. Footsteps echoed behind him and a tight sob escaped his lips. He emerged from the sidestreet and

43

knew there was only one way to go: away from the town and into the darkness beyond. Into the marshes.

The car park opened out to his left, a vast black pit, the waves pounding the beach on the other side of the sea-wall. Gravel crunched beneath his feet and his body was already damp with sweat. He took a swift, panic-stricken look over his shoulder and saw they were still following, their pace steady, unhurried, as if they knew he could not escape, that there was nowhere to run to.

He was beyond the car park, nothing ahead but darkness and stars. If he could reach the marshes he had an advantage: he knew the paths, they didn't. His feet slid from beneath him and he went slithering downwards, his body rolling over as he tried to grab at earth to slow his descent. His hands only closed around loose shingle, though, and he cried out, confused by what was happening. He came to an abrupt halt, soft mud cushioning the impact, and sat up almost at once. He quickly realised why he had fallen.

The road from the town turned into a raised track that ran along the coastline, the sea-wall and beach on one side, a steep embankment on the other. He had slipped down the embankment. At the bottom of the slope on this side was a boatyard, beyond that the quay to the harbour. The river headed directly inland from that point, winding its way through the marshes. A minor avalanche of shingle told him his pursuers had begun their descent, and once more he was on his feet, running, heading into the boatyard, hoping to lose them among the clutter of motor cruisers and sailing boats.

The two men steadied themselves at the bottom of the slope and watched him disappear into a channel created by two rows of boats. They glanced at each other, their eyes well-accustomed to the darkness by now, then moved forward, splitting up, one man following the same channel as their prey, the other taking a parallel path.

Trewick had a choice: hide in the yard itself, either beneath or inside one of the boats, or make his way into the marshes. His breathing was laboured, his throat becoming raw as though the air he sucked in was full of grit. He stumbled on, afraid of running into something in the dark, but equally afraid of giving the two men the chance to catch up. And in his haste, he did trip.

44

The grip end of the launching trolley had been carelessly left out of line with the boats it nestled between, and Trewick's left foot made contact. He flew forward, his lumbering form leaving the ground completely, and smashed into the earth with a force that jarred every bone in his body. He tried to stifle the cry that was squeezed from his chest, but was aware that the sound of his falling alone would bring the two men to him. Ignoring the numbness in his arms and knees, he pushed himself between the mounts of a medium-sized ocean racer. His eyes were blurred with tears of pain and fear, and he bit deep into his lower lip to stem the whimpers that rose like hiccups. He rolled himself up into a ball, keeping his face and hands tucked into his knees lest their whiteness show up in the dark. He waited and tried to listen over the pounding of his own heart.

Footsteps approached, not running, but slow and deliberate. He stopped breathing. They were closer, treading warily. He raised his head slightly to see, using just one eye, afraid to expose too much of his face. The footsteps stopped and he heard a shoe scuffle against metal. Silence for several moments and Trewick was forced to release air from his lungs. He did so as quietly as possible, then drew in a short, jerky breath. Footsteps again. A dark shape moved before him, not more than two yards away. He couldn't make out if it was two pairs of legs or just one. He tried to control his shaking, sure that even that could be heard. The legs moved on, out of vision.

His eyes closed and his sigh of relief was barely audible. Silent tears had made his face and beard damp and he brushed them away against his knees.

Then something prodded his back and a quiet voice said: 'Boo.'

The girl was lying on one of the caravan's narrow bunk beds, leaning on an elbow with her back against the wall as though he had roused her from sleep. There was no surprise in her expression.

'Kelly?' she said.

'Goldilocks?' he asked.

'With dark hair?' She swung her legs over the edge of the

bed, but remained seated. 'It is Kelly, isn't it? Or I should say Kelso. You match the description they gave me quite well.'

'Who gave you?' Kelso's hand was still on the light switch by the door. The door, itself, was open, ready for him to take instant flight should the occupant or occupants of his make-shift home have proved a threat. The girl didn't look threatening.

'Your people in the Central Drugs Intelligence Unit.'

'What the hell are you talking about?' His hand had dropped from the light switch and was pulling the door closed. His eyes stayed on her all the time.

'I've also spoken to your immediate superior, Detective Superintendent Barrie of the Drugs Squad, who passed me onto your governor, Detective Inspector Wainwright. As usual with the Yard, they were cagey at first.'

Kelso walked further into the caravan and leaned against the open doorway leading to the sleeping quarters. He flicked on the light switch in that section to get a better look at the girl.

She wore jeans and a dark blue crew-neck jumper, the sleeves pulled up to her elbows. Long, brown hair hung loosely over a shoulder; hair on the other side of the parting was tucked behind her ear as though she had quickly pushed it back out of the way when he had entered the caravan. Clear blue eyes appraised him in the same way he was appraising her.

'I still don't know what the hell you're talking about. And how did you get in here?'

The girl smiled and, strangely, it hardened her features rather than softened them. 'That door wasn't locked.' She reached out for a bag lying in the dressing-table unit opposite the bed. His hand closed around her wrist.

'I've got my ID inside the bag,' she said.

'Just tell me.'

'Ellie Shepherd.' She tried to pull her wrist away, but his grip tightened. 'I'm an investigation officer with Customs and Excise.'

He raised his eyebrows. 'Yeah?'

'Yes.' She pulled her arm away.

Kelso reached for her bag, opened it and riffled through the contents until he found what he was looking for. He held the wallet up and looked enquiringly at her.

She nodded.

He opened the wallet, studied the inside for a few moments, flicked it shut and tossed it back into the bag. 'Coffee?' he asked, placing the shoulder-bag back on the unit and turning away from her to walk through to the kitchen area. She followed him out and watched him fill the electric kettle in the compact sink. He took a mug from the cupboard above the sink and placed it next to the one standing on the draining-board.

'How d'you like it?' he asked, reaching for the coffee jar.

'Strong. Black.'

He grinned to himself and scooped the instant into the mugs.

'Aren't you going to ask me why I'm here?' the girl rested against the wall, her arms folded.

'Figured you'd tell me.' He turned to face her and she saw a weariness around his eyes that had nothing to do with physical fatigue.

'Have you come up with anything yet?'

He shook his head. 'You give me some information first.'

'Okay, here it is. For some time now, my department has been working closely with the Military Police at the NATO base at Bentwaters. You probably realise by now that it's one of the biggest combined defence installations we have in this country.'

'Yeah, I've seen enough A-10s flying over to start World War Three.'

'Not quite, but it has a high strike potential.'

'You said it was for defence.'

'Same thing.'

'Of course.'

'There's always a slight drugs problem on any American base, no matter where it is. It goes on, and those caught get discreet but rapid court-martials; of course, there's no way it can be controlled completely. Soft drugs have been a source of irritation to the US military since Vietnam. An irritation, but never a threat. Until now, that is.'

Kelso poured boiling water into the mugs, his interest aroused. 'You're telling me there're junkies flying those planes up there?'

She smiled, and this time the smile softened her face. It was an improvement.

'No, it could never get that serious. But the airmen are becoming . . . well, over-supplied, if you like. We think most of it is coming in through Harwich and passed on to the local towns where the airmen spend much of their spare time.'

'Shouldn't the local Drugs Squad be involved in this?'

'We keep them informed, but you know yourself how stretched they are. The trouble is, they very often don't bother to inform us of their own operations. We only found out about you by chance.'

Kelso placed the two coffees on the small dining-table and nodded towards the bench seat behind it. The girl slid into the seat and rested her elbows on the table's surface while he tossed his coat through the doorway on to the bed she had just left. He sat on a stool opposite her.

'You're not saying there's a connection between your investigations and mine?'

'There may be.'

'But you said the problem with the airmen was soft drugs.'

'Mostly Class B drugs, yes. Amphetamines and various combinations with barbiturates are included in that category.'

'My case is acid poisoning. A normal family, father, mother and child, all hallucinating from the effects of LSD.'

'Yes, I've been told. I'll be working with you from now on.'

'You're kidding.'

She shook her head. 'There's also a letter in my bag signed by Detective Chief Superintendent Stone of the CDIU instructing you to co-operate fully with me. Do you want to check it?'

He left her at the table and walked back into the bedroom area. She sipped her coffee and grimaced at the taste. Kelso returned, a frown of concentration on his face as he studied the letter in his hand.

'Your coffee's terrible,' she commented.

'My budget doesn't allow for the real thing,' he said distractedly, spreading the letter before him on the table. 'I'll have to verify this by phone.'

'Of course. I'll get some better coffee tomorrow – our expense allowance is a hell of a lot better than yours.'

He looked up at her in surprise. 'What are you talking about?'

'I'm staying.'

'Here?'

'Here.'

'You're crazy.'

'My God, I never thought you'd be a prude.'

'That's got nothing to do with it! I work best alone, that's all.'

She saw something more than just anger in his eyes. Was it apprehension? No, more. There was fear in them.

'Look, it's the perfect cover, don't you see? I'm your girl-friend. I've come down to be with you while you're working on your conservation project.'

'It's impossible.'

She leaned across the table, glaring at him. 'Why? Because I'm a woman? You think I'll be a hindrance?'

'It isn't that . . .'

'Do you remember Operation Julie a few years back – the drug syndicate that was busted in Wales? Two of the investigating detectives sharing a cottage in Blaencaron and working undercover were getting nowhere with the locals until they discovered they were regarded as a couple of homosexuals. Things soon changed when they shipped in a policewoman to act as secretary to one of them. It has to be a woman, don't you see.'

He was silent.

'Then you think I'm not good enough.'

Still he said nothing.

'I'm part of Bravo Squad.'

There was little love lost between Customs and Excise Drug Investigation Units and the police Drug Squads – both organisations were too busy trying to grab the glory for themselves – but there were two Customs teams well respected by every police division in the country: Bravo and Charlie squads.

If she belonged to Bravo, she had to be good.

'I was involved in "Operation Wrecker".'

She *was* good. In 1979, an eighteen-month investigation by Customs and Hampshire police had resulted in one million pounds' worth of cannabis seized and twenty-three arrests in the South.

'And I was there when they brought in the *Guiding Light*.'

One and a half tons of hashish worth £2 million on the streets had been its cargo. The final take after more raids on various locations – again in the South – had amounted to nearly £10 million's worth of cannabis.

'And when I say involved, I mean *involved*. I wasn't there to

49

make the tea and take notes.'

He held out a hand towards her. 'Okay, you're good at your job.'

'There's more.'

'I believe you.' He gulped his coffee. 'I didn't mean to offend. All I'm saying is that this . . . ' he waved a hand around the caravan ' . . . is no place for a woman. They shouldn't have sent . . . '

'You're not afraid I'm going to seduce you, are you? Because if you are, you needn't worry on that score. You're not my type.'

'That doesn't mean you're not mine.'

Some of the anger left her. 'I can take care of myself.'

'I wish I could say the same for me. It's kind of cramped in here, you know. We could get in each other's way.'

'I'll try to think pure thoughts.'

He grinned, but she could still feel his unease. He was worried about something and it was more than just the male/female or Customs/police relationship. She wondered if it was anything to do with his reputation. Did he believe in it himself? She'd had little time to find out much about him, but a contact she had in the Yard's CID had filled her in on his general background. She had dismissed her contact's insinuation as nonsense. Stupid nonsense. But was it affecting him? She hoped he hadn't become full of neuroses because of what amounted to no more than just bad luck.

'We're worried, Kelso.'

He looked at her curiously.

''79 and '80 were great years for drugs busting. Our combined forces virtually wiped out trafficking in the South of England, but we know it's still coming into the country. We're still the major staging post for the States and Europe. So how is it getting in?'

'The whole coastline of England is ideal. It could be anywhere. Probably everywhere.'

'No, the east coast is the most ideal. Heavy shipping lanes, a short hop across the Channel, lots of isolated areas to bring boats and light aircraft into.'

'And lots of coastguard patrols.'

'But they're getting through. Admittedly, we've stemmed the flow, but it's still a big problem. And every indication is that it's a problem that's growing.'

'Where does my investigation come into all this? It's kind of low-key, you know.'

'Most of our leads have come through minor events; a small slip by a trafficker, information picked up at pop concerts – or freak "accidents".'

'Like the one in this town? The Preece family?'

'Precisely.'

'Look, I may as well tell you: nobody expects anything to come out of this. They shifted me out here because I'm used to undercover work and because they wanted me away from London for a while.'

The girl wondered if she should tell him she had heard of his reputation as a jinx, and decided not to; if he wanted her to know, he would tell her in his own time. At this stage, it might make their working relationship even more awkward. 'Like I said, a tiny incident, isolated though it may seem, can often lead to something bigger.'

'Sorry, I don't buy that. There's something you still haven't told me.'

'All right, I was getting to it. It may have no bearing on what happened here – in fact, it probably hasn't but we have to be sure.'

'Go on.'

'Five days ago, an A-10 from the NATO base at Bentwaters went down in the North Sea.'

'I haven't seen any news on it.'

'You won't – the authorities are keeping it quiet. Officially, the reason for the crash has been put down to engine malfunction. Unofficially, the pilot went berserk and aimed it into the blue.'

'Berserk?'

'He tripped out. Freaked. He was on a mind-bender, a bad one.'

Kelso shook his head in disbelief.

'They recovered the plane and found the dead pilot floating in the sea two days ago – he must have ejected before the aircraft hit the sea. When they opened him up they found enough lysergic acid still in his system to kill ten men.'

April, 1953

HE'D PUT his bloody boot through the wireless set if he heard
Guy Mitchell belting out 'She Wears Red Feathers' once more.
Didn't people know there were other, nicer songs around? That
Frankie Laine did a nice tune. Made old Moaning Minnie –
Johnny Ray – sound like a bad case of asthma. Nice bit of
crooning he liked; old Bing and Perry were favourites for that.
He stuck a Player's into the corner of his mouth and tore a strip
off his Daily Sketch. He learned forward with a grunt and
shoved the paper into the fire's dying embers, then lit his cigar-
ette with the flame.

Sammy Fish stretched his limbs, letting the newspaper slide
onto the lino floor. He removed his wire-framed National Health
spectacles and huffed on them, wiping away the vapour mist on
the lenses with his sleeve. *Family Favourites.* Must be nine
o'clock. Time to do his rounds. Get away from fucking 'Red
Feathers'. He'd have to send off a record request for himself
one day – at least he'd choose something tasty. Bit of Lita Roza.

He stood and scratched his grizzled chin, then pulled the
folds of his baggy trousers out of the crease of his buttocks.
Don't know why I've got to look after the bloody little baskits,
he grumbled to himself. And that's what a lot of them were –
real little baskits, no dads, some with no mums, even. His job
was to look after the boiler and do the odd jobs around the
home, not play nanny to all those miserable bleeders. With a
back like his, he shouldn't have to work at all.

He cursed the principal, Mr Bailey. And his staff. Lazy lot of fuckers. Oh, couldn't do enough for the kids, but ask any of them to give him a hand lifting or mending and they didn't want to know. Scared now, though, weren't they? Frightened the LCC was going to close the orphanage. All run off to the council meeting tonight, didn't they? Serve the buggers right if the Council did close the place. Mind you, he'd-be out of a job for a start. Bugger that.

He shuffled across the kitchen, the cigarette never leaving his lips for a moment. They were saying now that fags could kill you, but it was all bollocks. They'd ban them if they really could.

Sammy Fish had worked in the orphanage for eight years, joining it just after the war. Unemployment was the order of the day and he considered himself lucky to have a job; there had been a lot of younger men, all freshly demobbed, looking for work. He had been all right *during* the war when labour was short, but when the fighting stopped, the employers could be more choosey. His one qualification was that of a handyman, or more accurately, a general dogsbody. His big *dis*qualification for the job in the orphanage was his hatred for kids. But that he kept to himself. Lots of children's homes had sprung up after the war – there was a big need for them – but now the local councils were trying to control them, bring them under their own umbrella. Mr Bailey's home was too small to contain thirty children. The maximum he should have been allowed was twelve. The old, Victorian house itself was big – but thirty kids? Too many. Bailey was in trouble.

Fish climbed the stairs, still grumbling, leaving thick billows of cigarette smoke behind to disperse into the shadows. They'd better all be asleep, he told himself. No, that was too much to ask for: the older ones would still be awake larking about. He was in no mood for any monkey business tonight, though. They'd feel the back of his hand around their chops if they gave him any nonsense. He wanted to be back downstairs in time for Wilfred Pickles on the wireless at half-nine.

To his surprise, the children in the first bedroom he poked his head into were all asleep – or pretending to be. They were all girls in there, thirteen packed into one large room, their ages ranging from five to fourteen. The boys – a right unruly bunch who sounded like the bloody Mau Mau sometimes – were on the floor above; next door was the nursery. Bailey thought that having them close to the infants would keep the boys quiet at night. That was a laugh: many a night he'd heard Bailey or his wife pounding up the stairs to stop the noisy skirmishes going on in this room. Still, there was no ruckus tonight, he mused as he trod the stairs to the second storey. That, of course, was because they knew *he* was in charge. They didn't mess about with him. He dealt out a few good hidings with the threat that they would get worse if they tell-taled to Mr Bailey. He chuckled as he remembered getting hold of one of the little baskits – saucey little fucker – and dangling him over the bannisters by his legs. Said he'd drop him if he didn't behave. Funny thing was – although not funny at the time because he'd almost given himself a heart attack – he nearly *had* dropped the blighter, the kid had screamed and squirmed so much. It was lucky Bailey and his missus had been out that night as well. Mind you, there'd been no more trouble from *that* kid again. He silently pushed open the door to the older boys' dormitory, half-hoping to catch one or two of them out of bed so he could mete out some punishment. He scowled in disappointment when he saw they were all in their places. Fish stood there for several moments waiting for the sound of giggling or whispering; all he heard were a few nasal snores.

The light in the hallway was dim: Bailey was always skimping on electric and coal. He even had bloody inquests on the gas bills. He probably wouldn't have had a light up here at all if the kids didn't have to use the lavatory during the night. He shuffled along the landing, his breathing heavy after the long climb up the stairs. The door to the nursery was slightly ajar; it always was, just in case one of the brats started bawling during the night. There were ten littl'uns in there, boys and girls, their ages from two to five years old. Whiney little baskits.

Fish stopped when he heard voices. Or was it just the one voice? He listened outside the door.

Baby talk. One of the nippers was having a right old conversation with hisself. Fish poked his nose through the doorway. He could barely see the outlines of cots and small beds in the gloom, but the voice was coming from a position opposite the door. He pushed the door open wider to allow more light into the room.

He was surprised when he saw who it was talking.

The boy sat upright in his bed, his toes still tucked beneath the sheets. He seemed oblivious to Fish standing in the doorway. Tiny hands were tucked into his lap and his head leaned forward as though he was studying something on the bed with him. But although he chatted away, the conversation was one-sided, for there was no one else there.

The caretaker was surprised not because of that fact – he had become used to children's fantasies by now – but because this particular kid had barely spoken to anyone since he'd been in the home. Fish knew the staff had been worried at first, thinking the boy might be retarded, but he had proved bright enough. Just timid. No, that wasn't the word they used. Withdrawn or something. Something like that. And now here he was talking ten-to-the-dozen. Well, he'd get what for if he woke any of the others.

Fish entered the room, angry, but forcing himself to tip-toe. The boy only became aware of him when his shadow fell across the bed.

'Right, you little orror, what's this about?' Fish whispered fiercely.

The boy looked up at him, his eyes becoming wide. The sides of his mouth dropped and his lower lip instantly began to tremble.

'Come on, what d'you think you're up to this time of night? You want to wake up all the others?' Fish stood over the boy menacingly, enjoying himself.

The boy began to shiver, but said nothing. He blinked as his eyes became watery.

'What's your name? Jimmy, innit? You wait till I tell Mr Bailey about you disturbing the other kids.' Fish's nose twitched and he raised his head, turning it in each direction and sniffing. His gaze fell back on the child before him.

'Have you messed yourself?'

The boy said nothing.

'Come on, answer me. You had enough to say for yourself a minute ago.'

The boy began to draw his little body into a ball, his head sinking down onto his knees, hands tucked into his lap.

'You little bleeder!' Fish cuffed the back of the boy's head. He kept his voice low, but its gruffness was effective. He pulled at the boy's shoulders, lifting him up and turning him around to examine the back of his long nightshirt. The boy cried out and the sound was no more than a tiny yelp, but Fish cupped a rough hand over his mouth anyway.

'You bugger! Don't you dare make a sound!' He examined the nightshirt by the poor light shining through the doorway and was almost disappointed to find no dampness, no stains. He grunted and let the infant collapse back onto the bed, but not before he'd dealt his bottom a hefty whack.

'Now get into bed and no more noise. Mr Bailey'll deal with you in the morning.'

The boy pulled the sheets up around him, covering his head so that only a small clump of hair was visible. The bedclothes shuddered spasmodically as he fought back the sound of his sobs.

Fish looked around the room once more: one of the other perishers must have done a packet. Or been sick. It was a funny smell. He shuffled out of the room, muttering to himself in low tones. He left the door ajar as was usual – didn't want Mr Bailey telling him off again for being careless – and crept stealthily towards the stairs.

He was on the first step going down when he thought he heard soft footsteps padding behind him. He half-turned and just caught sight of the tiny figure which had emerged from the shadows of the now wide-open doorway; then small hands were pushing at his hips, powerful hands, and he was toppling forward, the stairs rushing up to meet him.

He bounced down the staircase and, if his limbs had been less brittle with age, he might have survived. But his head came to rest against the wall at the bend of the stairs and his neck snapped like a frozen twig, his wire-framed spectacles slipping from his nose to swing casually from one ear.

At the last moment, just before all his senses had their lines to the brain cut, he was able to see the landing at the top of the stairs. And there was nothing there. Nothing at all.

SIX

Kelso sipped his second cup of coffee and held the gingham curtain away from the window. It was a bright day outside, giving the assertion that spring really had arrived after all. He watched Ellie Shepherd trudge her way along the lane between the caravans, a full shopping-bag carried against her stomach with both hands. Her dark hair was tucked beneath a bright red and white scarf, the scarf's knot tied at the back of her neck. A fawn raincoat that had seen better days covered her jeans. She caught sight of him at the window and flashed a smile. A *definite* improvement.

He opened the door for her and she brought in the smell of fresh, sea air with her.

'I didn't hear you leave,' he said.

'No, I didn't want to disturb you. You were snoring like a pig.' She dumped the shopping-bag on the draining-board and began to unload. 'I looked through your cupboards this morning. What are you? Some kind of anti-food freak? You don't like to eat?'

'I, uh, didn't realise I was so low. I usually restock every week.'

'I think you would have starved to death if you'd waited. Like some breakfast?'

'I've just had it.'

'Coffee?' She pulled a disgusted face. 'You'll never grow into a big boy.'

'I don't usually eat in the morning.'

'No, it shows. Well I'm hungry – maybe you'll join me.' She cluttered in the cupboard beside the sink and drew out a pan. Soon the delicious aroma of frying bacon, spiced with wafts of freshly brewed *real* coffee and toasting bread aroused juices even in his morning-delicate stomach.

'You sleep okay?' he asked after yawning and realising he hadn't.

'Fine. Those bunk beds are more comfortable than they look. How was the couch?'

'All right. It's meant to be a spare.'

'You could have taken the bunk above mine, you know. It wouldn't have bothered me.'

'Yeah, but it would have bothered me,' he mumbled.

'Sorry?'

'I just said my snoring would have kept you awake.'

She grinned. 'Maybe.'

Three slices of bacon crammed between two toasted doorsteps was placed before him.

'I told you . . . '

'Nonsense. Anyone can eat in the morning if they make the effort.' She grabbed his coffee mug and emptied the lukewarm dregs, replacing them with piping hot coffee. The ashtray by his elbow, full to overflowing, was whisked away and its contents emptied into the bin. 'Thanks, Ma,' he said, as she returned it.

'Just because you snore like a pig, it doesn't mean you have to live like one. How's the sandwich?'

He tried to swallow so that he could reply, but failed to clear his throat completely.

'That grunt means it's good, eh?' she said.

He nodded, then gulped the remnants in his throat down with coffee. The coffee burnt his lips.

'How come you're not married?' he finally managed to say, having already inspected her third finger, left hand, the night before.

'How do you know I'm not? The absence of a ring could be part of my guise as your girlfriend.'

'Are you?'

She shook her head and joined him at the table. Her sandwich almost matched his in size. 'How come *you're* not?'

Again she saw that troubled look appear in his eyes, but it was no more than a flicker.

'Does it show?' he asked, and she felt him making a conscious effort to relax.

'What? That you're not married? Yes, it shows. But I was told about you in my briefing.'

Kelso frowned. 'What else were you told?'

'Oh, just your general background. You're good at under-cover work.'

'Nothing more than that?'

'Is there anything else?'

He looked down into his coffee mug. 'No, there's nothing important.'

She studied him for a few moments, biting into her sandwich. She swallowed, then said, 'Okay, what's our routine for today?'

Kelso folded his arms on the table. 'Well, like I told you last night, so far I've come up with zero. The town is quiet, friendly – and doesn't seem to have any criminal activity.'

'It's a nice place. I walked through it this morning when I was shopping. The groceries go on my account, by the way; as I said, our allowances are a bit more realistic than yours.'

'I won't quarrel with that. Now, there's a river inlet that runs parallel to the coast for seven miles or so before turning inland. The distance between the river bank and the sea is no more than a couple of hundred yards in places. It's perfect for boats to come in through the channel and make their way inland. It'd be perfect for smuggling contraband or whatever, except that every boat is carefully monitored by the coastguards. Anything suspect would be pounced on immediately.'

'They couldn't unload on the beach, carry it across to the river?'

'Impossible. They'd be seen. Even at night the risk would be too great.'

'Who uses the river?'

'Mainly pleasure-boats. A couple of fishing drifters use the harbour where the river turns inland; their boats are too big to beach.'

'Couldn't they bring drugs in?'

He shook his head. 'It's unlikely. They've been watched, even searched. All they've brought ashore is fish. Something funny happened last night, though, but it could amount to nothing.'

'Funny?'

'Yeah, strange. Nothing much, just a little incident in the local pub.' He quickly recounted his meeting with the young, bearded fisherman and his hasty departure at the arrival of the man in the leather jacket. 'Like I say, it isn't much, but it's about the only interesting thing that's happened since I've been here.'

'What did he look like, this man?'

'Not like a local. He looked as though he would have been more comfortable drinking in the Green Gate at Bethnal Green. And, oh yeah, the little finger of his right hand was missing.'

Ellie's face was half-buried in her sandwich, but she nodded for him to go on.

'That's it, there is no more. Trewick bolted from the pub and I waited for chummy to follow. But he didn't. Just carried on drinking.'

The girl chomped on her food for a while, then said: 'Not much to show for three weeks' work, is it?'

'I've been telling my guvnors that in my weekly reports. Casing this back-of-beyond place isn't my idea.'

'Sorry, I wasn't criticising.'

He reached for a cigarette and lit it. As an afterthought he pushed the pack toward her. She shook her head.

'The funny thing is,' he said, exhaling smoke, 'I *feel* something is going on. Call it intuition, a hunch, or what you like. The place is almost too respectable, too perfect. And there has to be some explanation for what happened to the Preece family.'

'And the American pilot.'

'You really think there's a connection?'

'Both incidents involved LSD, and both involved unlikely victims. It's a coincidence that makes you wonder, isn't it? Of course, yours isn't the only lead we're following – you can imagine the furore that's been caused. A pilot overdosing while in control of a jet plane doesn't go down too well with the powers-that-be. The Wing Commander at Bentwaters has a lot of explaining to do.'

'I'm not surprised. How can a junky be allowed to fly a plane? I take it the A-10 was armed?'

'They're not saying.'

'No, I don't suppose they are.'

'As for the pilot, he obviously had no record of drugs. They're going over his background now with a fine toothcomb.'

'It's a little late for that.'

'They may turn up something useful.'

'I still don't see how he even got on board the aircraft if he was that hyped-up.'

'That's just the point: he wasn't. He acted normally. If he'd taken it by mouth in liquid or powder form it could have taken almost an hour to take effect. Injected straight into the bloodstream, a lot less. And with the massive dose he took, the reaction would have been immediate.'

'So he injected himself when he was up there.'

'That's it.'

'Christ, it's lucky he chose to dive into the sea.'

'That's the general agreement. Anyway, officially, we're not part of the military's investigation. It was only because of my department's probing into the soft drugs problem on the base that we got involved at all; I think the Ministry of Defence would have liked to have kept the whole matter under their own supervision. Really, we're only running around the edges of it and trying not to step on any toes.'

'I see.' He watched her thoughtfully as she drank her coffee.

'You were going to tell me what you had in mind for today,' she prompted.

'I thought I might casually bump into Trewick again. He could be worth getting to know.'

'Good, I'll come with you.'

'Well, I have to go into the marshes first just to make my cover look good. I want to take a walk along the riverbank anyway and look at some of the properties there. It's just an idea but if drugs are coming up the river – though God knows how – then they have to be unloaded somewhere. It might be worthwhile checking for likely places.'

'The river stretches for miles doesn't it?'

'Yeah, but it narrows down the further inland it gets. I think we can concentrate on the wider stretch for now, see what we find. I spent the first couple of weeks here trudging up and down the coastline looking for suitable isolated spots and my conclusion is that if trafficking is going on, the goods have to be landed upriver – the coast is too exposed.'

'Okay, let's make a start.' She gathered up the plates and mugs and dumped them into the sink.

'I, um, want to make a call first,' Kelso said.

She turned and smiled at him. 'They won't do it, you know.'

He raised his eyebrows. 'What?'

'They won't get me off your back. I'm afraid you're stuck with me.'

We'll see, he thought. 'I have to verify what you've told me.'

'H'mn,' she said.

'I won't be long.' He checked the weather outside and grabbed a light, waist-length jacket.

'Hey,' she called after him.

He turned at the door.

'You going to shave today?'

He rubbed his chin and felt the rough bristles. 'It's not Sunday already, is it?'

He closed the caravan door behind him and began to whistle as he headed towards the site entrance.

He heard the girl curse and turned to see her sliding down the grass embankment. Kelso stood and watched as she came to rest below him. She looked up and frowned at his smug grin.

'You're lucky you didn't go down the other side,' he called out. 'You'd have been in the river.'

'Why the hell did they make a footpath ten feet above ground level?' She pulled herself upwards, the wellingtons she had bought in town on his advice sinking deeper into the marshy soil.

'This embankment acts as a flood wall. The river's only about six feet below on the other side and when it swells, the embankment stops it spilling over.'

'It can't always have been successful judging by these marshes – there can't be a firm piece of soil for half-a-mile or so.'

'There is. You just chose a particularly bad stretch to fall into.'

'Uh-huh, that sounds like me.' Ellie managed to pull herself

64

from the mud and climb a few feet up the slope. Unfortunately, one of her boots had stayed behind, buried up to the ankle in oozing soil.

'Those canals crisscross the marshes and drain off most of the water,' Kelso told her, squinting his eyes to study the town in the distance.

'That's nice,' she said, concentrating more on the attempt to retrieve her boot than his remarks. Ellie finally wrenched the wellington free and pulled it over her foot. She began to crawl back up the slope.

Kelso reached down and she took his hand, covering the last few steps in a rush with his help. He steadied her at the top to prevent her slipping down the other side into the river, his hands clenched tightly around her upper arms.

For a moment, he seemed uncertain of himself and his hands dropped away.

'Thanks,' she said.

He turned from her and pointed ahead to where the river snaked back on itself, almost in a U-turn. 'I want to get round there, see what's beyond. According to the map, that's where the houses begin – or I should say, estates. They back on to the river.'

'They're marked on a map?'

He dug a hand into the bag he carried over his shoulder and produced a folded white sheet of paper. 'Drawn by a local artist,' he explained, as he opened it up. 'Much more useful than the ordinary printed maps. It has more details – footpaths, boundaries, old disused railways, even television masts. Look, it gives the names of private estates along the river.'

'What's this further up, where a main road crosses the river?'

'It's a maltings.'

'A what?'

'An animal feedstuff mill. They convert grain, barley, turnips and suchlike into food for livestock.'

They studied the intricately detailed map in silence for a few moments, a light breeze ruffling one corner of the paper. Kelso was right, the girl thought. The waterway provided an ideal road inland from the sea. Secluded, not too much traffic but enough not to draw attention to individual boats. The only drawback was that the entrance to the channel would be closely watched, the coming and going of boats noted and those whose movements were suspicious would undoubtedly be searched from time to time. She knew a vigilant watch was always kept for illegal immigrants and unquarantined pets along the coastline and, now that the authorities in Spain and Portugal had clamped down so heavily on drugs smuggling, making Britain a little *too* popular as a clearing-house, the scrutiny of vessels had become even keener.

'Do you mind if we sit for a while?' she said.

'Of course not. I should have told you the going would get rough.' He tucked the map away and sat down on the footpath, legs dangling down the slope facing the river. She sat next to him and watched the languid flow, enjoying the sun on her face, its warmth tempered by the mild April breeze. Two white swans drifted by.

'What did your boss have to say when you phoned?' she suddenly asked.

Kelso shrugged, 'He told me to stop belly-aching and get on with the job.'

Ellie laughed.

'He said you were good. Professional.'

'I am.' A small motor launch on the far side of the river moved smoothly upstream, the noise from its engine somehow muted across the wide stretch of water.

'He said your people wanted to flood the area with investigators.'

'Over-reaction, that's all. In the end they saw it would have done more harm than good. It would have queered your pitch.'

'So they sent you instead.'

'I'm all your department would allow.'

They were silent for a while, she recovering from the rough hike he had brought her on, he lost in his own brooding thoughts. Finally, Kelso said: 'What made you come into this game, Ellie?'

'Customs and Excise?'

'Drugs investigation.'

'I don't like what they do to people.'

'Even marijuana?'

She studied his face, then looked back across the water. 'There's a lot of rubbish talked about just how harmless it is.'

'Oh, I don't know. Even in the police we're a little cynical about the laws against it. They're pretty harsh, considering.'

'Considering the effects are no worse than having a few drinks?'

'Some say the effects are a lot better. Kids have seen what booze can do to their elders, and they don't like it. Make peace, not trouble. At least marijuana calms people, makes them friendly. You know, there's supposed to be over two hundred million people using it today, religious and medical groups included. They can't all be wrong.'

'And how many will eventually be turned on to hard stuff? One in every hundred? One in every thousand? Even one in every million would be too much!'

'Hey, come on.'

'I mean it. It's this bland acceptance of so-called soft drugs that gets me. More deaths and damage are caused by barbiturates and amphetamines than heroin and other narcotics.'

'Yeah, I've done my training, too.'

'Then you should know how kids get hooked. They see their parents taking pills – headache pills, sleeping pills, slimming pills – and they experiment themselves. Ever heard of a "Drug Salad"?'

He shook his head, surprised at her anger.

'Kids steal whatever pills they find lying around in the home and mix them together with whatever their friends have found. The idea then is to dip in and swallow whatever comes out. Can you imagine what a combination of certain tablets can do? In the States, mothers pack vitamin pills into their children's lunchpacks; some even dust their sandwiches with penicillin powder to keep the germs away. The next step for kids is grass, or maybe speed – whatever fancy name they give to dope to make it sound more friendly, more acceptable to themselves. When the kicks no longer come so easily with what they're used to – with what their own metabolism has learned to resist – they go for something harder. Cocaine, opium, heroin. Or synthetic substitutes like Physeptone. Or maybe they'll go for LSD and THC. It depends what they can afford. And remember, heroin is cheaper on the streets nowadays than cannabis. If they haven't got the money, they find ways.'

'But that's like saying you should never take an aspirin for a

67

headache, because eventually one won't be enough. You'll need two. Then maybe three.'

'We're talking about kids, where moderation isn't an easy word. I agree that if everyone was sane and sensible marijuana would be no problem. But not enough people – not enough adults, let alone youngsters – are that rational. It's also now believed that cannabis may linger in the body in a harmful way for weeks after it's inhaled.'

'But doesn't banning the drug make it all the more desirable.'

She groaned. 'Not that old "prohibition" chestnut.'

'It's true, though.'

'Sure it's true. But it's the only control we have, inadequate though it may be. Look, if the Law turned around and said it was okay to rape, do you think the novelty would suddenly wear off. Christ, Kelso, you're in the Force, you know just how thin that barrier between civilisation and naked animal behaviour is.'

'We were only talking about smoking grass.'

'But a line has to be drawn somewhere, for all our sakes.'

'It's where you draw the line.'

'You can't let grey areas blur its edge, you know that.'

He held up his hands. 'Okay, I give in – with reservations. I only want to nick whatever villains the law tells me to, anyway.'

Her body seemed to relax. 'I'm sorry, I didn't mean to lecture you. It's just that I've seen what drugs can do.'

Kelso's voice was soft. 'So have I, Ellie.'

'But to someone you've known, someone close to you?'

'No, I couldn't say that.'

'I shared a room with a girl at university. We were good friends. She was quite brilliant, one of those infuriating people who never seemed to find it necessary to cram knowledge into her head. Once she was told something, or read something, it was there, locked inside her brain ready to be used the instant she needed it. She was a little younger than me – a child prodigy, really. Her father was a grocer in Sutton and he was so proud of his girl. I stayed at her home one weekend; he couldn't stop talking about his Ginny and how proud he was of her achievements. Every time she went out of the room, he'd grin from ear to ear and tell me how marvellous she was. And she was, too; it was no idle boast.

'It was the end of term, we'd finished our exams, I was worried, she was buoyant. We went to one of those end-of-term parties – I had to persuade her to go because she thought all those yahoo students were a bit wet. They were smoking pot, someone had some coke, "borrowed" from his rich parents, others had pills. Plenty of drink, too. One idiot arrived with pills and wouldn't tell anyone what they were. Most of them there knew, but me and Ginny, we were a little naïve about such things. He persuaded Ginny to try one. I told her not to, but I suppose she felt she had to accept the dare. It turned out to be LSD. One lousy little tablet killed her. Just one.'

She wasn't looking at Kelso, but staring back down the river, the way they had come.

'The effects of that tablet scared her so much she went into extreme hysteria. She died of asphyxia.'

There wasn't much that Kelso could say. He wondered if Ellie was weeping, but when she turned to face him there was only anger in her eyes. 'You've obviously had to study reports on drug abuse. You must know the damage they've caused, particularly to young lives. So how can you be complacent?'

'I'm not, Ellie. I'd just rather see real villains in the dock than some silly sod who hasn't the sense to confine his pot smoking to his or her own home. The joke is that a lot of those students and undergraduates who are smoking now are eventually going to be lawyers, barristers, and a few of them judges; that's when the law will be changed.'

'You may be right. I hope not, but you may be.'

'Is what happened to your friend the reason you joined Customs?'

'No, it had nothing to do with it. It seemed an interesting job when I left university, but it was only later that I got involved in investigation. They keep an eye out for any of their employees who have an investigative flair; I guess I had. The more I learned just how corrupt and vicious the whole smuggling scene was – not just drugs – the more I wanted to do my bit to stamp it out. It will never happen, of course, but at least we're controlling the situation to some extent. Not that we get much help from your lot.'

Kelso smiled. The rivalry between Customs and Excise and the police was notorious and often a source of embarrassment to both organisations; he'd heard many stories of Customs investigation officers being arrested by the police and police undercover agents being followed by Customs officers.

'Maybe we can really work together on this one?' Ellie said and was surprised to see Kelso's smile fade.

'Let's move on, shall we?' He stood and she, too, got to her feet.

They walked on in silence and Ellie resented his sudden aloofness. Did he think she was just a dead weight, a nuisance to be tolerated, but not accepted? Or did he believe his own publicity? Well okay, if that was the way he wanted it, then that was how it had to be.

And then she was laughing as she watched him slip and roll down the embankment into the mushy earth below.

It was late afternoon and Ellie felt hot and sticky. It wasn't the weather, for a cool breeze had struck up again; her discomfort was because of the wearing route march he had led her on. She was hungry, too.

'Hey,' she called out to him. 'Don't you ever eat?'

They were using a narrow track leading across the fields which backed on to the outskirts of the town. He turned to look back at her and she could see his surprised expression. 'I'm sorry,' he said, when she caught up with him. 'I forgot about food.'

'Well your stomach should have reminded you.'

'Are you tired?'

'My spirit is willing.'

He chuckled. 'The going's easier now. It won't take us long to get back. I'll cook us something while you take a shower.'

'Oh no. If lack of food doesn't concern you, I'd hate to think what your cooking's like. I'll handle the eats.'

'Suits me,' he said.

They continued walking, Ellie keeping pace with him now she knew a goal was in sight. 'You're right about the river,' she said after a while. 'It's a natural.'

'Yeah, but no signs of trafficking. How many boats did we

see using the river today? Two, three?'

'There are plenty moored out there.'

'Not many actually go out to sea, though. They mainly use the waterways.'

'Maybe we'll turn up something when we find out who the owners of those properties along the banks are. You never know, some of them could have criminal links.'

'It's worth a try. I'll check with Lowestoft – they may come up with something.'

'Wouldn't the local bobby be better?'

'No, he doesn't even know I'm here. We thought it better to keep it as quiet as possible.'

They crossed a footbridge, the grassed-edged canal beneath them shallow and slow-flowing. The path cut across another field and Ellie saw the allotments leading up to buildings just beyond.

Kelso indicated with a nod towards a group of small red-bricked houses directly ahead of them. 'That's where the Preece family live.'

'Not exactly the kind of people you'd expect to be turning themselves on.'

Another straight, manmade canal edged the field, and a foot-bridge ran across it to the path leading around the allotments. They took it.

'The woman jumped into that,' Kelso said, pointing down into the water.

'She was lucky it's so shallow.'

'They still had a job pulling her out, though. Apparently she kept trying to lie on the bottom. She wanted to drown.'

Ellie shuddered. 'We've got to find these bastards, Jim. They've caused one death, they could have easily caused more.'

'If they're the same people. What happened to the pilot and this family could be unconnected incidents.'

'Yes, but I think you have the same feeling as me. I wasn't sure when I came yesterday – I'm not absolutely sure now, but somehow I *know* there's a link. Call it experience, or just plain woman's intuition, but I feel certain the LSD came from the same source.'

Kelso said nothing, but he understood her instinct and thought he could explain it. Any extraordinary event in this part of the

71

country was completely out of character; two extraordinary events of a similar nature and you had to assume there was a link. Yet, it didn't necessarily make it so. Ellie moved closer to him and slid a hand into his. He looked curiously at her and she inclined her head towards an old man who was working in one of the allotments. The gardener glanced up at them as they passed.

'We're supposed to be in love, remember?' she whispered.

They cut through an alleyway leading directly into the town and Kelso brought her to a halt at the end of it.

'Look, I'm going down to the quay to see if Trewick's drifter has come in. Why don't you head back to the caravan, take your shower, and then get some food underway?' He handed her the doorkey.

'Yes, Master.'

'I won't be long. I'll just try and fix up a drink with him for later tonight, if he's there.'

'Only if I can come along for the drink too.'

'Of course. We're in love, aren't we?'

She leaned forward and kissed the tip of his nose. 'That's for effect,' she said, and her eyes were laughing at him.

He watched her cross the road and turn to wave before she disappeared into a sidestreet. He was frowning as he walked towards the quay area.

Kelso's pace quickened when he saw the fishing boat was there, half its catch already loaded onto a waiting truck. He slowed down as he drew near, not wanting to appear over-anxious. Two deckhands were loading long boxes crammed with whiting, cod and sprats; another man, older, thick grey sideburns almost meeting beneath his heavy chin, watched them from the drifter's deck. He eyed Kelso suspiciously when he sauntered over.

'Good catch?' Kelso asked.

The fisherman stared at him briefly, then shouted at the two men loading the truck. 'Come on, you dozy bastids, we haven't got all day!' Even the Suffolk accent failed to soften the gravelly harshness of his voice. He regarded Kelso once more, not bothering to conceal the disdain he obviously felt. 'No good fishing in these waters anymore, mister. Fur'ners cleaned us out. Bastids!'

He spat onto the dock, a gob of yellow phlegm landing only a few feet away from Kelso's boots.

'Yeah, bloody thieves,' he agreed. 'Andy's not around, is he?'

The fisherman's face darkened and his scowl made the two men loading fish work even harder. 'No, he ain't around, that no-good fucker! Been to another one of his parties last night, I suppose. Let us down badly again. I'll kill the fucker when I get hold of him.'

Sorry I asked, Kelso thought.

'You weren't with him last night, was you?' the fisherman accused.

'Me? No. I saw him in the pub, but he left early.'

'Well he's done this once too often, he's forrit this time.' The fisherman jumped up onto the quayside with an agility that was surprising for a man so heavily built. He strode over to Kelso and a stout finger stabbed the air in front of the detective. 'If you see him afore I do, being one of his mates . . . '

'Wait, I'm not . . . '

'If you see him, you tell him from me, I'll knock his blasted head off when I get hold of him.' He whirled away, no longer interested in Kelso, and scooped up one of the fish boxes and hurled it into the back of the truck over the heads of the two loaders. 'No-good little bastid!' Kelso heard him mutter.

Kelso walked back to the high street, his mind busy with fresh thoughts. So Trewick hadn't turned up for work this morning. He'd left the pub in a rush last night and hadn't turned up this morning. Again, maybe nothing, but maybe *something*.

By the time he reached the caravan site he was wondering if sheer desperation was making him exaggerate the significance of what was, after all, a minor event. But when he found Ellie's slumped body lying on the caravan's floor, he realised that things were taking on a new pace.

SEVEN

KELSO QUICKLY examined the girl and his probing fingers found
a swelling beginning to rise at the back of her neck. He brushed
her hair aside and saw a patch of redness beneath the roots;
whatever had hit her had not been sharp, for the skin was
unbroken. Ellie groaned as he touched the wound once more.

'It's okay, Ellie, it's me, Kelso. I'm going to get you onto
the bed.'

He quickly ran his fingers down her arms and legs, pressing
lightly, searching for more injuries. Satisfied that the blow on
the head was all she had suffered, he gently turned her over and
slipped his arms beneath her shoulders and legs. He carried her
through to the caravan's bedroom and placed her on the lower
bunk. She groaned once more and reached round to touch the
area of throbbing pain. Her eyes opened and for several seconds
she seemed confused. Then she focused on Kelso and tried to
sit up.

'Stay there,' he ordered. 'I'll get something to ease the pain.'

He returned to the kitchen area, quickly scanning the caravan's
interior, making sure there was no one lurking inside. Then he
ran cold water over a tea-towel, wrung out the excess, and went
back to the girl, who was now resting on her elbows. She yelped
aloud when he placed the sodden wrapped towel against the
swelling.

'Lie back,' he told her.

'No . . . I'd rather sit.'

She gingerly swung her legs over the side of the bunk and he let her hold the towel herself against her neck. 'Christ,' she said, 'what hit me?'

'I was going to ask you.'

Ellie shook her head, then regretted the movement. He studied her eyes for a few moments. 'What's your name?' he asked.

'What?'

'Tell me your name.'

'Oh Chri . . . I'm okay. My name's Ellie Shepherd, you're Jim Kelso, alias Jim Kelly. I'm not concussed, just a bit heavy-headed.'

'Can you remember what happened?'

'I can remember.' She twisted her neck in a slow, circular movement, wincing as she did so. 'Bastard!'

'Did you see who did it?'

'No, it happened too fast. I got to the caravan and found the door unlocked. I thought maybe you'd forgotten to lock it on our way out. I came in and all I remember was hearing something come up from behind and then I went completely numb, The bastard hit me.'

'You didn't see who?'

'It happened too fast. I half-turned but all I remember was a big, dark shadow looming over me. Have you got any ideas?'

It was one of those moments again, one of those brief instants when she saw that strange turmoil going on in his eyes. It was almost a suppressed panic. Then it was gone and replaced by a cold hardness – and this was another reaction she was coming to recognise.

'Someone must be curious about me. Either that, or it was simply a case of burglary. I'll have a look round in a minute, see if anything's missing.'

'Who would want to know about you? Do you think somebody suspects you're the Law?'

'Perhaps. Or maybe . . . maybe . . . ' His voice trailed off. He stood and said. 'You look as though a stiff drink might help.'

'It would. But what were you going to say?'

He went into the kitchen, leaving her staring after him. She watched through the doorway as he quickly examined the interior of the caravan, checking drawers and cupboards, often just staring at objects as if they could give him a clue as to who had broken in. Finally he returned with a bottle half full of scotch and two tumblers.

'This be okay?' he asked, holding the whisky towards her.

'I'll need a little water with it.'

He poured two measures and went back into the kitchen to add water to hers. He handed her the scotch and watched her take a sip. She grimaced.

'Your head?' he asked.

'The scotch,' she said.

He took a large swallow of his own drink and Ellie shuddered inwardly.

'We've been searched,' Kelso announced.

She was taken aback, but waited for him to go on.

'I always make a point, when I'm working undercover, of placing things in certain positions. You don't need strands of hair stuck over closed doors or fine powder sprinkled around the room: all you need is a shoelace lying across a shoe in a certain way, a tie hanging loose over a drawer, but at an angle. If anything is moved, I'll know. You had no chance to touch anything when you came in, so it had to have been our intruder.'

'What could they have found? Your ID?'

'I never leave that lying around.'

'Anything else? Papers, your reports?'

'Don't keep them. There was nothing for them to find and you probably disturbed their search anyway.'

'You were going to say something a minute ago. Why they would have broken in . . . '

Kelso was sitting on a stool opposite the bunk, and now he leaned closer to her, elbows on his knees, tumbler held in both hands. 'This Trewick, apparently he didn't show up at the boat today. His skipper was blazing mad; seems Trewick has a reputation for being unreliable. Last night, he was frightened – I could feel it. Almost scared for his life. And I'm still sure it was the man in the leather coat who scared him – Trewick ran out so fast I felt the draught. I told you last night this character who came into the pub looked like an out-and-out villain, hardly the sort that hangs around in little fishing towns.'

'But he didn't follow Trewick out.'

'Maybe he didn't have to. He may have known he could find him later. Maybe he was more interested in me.'

'Why should he be? That doesn't make sense.'

'Because I was seen in deep conversation with Trewick before he scooted. If Trewick had upset someone – *some organisation* – in these parts, they may be wondering who-the-hell I am and just what I was doing talking to Trewick.'

'They think you're involved with him?'

'It could be. Anyway, they'd want to find out.'

There was a new tenseness in Kelso and she knew it was because he felt things were beginning to move; the other side had shown a face, they were no longer an imagined nor inanimate entity. Kelso was beginning to enjoy the situation and she felt the same excitement, despite the throbbing ache in her head.

'So what happens now?'

'I carry on in the same way.'

'What about me?'

'I want you out of it.'

'No way. You can't unload me.'

'Ellie, I think it really could get dangerous.'

'It wouldn't be the first time.'

The determination in her voice told him that there would be no point in arguing. Later he would try to get his DI to haul her off the operation.

'Okay,' he said, avoiding her look by sipping his drink.

'Do we go to the local police, report an attempted burglary? That would be the thing to do in normal circumstances.'

'No, we keep it to ourselves. I think we'll be watched, so let's give them a little mystery. If I'm mixed up in some shady business with Trewick, the last thing I'd do is go to the pigs. Let's lead them on a bit, see how they react.'

'It's risky.' She saw him ready to pounce and quickly added, 'But okay, I'm game.' She smiled smugly to herself when she saw his disappointment; she wasn't going to give him any excuse to ease her out.

'Why don't you rest? I'll have a snoop around outside, see if there's any bogeymen.'

There were no protestations and he guessed she was more groggy than she was letting on. He left her and stepped outside. The breeze had a definite chill to it and the falling sun had no warmth. Kelso strolled across to the blockhouse containing the toilets and showers, peering into the segregated sections to check that they were empty. He toured the perimeter of the site, then went out into the street beyond. From there he had a view of the sea, its blueness made sombre by the silt suspended in its depths; a few people trudged along the shingle beach, and one or two anglers sat patiently waiting for something to bite. The road opposite leading back to the town's high street was deserted save for a single dog who sniffed its way along the gutter.

Kelso went back into the site and surveyed the twenty or so caravans there. He knew that only two others were occupied, the rest empty and waiting for seasonal clients. At least, they were supposed to be empty.

The tension was tightening his spinal cord again, and he knew it wasn't just because any one of the trailers could be hiding watchful, suspicious eyes, nor because he was sure things were beginning to break at last. It had more to do with the old, familiar tension, the mounting unease that had visited him many times in the past. The unnatural malevolence that had caused so much destruction in his life.

He went in first and held the door open for Ellie. Many heads turned and watched her with interest as she linked Kelso's arm and went with him to the bar. She smiled at one or two of the less discreet customers and they grinned back, pleased by her attention.

'Don't overdo it,' Kelso whispered. 'They'll have you on your back behind the bar if you're not careful.'

'Just trying to be friendly.'

'Some of these characters might see it differently. What'll you have?'

'I'll stick to scotch.'

Ellie felt a lot better, having rested earlier, showered, and eaten. Kelso had cooked the meal and it hadn't turned out half so bad as she'd expected. Not good, but not that bad. They had walked along the beach before turning off into the town at the appropriate sidestreet, and the cold air had blown away the last of the fogginess from her head. It was dark out, almost black along the shoreline, and each wave was a lonely sound as it crashed against the beach.

'Evening,' the barman said, eyeing Ellie with undisguised appreciation. 'Pint of Old for you, then, and what'll it be for the young lady?'

'Scotch and water.'

'Soda.' Ellie quickly put in, flashing a smile at the barman.

'Soda it be.' He drew a pint of beer from the pump and, as the glass was being filled, Kelso leaned forward on the bar.

'Seen Andy tonight?' he asked casually.

'Andy?'

'Andy Trewick.'

The barman frowned. 'He ain't been in here tonight. No, ain't seen him in here.' He placed the dark liquid on the bar before Kelso and said in a confidential tone, 'And to tell you the truth, he ain't been missed. 'Cept by his guvnor, of course.'

He turned his back to Kelso and shoved a small glass under the whisky optic. He allowed Kelso to add the soda and leaned on the bar. 'Old Tom Adcock's been in a couple of times tonight looking for him. Seemed a bit anxious, too.'

'Tom Adcock?'

'Skipper of the *Rosie*. Trewick's skipper. Called him some names, all right. Didn't turn up for work today, left old Tom short-handed. Why was you looking for him, then?'

'Oh, nothing really. We'd just arranged to have a drink tonight, that was all.'

'Well, you don't want to be drinking with his sort, if you don't mind my saying so. Nothing but trouble, that lad. If I was you, I'd stick with your bird-watching and let well alone. Plenty of nice people around here without getting involved with the likes of him.'

'The likes of him? What d'you mean?'

'Oh, I don't want to be saying. But he likes a good time too much, that lad. He's got a reputation.'

'What for?' Kelso pressed.

'I told you, I'm not saying. He spends too much time with those Yanks, for a start.'

'Yanks?'

'That's right.'

Kelso looked quickly at Ellie and saw she shared his sudden interest. 'From the base?' he said to the barman, but he had gone to serve another customer.

Ellie found it difficult to keep her excitement from showing. 'You're not thinking what I'm thinking, are you?'

Kelso reached inside his reefer jacket for his cigarettes. She refused and he lit one for himself.

'Well?' she persisted.

He blew out the smoke in a long sigh and said, 'It looks interesting, doesn't it?'

'Interesting? You were the . . . '

He looked around and she took the hint, keeping her voice low. 'You were the one looking for a connection.'

He nodded. 'Come to think of it, I've seen him in here a couple of times talking to Americans. I didn't think it important till now.'

'A lot of engineers and suchlike from the NATO base live in flats or houses in the area; there's just not enough room for everybody at the airfield. Some of the unmarried ones move in with local families or share a place in a group. That kind of set-up is ideal for drug parties.'

'And Trewick could be a supplier? It doesn't make sense, though; he's a bloody fisherman, not exactly the type to be a pusher.'

'At least it's a job where he goes out to sea every day. It's an opportunity . . . '

'Wait. Let's move away from the bar.'

Ellie was attracting too many interested glances and he was afraid their conversation would be overheard; he led her through the crowd towards a quiet corner. 'Watch your arse,' he warned her over his shoulder, and she was glad to see his humour had returned; he had seemed strangely moody since the incident in the caravan.

By the time they reached the corner, she had seen the wisdom in his remark. 'What are they, all sex-starved in these parts? Haven't they ever seen a woman before?'

'Arh, but you be a stranger, m'dear. Don't get many strangers 'round here.'

'Your accent's terrible.'

'So's moi lust, m'dear.'

There was a moment's silence between them and he realised there was some truth in his jest. She was a good-looking woman and it had been a long time . . . He pushed the thoughts away, but he knew she had read his mind.

'Er,' Ellie began to say and she was embarrassed by her own stammer. 'Er, I was saying, Trewick has the opportunity . . . '

'Yeah, he gets trips out to sea. But the drifter is watched. It's been searched more than once. There's no way they could risk it.

'It might be worth keeping an eye on the boat for a while, though.'

'I agree. Let's take a walk down to the harbour later, have a nose around. You never know.'

His eyes swung towards the double-doors as they opened: two ruddy-faced men walked in and were greeted by others in the bar. Kelso had almost expected Trewick to arrive. Or maybe the other one, Leather Jacket, It would be interesting to see him again.

But neither man came into the pub that evening and by half-past ten, Kelso felt sure they wouldn't.

'We may as well leave,' he said to Ellie, who was engrossed in a series of framed photographs on the wall behind them. They were pictures of the town under at least four feet of water, several showing small boats being rowed along the high street, others of people being led to safety from their homes across wooden planks; surprisingly some of those being evacuated were smiling as though the whole business was something to enjoy. One or two prints were of great white waves lashing the sea-walls, breaking through.

'That must have been something,' Ellie said. 'When did it happen?'

'1953,' Kelso answered. 'The Coastguard Sector Officer here told me the whole of the east coast was hit by a North Sea storm surge. They reckoned the damage to homes, agricultural land and industrial sites came close to £50 million; that was a hell of a lot of money in those days.'

'Maybe I'll forget about retiring to a little bungalow by the sea.'

Kelso grinned. 'Don't worry, it doesn't happen that often.'

'Once in a lifetime would be enough.' She drained her glass. 'You want to go?'

He took her glass and placed it with his own on a table nearby. 'Let's go down to the harbour and have another look at that drifter.'

She hung on to his arm as they made their way through the crowd towards the exit, clinging close, more for her own protection than to give the impression that they were lovers. It had grown even colder outside, but Ellie was relieved to breathe in deep lungfuls of fresh air after the smoky atmosphere that they had just left. The quietness, too, was refreshing.

There were no lights in the harbour, but clinking sounds drifting across the water gave evidence of the boats moored in its darkness; the bulky black shapes of the two fishing vessels at the quayside were visible in the light from the quarter-moon.

'Should we risk searching Trewick's boat?' Ellie asked.

Kelso shook his head. 'No point. We'd need flashlights for a start, and they'd hardly leave anything incriminating lying around.' He scratched his rough chin and gave an exasperated sight. 'The more I think about it, the more I'm convinced we're barking up the wrong tree. The skipper of this boat, Adcock, is a real old sea-dog, not exactly the type to be mixed up in drugs smuggling. Booze, the odd immigrant every now and again, but not something as heavy as drugs. It doesn't fit.'

'Perhaps times are hard for him.'

'Funnily enough, he said as much today. It still doesn't gel, though. He's too . . .' Kelso searched for the right word ' . . . too bloody *traditional*!'

'Times are changing, Jim, or hadn't you noticed? Nobody's what they seem nowadays.'

He looked sharply at her, but the moonlight was not enough to reveal her expression.

'Let's get back,' he said and walked away from the quayside. Ellie took one last look across the waters of the harbour, then turned and followed him.

The case was even more frustrating to Kelso now; he felt sure things were beginning to move, but there was no other action he personally could take. He had to wait for them – whoever *they* were – to make another move. The question was, would they? His caravan had been searched, Ellie attacked. Would it be left at that? He hunched his shoulders, his mood darkening once more.

'Hey, wait for me!' The girl caught up with him and linked his arm. 'We're supposed to be in love, remember?'

'There's no one around,' he snapped and she flinched away

from him.

Oh go to hell, she thought, keeping a distance of two feet between them. Then, for some reason, he was looking back into the car park they had just passed, craning his neck as though he thought someone was hiding there. She decided not to ask what was wrong, a little tired of his sudden changes of mood by now.

They continued walking, neither of them speaking, keeping to the centre of the narrow backstreet, for there was no room for pavements along its length. It was dark and the only sound was that of their footsteps. Kelso stopped, suddenly alert.

Ellie stared at him and she, too, became aware of the tension in the air. She looked around, the feeling of being observed acute, but she could not see into the shadows.

She cried out when bright light flared from above.

Kelso put a protective arm around Ellie's shoulders and quickly drew her away from the overhead telephone lines. Sparks showered down, each one extinguished before it reached the ground, and the smell of ozone filled the air. The faulty white terminal at the top of the telephone pole spluttered into lifelessness with one final surging flash.

Ellie was shaking, her face buried into his chest, only cautiously looking upward when the crackling and fizzing sounds had stopped.

'What on earth caused that?' she said, still hugged close to Kelso. There was no reply from him. Instead, he led her around the pole, keeping well to the other side of the street, both of them watching the terminals above with nervous expectancy. Ellie breathed a sigh of relief when they were clear. 'Can you still feel it? The air – it seems charged somehow. Filled with . . . with, I don't know – electricity!'

'Static's been discharged into the atmosphere, that's all.' There was a peculiar numbness in his tone.

'I'm not sure that's possible, but if you say so . . . '

'It is. Come on, let's get back.' This time he held on tight to her, his footsteps rapid so that she had to trot almost to keep up with him. His pace slowed only when they were near to the caravan site and, by this time, they were both panting slightly. He quickly scanned the entrance before going in. He dropped his arm away from her as they approached their caravan and she saw he was looking from left to right, searching the shadows for any intruders. He seemed relieved when he tested the door and found it locked. He used his key and put an arm through the open doorway to switch on the light. Ellie blinked her eyes against the sudden glare, then saw the folded white sheet of notepaper lying just inside the doorway.

Kelso ignored it and stepped up into the trailer, making sure it was empty before indicating for her to come in. She picked up the piece of paper and handed it to Kelso. He opened it up, his brow furrowing into a frown as he read the contents.

'What is it?' she asked, eager to know.

There was a half-smile on his lips when he replied, a smile that was not reflected in his eyes. 'It's an invitation,' he said.

EIGHT

ESHLEY HALL was a stark, grey-stoned manor house, impressive when seen from a distance, but disappointing on closer examination. The elegance of the two rows of tall windows along the façade was spoiled by the top storey which seemed somehow truncated, meanly proportioned compared to the building's otherwise generous structure. The effectiveness of two statues mounted on the roofline was impaired by chimneys that seemed added as essentials with no thought given to design harmony. The drive swept round before the building and the wide stone steps leading up to the main entrance restored some sense of splendour. Kelso almost felt obliged to park the battered Ford Escort, on loan from the Suffolk Constabulary, somewhere out of sight from the house. But he didn't; he brought it to a halt directly below the stairway.

He was relieved to get out of the car, for petrol fumes filled the interior to such a degree that he thought it might even be dangerous to smoke inside. He mounted the steps and was reaching for the large brass doorbell when the heavy oak double-doors opened. A thin-faced man, about Kelso's age, wearing a grey business suit and navy blue tie, stood just inside.

'My name's Kelly . . . ' Kelso began to say.

'Yes, we were expecting you. I'm Sir Anthony's personal secretary, Julian Henson. Would you follow me.' It was a command rather than a question. To Kelso's surprise, the grey-suited man stepped out and closed the door behind him. He scrutinised Kelso briefly as he walked past him down the stairs.

'Sir Anthony is in the garden,' he said over his shoulder.

Wonderful, I'd hate to get your house dirty, Kelso said silently, conscious of the stained sneakers and faded denims he wore.

A broad terrace ran the length of the house at the back, with two sets of steps facing each other leading down into the gardens. Kelso paused for a moment at the top of one flight and looked out across the long sloping lawn. The river glistened like blue silver, the forest on the opposite bank a dark contrast against its sun-reflecting surface. Beyond were fields, their undulations gentle, never rising to any great height. The whole garden area was bordered on two sides by square-shaped hedges which were at least seven feet in height; the lawn itself stretched as far as the riverbank, a broad path to one side leading down to a building at the water's edge which, from that distance, looked to be constructed in the same style as Eshley Hall itself. Kelso guessed it was an elaborate shell disguising what could only have been a boathouse. A figure, dressed in blue, caught his eye; the man was sitting in a spot halfway between the house and river, two white, round tables set out before him, one shaded by an umbrella.

'Mr Kelly?'

Henson stood at the bottom of the stairs impatiently looking up at Kelso.

'Sorry.' Kelso descended to the lawn and unhurriedly followed the grey-suited man, who was already far ahead, striding towards the seated figure. He saw the two men briefly conversing, then both heads turned in his direction. The seated man, whom Kelso realised was wearing a blue tracksuit with a lighter blue stripe running down the sides, turned back to the papers he had been studying. Henson kept his eyes on Kelso, his expression grim, as though he disliked everything about the scruffy individual strolling towards them, particularly the length of time it had taken him to cross the lawn.

'This is Mr Kelly, Sir Anthony,' he said crisply at Kelso's arrival.

Sir Anthony pointed towards a chair at the other table without looking up from the document he was reading. Kelso slumped into the seat and looked inquisitively at his host. He was a small man, his appearance neat even in the tracksuit; a white towel was draped around his neck, the ends tucked into the tracksuit's top.

'Some fresh orange juice for Mr Kelly, Julian; he looks as though it might do him some good.' Still he kept his eyes on the paper before him.

'Thank you, Julian,' Kelso said as the personal secretary poured orange juice from a beaker. Ice clinked against glass and Kelso glanced at the remaining debris of what must have been Slauden's breakfast: orange peel, grape stalks and two uneaten figs. He sipped the orange juice and returned his gaze to the man before him only to find two sharp gimlet eyes watching him.

Slauden's features were as concise as his figure, only the nose, bent at its bridge, marring its proportions. A thin, black moustache ran the length of his upper lip, and his hair, scant at the top of his head, was just beginning to grey at its edges.

'I'm glad you accepted my invitation, Mr Kelly.'

I'm almost glad I shaved, Kelso thought, a little uncomfortable under the close inspection he was receiving. 'I'm surprised you know about me.'

'Adleton is a close-knit community; there's always a mild interest in the presence of strangers in the locality – outside of the holiday season, that is. A town councillor, in fact, told me of your particular interest in the area.'

'Your invitation said you might be able to help.'

'Yes, that's possible.' Slauden turned his attention to his personal secretary. 'These seem to be in order,' he said, indicating the mass of documents before him.

'You've studied them all, Sir Anthony?' Henson asked, seeming surprised.

Slauden nodded. 'Every one. Put them in my briefcase and we'll discuss them on the way to London.' He glanced at his wristwatch. 'We'll leave at half-past ten.'

Somehow Kelso knew it would be exactly on the dot of half-past ten. The little man exuded authority, efficiency and exactitude. Beside him, even the crisp-mannered Henson was a slouch.

The papers were gathered up and the secretary departed, striding across the lawn as though he were on his very own marching parade.

'Now, Mr Kelly, I understand you are making a study of the

birdlife in this area.'

Kelso nodded. 'That's right.' He reached for his cigarettes and began to take one from the pack.

'I'd rather you didn't.' A command, not a preference. 'I spend a great deal of my time in the City – in my office, or at various functions – and I'd rather breathe in poison only when the occasion renders it unavoidable.'

Kelso put the cigarettes away.

'Thank you. Your research has been commissioned, or is it merely an indulgence on your part?'

'Oh, yes, I've been commissioned to do it.'

'May I ask by whom?'

'It's a conservation group; I don't think they'd want me to say exactly which group. They'd rather wait until their paper has been published.'

'I see. Has their secrecy any particular purpose?'

'Oh, there's no real secrecy involved. It's just that certain authorities and organisations have a way of being obstructive when they think they're under some kind of investigation.'

'You're not employed by a left-wing group, are you?'

Kelso laughed, but he was beginning to feel uncomfortable; their discussion was rapidly developing into an interrogation. 'No, they're nothing like that. Just people with a conscience, that's all. Conservationists, no more than that.'

'What *is* their view, then?'

'Their view?'

'Yes. Why the research in this area. What is it that disturbs them?'

'Oh, it's not that they're disturbed. They're just trying to find out if there's anything to be disturbed about. They're worried about pollution in the rivers and estuaries driving the birdlife away.'

'Surely you're thinking of the Norfolk waterways. In that I can understand your concern. Summer always finds the rivers and canals of the Broads teeming with human life and all the excreta it brings. Yes, it is an immense problem there; but this is Suffolk, Mr Kelly, a vastly different environment.'

Kelso was thinking fast, not wanting his cover to seem lame. 'Well, it's not just that; it's a combination of things. There's the various air force bases in the area, aircraft flying low overhead.

90

How does the noise affect the birdlife? Then there's the gradual but steady erosion of the coastline, land being eaten away or reclaimed by floods.'

'Ah yes. Well, I think there is little for you or your group to worry about. The noise from aeroplanes, jets or otherwise, doesn't seem to bother our bird colonies one iota. And as for the flooding which, I must admit, has been severe in these parts in the past, you'll find that most wildlife adapts pretty well under any circumstances.'

Slauden stood and was even smaller than Kelso had imagined. 'Come along with me, Mr Kelly, and let me show you something.'

The detective followed him towards the water's edge, his strides long to keep up with Slauden. Everybody seemed to walk in double-time at Eshley Hall.

'Wonderful time of year, don't you agree?' the little man said. 'Full of new life, fresh vitality. You can feel the sap stirring, beginning to rise. The very earth comes alive with thrusting shoots eager for sunlight. The animals have a new urgency. Even the birds lose their timidity. Look at those two there, Mr Kelly, showing off for all the world to see!' He pointed at two birds swooping low over the reeds by the water's edge, searching for dragonflies. 'Wagtails, aren't they?'

'Yellow wagtails,' Kelso answered. 'And they wouldn't be so happy if they saw the marsh harrier over there on the other side of the river.' His homework on the feathered species was paying off; he even sounded good to himself.

The harrier came skimming across the river and the two birds fled, shrieking their shrill warning to others.

'There, Mr Kelly.' Slauden was pointing again. 'Can you see the coot nesting among the rushes. He's lying low because of the harrier.'

'I see him.'

'You'll see much more.'

'I already have. I've been exploring the marshes for three weeks now.'

'Then you'll have found redshank, ringed plover, the oyster-catcher, dunlin . . . so many different species. Even the bearded tit, I'll warrant.'

'Not to mention the avocet.'

'Ah, yes a rare creature indeed. You'll find many – and others

– in my own private bird sanctuary, Mr Kelly.'

'Your own sanctuary?'

'Why, yes, that's why you were invited here. If you follow this path along the riverbank, it will take you beyond my grounds to a heavily wooded area and there you will find all kinds of wildlife, let alone varieties of our winged friends. Investigate, Mr Kelly, then let me know if you're still concerned over pollution and noise in this area. Let me know what you think of my honey buzzards and sooty terns. Try to find the storm petrel, who returns every year to breed. Then I think you will realise your fears are groundless.'

'That's very kind of you . . .'

'Not at all. But please be careful as you approach the woodland; I have a very special visitor indeed nesting in the reeds. He's well hidden, but I spotted him down there just the other day, tunnelling himself in. A goosander, Mr Kelly. Extremely rare in these parts, wouldn't you agree?'

'Yes, yes, very unusual.'

He felt suddenly awkward under Slauden's gaze and turned towards the path he had indicated. 'Down here, you say?'

'You go ahead. I have to get changed for my trip down to London. Snoop around as long as you like, Mr Kelly; I'm sure you'll find much of interest.' With that, Slauden wheeled around and began to jog back towards the house.

He felt disappointed, too, having anticipated a more fruitful outcome to the meeting. Last night, the note pushed under the caravan's door had seemed like an invitation into the spider's web, because of what had preceded it, but now, in the cold light of day and in such natural surroundings, he realised his imagination had been running away with itself. Maybe Ellie, who was at that moment digging into Slauden's background, would turn up something interesting. In the meantime, he would do as the little man suggested: snoop around. He turned and walked along the pathway, away from the nearby boathouse and towards the woodland.

Ellie passed the empty quayside and looked across at the various yachts and motor launches tied to their buoys on the water's calm surface. Earlier, she had phoned the Customs and Excise London headquarters and requested information on Sir Anthony Slauden. She had rung back an hour later and was discouraged by what she learned. Sir Anthony was a well-respected figure in the City, the chairman of a large investment corporation and a director of five other companies, which varied from publishing to pharmaceuticals. He had been a colonel during World War Two, and had been decorated twice. A useful but undistinguished career in the Foreign Office after the war had eventually led to a position in the unit trusts and shares company, which eventually resulted in his chairmanship. The only slight on his name, if it could be called a slight – embarrassment might have been a better word – was that his knighthood had come from a certain retiring Prime Minister's honours list, a list that was regarded with suspicion by the public because of various honours bestowed upon businessmen of somewhat dubious reputations. However, that was hardly Sir Anthony's fault.

He owned three properties in Great Britain: one in Scotland, a small castle no less, Eshley Hall in Suffolk, and a terraced house in Westminster. He often holidayed at a villa he owned in the Algarve. There were no scandals in his life apart from a wife, now dead, who had divorced him seventeen years ago, and a father who had shot himself over a gambling debt when Sir Anthony was only seven. Slauden was sixty-one, played tennis, squash and golf, rarely drank liquor, did not smoke, and regularly gave to various charities. Sir Anthony Slauden merited ten lines in *Who's Who*.

So it looked like his invitation to Kelso had been perfectly genuine; the sequence of events had encouraged Ellie and Kelso to believe it had some special or sinister significance. Ellie turned away from the harbour and began walking back towards the town. On impulse she changed direction to cut across the fields, wanting to take another look at the Preece house. That family were the key to all this, they were the initial reason for the investigation. How had they become the victims of an hallucinogenic drug?

What she saw as she approached the allotments behind the houses made her stop and stare. With a rush of excitement Ellie realised she might – just might – have stumbled upon the answer.

NINE

'NOBODY THOUGHT of checking their food.'

Ellie studied Kelso's face, waiting for a reaction. He shook his head as though refuting her theory, but it did little to dampen her enthusiasm.

'Don't you see, if one of the Preece family had died, they would have had to perform an autopsy; I'm sure they would have found traces of lysergic acid in their digestive system.'

'But the whole canal would have been contaminated for . . . '

'Not necessarily. Look, when I crossed that field today, the old man, the same one we passed yesterday in his allotment, was dipping a watering can into the canal, stream or waterway, whatever you might call it. I spoke to him and he told me it was normal practice for gardeners to use that water for their vegetable crops.'

'But it drains from the marshes; it would be salt water.'

'No, that's just it. It isn't entirely a salt marsh. They's why there's such a mixed combination of salt- and fresh-water marsh wildlife there. Only the lower section has been penetrated by sea water. There *is* a stand tap the gardeners who work the allotments use, but it's further up towards the houses. Unless they want to hose their crops, they find it more convenient to use the canal.'

'It still doesn't explain why no one else was affected.'

'Preece was unlucky. I think the water he scooped up contained a minute sample of acid – it may have been in crystal form – but it was still undiluted enough to have effect. A million to one chance, I admit, but stranger things have happened.'

'You're saying he sprinkled acid on his own vegetables?' Kelso's voice was incredulous.

'That's my guess. And it's not so illogical, is it? Not when you give it further thought.'

He was already giving it further thought. 'Are you saying what I think you're saying?'

She smiled, and it was that hard smile, without warmth. 'You got it. I believe there's a drugs factory somewhere in the area.'

'But they wouldn't be stupid enough to deposit chemical waste, let alone pure acid, into the water system.'

'Of course not. It would have been an accident, a careless mistake that Preece and his wife and son paid for. I'll bet we find they had some nice spring vegetables for their dinner that night.'

'We'll leave the local police to find *that* out.' Kelso rose from the caravan's kitchen table and walked through to the lounge area to retrieve his shoulder-bag. He rummaged inside and came back to the table, laying out the carefully drawn map of the locality. 'Let's see where that waterway runs to,' he said.

Ellie moved her stool around to sit next to him and they both stared intently at the map. Kelso's finger found the waterway and traced its route, travelling away from the coastline. His hand stopped moving and he let out a deep breath. 'It's just open country.'

'Wait a minute. Look here, another waterway runs into it.' She pointed eagerly at the junction and Kelso quickly followed the other waterway's route. 'I don't believe it.' He looked at Ellie, his eyes wide.

'What is it?' she asked impatiently.

'You see where it runs through the wooded area? That's part of Slauden's estate. The waterway passes near to Eshley Hall.'

They stared at each other, neither saying a word. Then Ellie giggled and Kelso's eyes began to narrow and he was grinning, beginning to laugh, himself.

'D'you think it's possible, Jim?' Ellie had stopped laughing, a little wary now of the implications of their suspicions. 'I mean, he's *Sir* Anthony Slauden, a war hero, a patron of the arts, the chairman . . . oh my God. Something else I learned today: one of his businesses is a small pharmaceutical company.'

'So it would be no problem to get hold of large quantities of calcium lactate or any other precursors he needs.'

'Oh Christ, I can't believe it myself now; it fits too well.'

'No, it doesn't. It's all circumstantial. The very character of the man goes against everything we suspect. He's a leading figure of the Establishment. He owns his own bird sanctuary. He's even a bloody health fiend!'

Their elation was beginning to dwindle fast.

'Circumstantial or not, Jim, it does seem to point a finger.' Ellie's tone was insistent. 'Doesn't it?'

'It's worth checking out. We'll keep this to ourselves for now – I'd hate to look stupid – but I think we'll have a closer look at Sir Anthony. Let's take a walk along that waterway tomorrow, see where it goes to in his estate. It might just turn up something.'

'You didn't find anything suspicious today?'

'Not a thing. Of course, I wasn't invited to snoop around near the house; I also had the impression I was going through some kind of interrogation. But then, maybe I'm not the type he likes wandering around his estate – I guess I look a bit radical for his tastes.'

'You don't look like fuzz, that's for sure.'

'I'm a long way from Hendon.'

'I bet they're pleased.'

Kelso grunted and Ellie wasn't sure there was a word contained in the sound. He began to fumble in his pockets for his cigarettes.

'You smoke too much,' she said.

'Yes, Ma.' He offered her one and she shook her head. 'Hungry?' he asked.

Ellie nodded. 'And thirsty. I took the trouble to eat today, but I suppose you didn't.'

'Uh, no.'

'Okay, let me freshen up and I'll cook us something.'

'Let's eat out, save you the trouble.'

'Deal. I'll pay, though; I feel like celebrating a little and I don't think police funds cater for my mood.'

'Let's not get carried away, Ellie.' His tone and expression were serious. 'All this may be just wishful thinking; we've no real evidence as yet.'

'I know, I know. But own up: it looks a little brighter since I came on the scene, right?'

He laughed aloud. 'Yeah, I've got to admit that.' Then he hesitated before speaking again. 'I rang HQ today on the way back from Eshley Hall.'

'Oh yes?' She became wary.

'Ellie, I tried to get you taken off the investigation again.'

'For Christ's sake, why?' she said angrily. 'I'm not incompetent, am I? I'm not getting in your way? What the hell did you tell them?'

'It doesn't matter. They refused, anyway. They said exactly as before: you're a good operative and our departments have to co-operate with each other. They told me to grow up, too.'

'Grow up?'

'I said it was awkward sharing a caravan with a woman.'

Her eyes rolled heavenwards. 'And they told you to grow up.'

'And to make the most of it.'

She flushed red for a moment. 'Did you report that I'd been knocked out by an intruder?.'

'No.'

'But . . . ' she began to say.

He leaned forward, elbows on the table, cigarette pointed towards her as though it were a full stop to her protests. 'If I had, they'd have sent a team down here. Softly, softly, would have become crash, bang. You know what they're like when women – ours or yours – are involved. Christ, they're bad enough when there's violence against one of their men. I couldn't take the chance of letting them spoil a low-profile operation. You understand that?'

'Yes, of course I do. I'm in agreement. So that's why you used the lame excuse of our sharing the caravan.'

'I felt pretty stupid.'

'It *was* pretty stupid. But let's forget it, okay? I told you before, you're stuck with me, so you might as well resign yourself to the fact. Now, let me get myself together and I'll treat you to a feast. You look kind of untidy yourself, by the way.'

'You're not angry?'

Ellie was standing, ready to move away from the table. She stared down at him. 'I'm angry; but there's no point to it.' She rested her hands on the table-top. 'Is there anything else on your mind, Jim? Anything else you're worried about?' Come on, she thought silently, bring it out into the open. You're no jinx; it's just a label others have stuck on you.

He drew in on the cigarette and avoided looking into her eyes. 'No, there's nothing. What else should there be?'

'Okay.' She turned away and closed the sliding door between the kitchen and sleeping quarters. Kelso ran a hand through his thick, dark hair and listened to her movements. His face was grim.

The restaurant, which was really part of an inn, was situated on a quiet road leading towards the main London route. There were few diners that evening and the atmosphere was relaxed, informal, the lighting subdued, the service unobtrusive.

Ellie looked across at Kelso, smiling as she watched him concentrate on the huge sirloin steak before him. He ate steadily, as though devouring the food was a task that needed all his attention and deliberation. The candle at the table's centre glowed warmly through the red glass in which it was encased, giving his face a rounded softness that usually was not apparent. With his hair neatly combed and wearing the only tie he owned – a narrow one which, he professed, had been in fashion when he had bought it, became dated with the advent of broader widths, and was the current height of fashion once more – he looked a world apart from the unshaven, tousled-hair character she had first met. His nose was slightly crooked, his chin only just firm enough, his lips about right; but it was his eyes that drew the attention. They were of the deepest blue, almost black in the subdued lighting of the restaurant, and were strangely both soft and intense when staring directly at her. They were framed by dark lashes that any girl would have envied and only his eyebrows, rising to sharp corners at their apex before descending towards his cheekbones, gave his features a harshness that was attractive yet a little intimidating. He reached for his wine glass and caught her gazing at him.

He smiled, raising his glass to her, and she quickly reached for her own wine, feeling her face flush red again, this time in schoolgirlish embarrassment rather than anger.

'How's your stroganoff?' he asked quietly.

'Fine. Your steak?'

'It's good. I didn't realise I was so hungry.'

'It seems you never do.'

He sipped the wine, watching her over the rim of his glass. 'You still haven't told me why,' he said, putting down the glass. She looked enquiringly at him. 'Why you're not married,' he said, cutting into the steak once more.

'Oh.'

'Any reason?'

'The usual. I'm still waiting for the right one to come along. I suppose I'm somewhat naïve.'

'I don't think so. Have you looked hard enough?'

'Haven't tried. I like my job too much, I guess; it takes up most of my time. Jim, I want to ask you something, and I'd appreciate a straight answer.'

'Is this Leap Year?'

'Be serious, just for a moment.'

He stopped cutting and laid his knife and fork down. 'Go ahead.'

She hesitated, then plunged straight in. 'When I was being briefed on this job, I made some of my own enquiries. About you.'

He picked up his knife and fork again and resumed cutting. She was undeterred.

'A friend on the Force told me you had something of a reputation.'

'Let's drop it, Ellie.'

'Don't be angry. I just want to find out if that's the reason you wanted me off this investigation. Whether it's that or it's just because I'm a woman and not up to your standards.'

'Your friend told you I'm a jinx. A Jonah, I think the popular word is.'

'He said a few of the operations you were involved in had ended badly.'

'Only a few? Yes, I suppose there were only a few; but that's all it takes for people to believe that you're bad news. Why do you think I got transferred to this detail? My last op. – a security van blag, – got fouled up. A policeman was shot, killed, and he was only a driver.'

'But that could hardly have been your fault.'

'It was, though. I had the gunman in my sights; I could have stopped him using his shotgun. My gun jammed and the driver was wasted.'

'How can you blame . . . ?'

'I know. It was the gun's fault, not mine. But other things have happened; this was just another piece of bad luck in a chain of unfortunate incidents.'

'This is silly, Jim. Do you think it could happen again? Is that what's worrying you?'

'Why should it stop now. It's dogged me all my life.'

'You're not serious. You can't really believe. . . '

'Ellie, I know certain things happen around me. Things that are inexplicable, bad things that defy logic. I just don't want anybody else to get hurt.'

'I've never heard such self-indulgent nonsense in all my life.' She felt angry, but her voice was restrained. 'Just because you've run into bad luck now and again, it's no reason to wallow in self-pity and imagine you're the cause of other people's mishaps.'

'I'm not wallowing in self-pity!'

'You listen to me!' Her glass thumped down on the table and heads were turned in their direction. 'You listen to me,' Ellie repeated, her voice softer, but still as harsh. 'There is no such thing as a jinx, or a Jonah. It's something people have invented to suit their own tiny minds, something that helps them put troubles and misfortunes into tidy little boxes. It's in the same league as curses and spells and witchcraft and ghouls. It has nothing to do with real life, Jim!'

'You don't understand. You don't know what's happened in the past.'

'So tell me. Maybe I can make some sense of it.'

He shook his head. 'I don't think anyone can do that.'

Suddenly, she wanted to reach out and touch him, to hold him close and tell him the only thing to fear was himself, that destructive part of his mind which made him believe he was cursed. Then she was holding his hand and his eyes were confused; for the briefest of moments – and she might have been mistaken – she felt pressure on her own hand as he squeezed it tight, but then he was withdrawing, pulling his hand free, picking up the fallen fork once more.

'Okay,' she said, emotion slowly draining away. 'Let's forget about it. I'd hate to intrude on your self-made misery. We've got a job to do, so let's just get on with it. No pocket-book Freud from me, no quirky misapprehensions from you. Strictly business, forget anything personal. Does that suit you?'

'Ellie, I . . . '

'Does it?'

'All right.' He began eating again and Ellie attacked her own food, not understanding the resentment she felt, the anger seething inside her. Disliking the feeling of rejection.

The rest of the meal was eaten in moody silence, save for the few formal courtesies of dining etiquette, and by the time coffee had arrived, Ellie was already beginning to regret her insistence on bringing up the subject. She hadn't meant to upset him, hadn't meant to upset herself. They worked well together, they might even achieve some results on this case. And there was something about him . . . she bit down on her lower lip. For Christ's sake, Ellie, shut up and drink up! She finished the coffee and picked up the bill that had been left on his side of the table. It had crossed her mind to slip the money to him beneath the table, but decided he would not have been at all embarrassed by her paying. She was right, he wasn't. He was too preoccupied with his own brooding thoughts.

They left the restaurant and drove back towards the town, the car's headlights cutting through the darkness like wide-beamed lasers through solid matter. When they reached the empty streets of the town he turned right towards the high street, away from the caravan site. 'I thought we'd have another look in the pub – maybe Trewick will be there tonight.'

Ellie said nothing, still a little perplexed by her own feelings.

The bar was crowded, the thick smoke rushing towards the door like swirling fog when they walked in. Kelso quickly and surreptitiously scanned the faces and was disappointed once more not to find Trewick's among them. It was strange, for up until last night, the young bearded fisherman was a regular patron of the pub; Kelso had seen him there on most of his visits. He wondered if Trewick had been absent from work again that day.

Ellie quickly moved to a vacant seat she had spotted while

Kelso pushed his way up to the bar. He leaned against it and waved a pound note in the air to attract the barman's attention, when he caught sight of a familiar face at the end of the counter.

It was Tom Adcock, skipper of the *Rosie,* and he sat staring down at his pint of bitter as though it contained the troubles of the world.

Ellie was puzzled to see Kelso winding his way through the crowd once more, heading towards the end of the bar. He stopped by a bulky-looking man with grey whiskers, a mean-looking individual who sat alone with both elbows on the counter, a sullen expression on his face.

'Just fuck off and leave me alone,' Adcock growled, then took a long swig of his beer.

'I only asked you if you'd like another drink,' Kelso said patiently.

'Why would you be buying me a drink?'

'No reason. It was just that we'd chatted yesterday and tonight you look as though you needed cheering up.'

'Well I don't. Not by you, anyway.'

'Okay, fair enough.'

The barman had reached Kelso by then. 'Usual, is it?'

'Please. And a scotch and soda.' He turned once more to Adcock. 'Sure you won't have one?'

A low growling noise was the only reply he got. The barman winked at Kelso and turned away, walking down to the pumps.

Kelso was almost afraid to ask but he knew he had to. 'I, um . . . you haven't seen Andy today, have you?'

The silence was as unsettling as the growling. Adcock slowly swivelled his head towards the detective and fixed him with his glare. 'Why are you so fuckin interested in Andy? What's he to you?'

'I told you yesterday: we were going to have a drink together.'

'Well he's not around. Not likely to be, neither.'

'What d'you mean?'

The fisherman ignored him and drained his glass in one mighty swallow. He slammed it down on the counter and bellowed. 'Let's have another one in there, Ron.'

The barman waved an acknowledgement and continued drawing Kelso's bitter.

'Where's Andy got to?' Kelso persisted.

'Away. Now fuck off and leave me alone, you snoopy little bastid. Likes of you got Andy into trouble.'

'What kind of trouble?'

Kelso felt his knees go weak as the fisherman slowly rose from the stool and towered over him. 'I didn't say nothing about no trouble. You just keep on, boy, and you'll find my fist down the back of your throat. Now get out of my way.' He pushed past Kelso, who staggered back against the bar, then thrust his way through the crowd, the more observant and wiser drinkers stepping back from his path.

Kelso turned as the barman placed the drinks he had ordered on the bar top. 'Doesn't take much to upset old Tom, does it,' the detective remarked, feeling a little shaken.

The barman chuckled and plucked the pound note from Kelso's hand. 'He's been in here all evening drinking hisself silly. I don't know what gets into him sometimes.'

Kelso took the drinks over to Ellie's table, not before he had gulped down some of the beer, though.

'What was all that about?' she asked as he slid onto the bench next to her. 'I thought he was going to eat you.'

'He didn't like my smooth manner.' Kelso drank more of the bitter and felt his nerves beginning to calm down a little. 'Come to think of it, I didn't go much on his,' he said.

'Who was he?'

'Trewick's skipper. And he said Andy isn't around anymore.'

'What did he mean by *that*?'

'He felt disinclined to explain.' Kelso frowned and put his glass down on the table. 'Strange, though. He got really upset when I asked about Trewick. Said I was the sort who got him into trouble. He'd ordered another beer, too, but didn't wait for it.'

'You think this Trewick has done something to upset him?'

'Well, maybe he's just skipped off for a couple of days and the old man feels let down.'

'Or he's got himself into trouble and his skipper's keeping quiet about it.'

'Could be. I'd like to know just what he's been up to, though. It might be interesting.'

They both sipped their drinks, then Kelso took Ellie by surprise by moving closer to her and putting an arm around her shoulders. She looked quizzically at him.

'We're supposed to be in love, remember?' There was a glint of amusement in his eyes. 'They should have sent someone less attractive; you draw too much attention.'

The stares and winks in her direction had not entirely gone unnoticed by Ellie. She kissed his cheek. 'Just to make it look good,' she explained.

He surprised her again by returning the kiss. 'That was because I felt like it,' he said.

Ellie gave a tiny shake of her head. 'You're a strange one, Jim. You change moods so fast.'

'I'm sorry about earlier. I know I'm difficult at times, but I promise you, there is some truth in what I told you.'

'Do you want to talk about it now?'

He paused and she knew he was trying to decide in his own mind. Finally he said, 'No, Ellie. I think we should do as you said, keep this on a professional basis. If it's any use to you, I think you're good at your job. And I also like your company.'

She smiled. 'Okay, you're the boss. What happens next?'

'I feel kind of beat. Let's relax and enjoy our drinks for a while, then we'll take another look at the harbour. There's something drawing me to that place like a bloody magnet, but I don't know what. Somehow I feel the answer is there, staring us in the face.'

Ellie frowned. 'I know what you mean – I have the same feeling. Maybe whoever lives in that – what was it called? The Martello Tower? – maybe they've seen something suspicious going on. They'd have a clear view of the estuary and harbour; they can even see a good stretch of the coastline from there.'

'I'm not sure there's anyone in residence at the moment. Anyway, we can hardly knock them up this late, and even if we did, what could we say? I don't think they'd welcome questions on birdlife this time of night.'

'True, but we could take a look, see what they're able to see. It might give us some ideas.'

Kelso refrained from telling her he had spent hours along that point and had found nothing to arouse his suspicions; instead he agreed they should take a look and then turn in. He was suddenly aware that having Ellie in the caravan with him tonight would be even more disturbing than on previous nights.

They continued chatting, keeping their conversation light and away from their investigation, discussing any topic that came into their heads. She enjoyed his quiet but wry sense of humour; and he enjoyed her appreciation of his quiet but wry sense of humour; she was an enthusiastic listener, with a ready laugh and, although there was still some reserve on his part, her natural affability was beginning to bridge the distance between them. Ellie now understood why he was a good undercover man, for he had a toughness about him – not obvious at first – that had to be respected, and a casual manner that must have made it easy for him to be accepted by members of the criminal fraternity. It was a pity that past misfortunes, exaggerated or perhaps exploited by others, forced him to back away so often, to hide behind a barrier of aloofness. The silly stigma that he had been labelled with – and one in which he seemed to believe himself – was enough to make anybody moody.

They left the pub half an hour later, both feeling more relaxed than when they had entered. Kelso held the Escort's door open for Ellie. She watched him through the windscreen as he walked around to the driver's side, his shoulders hunched against the light drizzle that had started, longish dark hair flowing over his upturned jacket collar, and smiled when he hand-leapt over the corner of the bonnet rather than walk around it. She was glad, at least, that he had broken out of the earlier sullen mood.

Kelso got into the car and switched on the ignition. He caught her studying him.

'You okay?' he asked.

'I'm fine.'

'Right.'

The car moved slowly away from the kerb, heading down the high street towards the harbour. Neither Ellie nor Kelso had noticed the car parked further along the road and the three men inside who had watched with silent interest as they had left the pub. It was only when Kelso's Escort was some distance away that the car moved out and began to follow.

April, 1960

THE LONE Ranger galloped over the debris, slapping his own backside for extra speed because there was no Silver between his legs. There were Indians all around, shooting arrows from the glassless windows of the bombed-out buildings, and he had to weave and dodge, calling for the invisible Tonto to do the same; if either one of them went down out here, there would be no hope – their scalps would be lifted. But The Lone Ranger did go down, for he had failed to see the metal piping protruding from the ground. He cried out as he hit the earth, scattered half-buried bricks making the impact even harsher.

He lay there stunned for a few moments, fighting back the welling tears, even thought there was no one around to see him cry. He finally sat up, no longer the Masked Man, but just a skinny kid who had come a cropper. He sniffed as he brushed the dust from his hands, then reached down and rubbed his sore ankle; he groaned not through pain, but because of the small rent in one knee of his jeans. Mum was going to be upset about that – not angry, she never really got angry with him. The jeans were only two months old, his first pair of long trousers, bought for him because he had told her the other kids laughed at his skinny white legs. Dad wouldn't be too pleased, either.

The boy got to his feet and gingerly tested his ankle. It was okay, it bore his weight. He examined the tear once more, holding the sides together in the vain hope they would stick. They didn't, as he knew they wouldn't. Mum would patch them and maybe Dad wouldn't notice, although, as a policeman, there wasn't much that got past him. He ran a finger beneath his nose, sniffing as he did so. Twerp, he called himself. He'd been warned not to play on the bomb-sites, now he'd paid the penalty. There'd be no *Gun Law* tonight.

He limped over to a pile of rubble and sat, stretching out his legs to dust the dirt from them. It was a warm day, the sun not fierce, but friendly enough. A single fly, deceived into birth by the fair weather, buzzed around his head; he snatched at it, almost sure its wings had brushed his palm at one point. The fly's antennae sensed a more interesting prospect and zoomed away to the drying human excrement just inside the open doorway of a gutted building. The boy scratched his cheek, then brushed his long, dark fringe away from his eyes. He knew he should hurry home, that Mum grew anxious when he was late and Dad, as always, would have a few little chores for him to do in the house; but it was nice sitting here among the dirt, nice being out of school, and nice feeling the sun's heat after such a long, dreary winter. The bright blue sky, with just a few puffy clouds hanging motionless, reminded him that the long, no-school, summer months were not far away. Weeks that seemed to stretch into years, days that wallowed in a vacuum of time. Playing, helping Dad, pictures at the Bug-hole on Fridays, helping Dad, shopping with Mum, helping Dad, playing and more playing and more playing. Then, with a bit of luck, if he had passed the scholarship, the new school. The grammar school. A uniform and homework. It must be funny to do schoolwork at home. All boys there, no girls. He quite liked girls really.

He noticed a line of ants passing by his right foot and jerked himself up so that his chin was touching his knees; he peered down at the ants, studying their black, scurrying forms with frowning concentration. There were two lines, in fact, both moving in opposite directions, so close it seemed each ant would bump into its approaching partner. None ever collided, though; they would stop and, it seemed to the boy, indulge in a quick excited conversation, then move around each other, journeying on to where the other had just come from. He picked up a chunk of brick that was lying nearby and, careful not to squash any of the little creatures, planted it firmly in their path, wondering how they would react. What would he have done if a ten-storey building had just been plonked down in front of him? Run a mile, that's what. The ants didn't; they weren't even puzzled by the massive object. They scuttled around it, both sides instinctively choosing the same route so their contact would not be broken. The boy smiled admiringly.

He whirled round when another brick, a whole one this time, smashed into his. Three boys leered down at him from the top of a mini-hill of stacked dirt and debris. He recognised one immediately: Billy Cross, same age as himself, in his class at school. The other two were older – about fourteen or fifteen, both wearing bum-freezer jackets, winklepicker shoes, and nasty grins. They ran down the rubble like three banshees, hooting and shoving, reckless in their descent. One tripped near the bottom and went scudding to his knees. He cursed as he rolled over in the dust, the other two skidding to a halt and laughing. The squatting boy nervously joined in the laughter.

'What you fuckin laughin at?' The fallen youth had picked himself up and was glaring at the boy.

'Yeah, what you fuckin laughin at, Kelso?' The one from the boy's class was standing over him, his podgy red hands clenched into tight fists.

'Nothing,' Jimmy Kelso answered, looking back down at the ants and seeing the crashed brick had disorganised their line, the flow panic-stricken now rather than swift.

'Who's he, then?' The other, older boy, the one who had been laughing at his companion a moment before, had come forward to stand over Jimmy.

'He's in my class – Jimmy Kelso's his name.'

Jimmy now recognised the older boy: he was Billy Cross's brother, Davey, a senior year pupil.

'What you doin here, kid?' Cross's brother asked, kicking dirt onto the fleeing ants.

'Nothing.' Jimmy tried to make his reply as friendly as possible.

'Nothing, nothing,' the older boy mimicked. 'You're not laughin at nothin, you're not doin nothin. Fuckin dead loss, int yuh?'

Jimmy kept silent, not enjoying the fluttering feeling inside his bowels. He didn't much like Billy Cross – he was one of those kids with fat fists and a fat head, who had a lot to say for himself in the playground, but little to say in the classroom.

Jimmy had fought him once, and lost – badly. He didn't feel like going through the same punishment again especially with Davey Cross there to help his brother just in case, by some miracle, Jimmy came out on top.

'What's this little cunt?' The other youth had joined the group and was brushing off dirt from his coat sleeves so it drifted down onto Jimmy's head.

'He's playin with the ants,' Davey Cross reached for the brick and held it high. 'Sputnik Three comin in!' He dropped the brick onto the ants once more, crushing several and laughing gleefully. Jimmy began to rise and rough hand shoved him back.

'Where do'you think you're goin?' Davey asked.

'Going home.'

'Oh, are yuh? You got any money?'

Jimmy looked up at him and shook his head. The two thrupenny bits felt like lead weights in his pockets. He was yanked to his feet.

'Oh yeah? Let's have a look, then.'

Jimmy pulled himself away and took a few steps backwards. 'Keep your hands off,' he warned.

'Saucy little git.' The other youth grabbed his arm.

'Wait a minute, Bri.' Billy Cross was grinning from ear to ear, enjoying himself. 'His old man's a copper. Don't think much of coppers, do we?'

The two older boys looked at one another and slowly shook their grinning heads. 'No, we fuckin don't.'

Davey Cross moved in closer. 'Turn out your pockets, you little copper's bastard.'

'No.' Jimmy's fists clenched tightly.

'Do as you're told.'

'No.'

Jimmy's shirt collar was grabbed and Davey pulled his face close to his own. 'If you don't, you little sod, I'm gonna smash your head in. You got that?'

The boy was too afraid to speak.

'Let's give him a touch of this,' Davey Cross's companion had picked up a short length of hosepipe and was twirling it around his head in his own impression of Lash LaRue.

'You want some of that, kid? You gonna do as you're told?'

Jimmy thought that Davey's sneering face was just about the

110

ugliest thing he had ever seen. He managed to jerk his head from side to side in a negative statement, and then found himself lying flat on his back in the rubble, wincing as sharp edges jabbed into his flesh. 'Leave me alone!' he shouted. 'I'll tell my Dad!'

The other boy and the two youths laughed aloud and this time Jimmy found it difficult to stem the tears that were brimming in his eyes.

'He ain't your dad, anyway,' Billy Cross taunted. 'Your mum told mine – you're adopted. You ain't their kid.'

'Oh, he is a little bastard, then? A right little bastard! I ain't surprised your own mother didn't want you. Still, what an ugly cow she must've been to drop something like you.' Davey's breath exploded from him as Jimmy's head connected with his midriff. They both went down in a flurry of arms and legs, the younger boy on top, hitting out with a fury that momentarily stunned his opponent. Jimmy couldn't see through his tears, but he felt his small fists connecting with firm flesh and occasionally with hard bone. The best Davey could do was to try and cover his face with his arms.

Jimmy felt his hair grabbed from behind and he screamed as he was wrenched backwards. He sprawled in the dirt and heard the whoosh of disturbed air, then, almost instantly, felt the shocking pain in his legs. He screamed again, but there was no respite from the rubber hose as it whacked against his thighs.

'Give me that fuckin thing!' Davey was on his feet and pulling the hose away from the youth named Bri. 'You asked for this, you little git!' He swung the length of hose over his head and brought it crashing down on Jimmy's shins.

The pain seemed to squeeze the boy's heart. 'Don't!' he screamed. 'Please, please don't!'

More pain was his answer.

He tried to rise and felt the lash against his buttocks, causing him to stumble forward onto his knees. Somewhere in the distance he could hear their laughter, the foul curses that accompanied each stroke of the makeshift whip. His hand groped around in the rubble beneath him, closed over something solid, a cracked piece of masonry that had once been part of a fireplace, and then he was blindly throwing it towards the source of his torment, hoping it would kill, maim, or at least stop the nightmare. The yelp he heard told him the missile had found a target. He was on his feet and running before they had got over their surprise.

Something thumped against his back, but he kept going, tears blinding his vision. Their wails of rage and the obscenities they called after him spurred him on; a hail of thrown objects caused him to stumble. He pushed against the ground to force himself up and a brick smashed into little pieces only inches away from his hand. He scrambled on and saw the dark opening ahead; he ducked into it as a length of metal crashed against the door-frame. The sudden gloom confused him and he slid to a halt, blinking furiously to clear the tears. He leaned against the damp wall of the corridor, huge panting breaths broken by painful sobs disturbing the silence of the ruined house.

Jimmy began to see more clearly and could not stop the whimper that escaped him. The corridor was blocked by rubble, timbers and masonry fallen from the floor above. There was no way out. The staircase, its bannister long since gone, many of the steps just open holes, was the only way to go. The shouts outside were drawing nearer, the footsteps louder.

He began to climb the stairs.

'I'll kill the fuckin bastard!' Davey sucked blood from the grazed knuckle which had been struck by the missile Jimmy had thrown. The length of hosepipe was curled into a loop in his other hand, ready to be used again and this time with even more force. He'd teach the skinny little git. He'd pulverise him.

They stopped just a few yards from the opening the boy had fled into and warily looked up at the building, examining its crumbling state before entering. Billy Cross picked up more stones and bricks and began hurling them into the dark corridor. The two older youths joined in, screaming and whooping with the thrill of it all. When no cries replied to their onslaught, Billy and Bri turned to Davey, who drew up a gob of phlegm and spat it into the doorway.

'Come on,' he said to the other two, 'let's go in after him.'

'I don't know, Davey. Those old dumps are a bit iffy.' Bri shook his head as he studied the black, glassless windows, secretly shuddering because they reminded him of a face with the eyes torn out.

'Fuckin chicken are yuh?' Davey scowled at his companion.

'Not me, Davey,' his younger brother piped up. 'I'll come with yuh.'

'You comin, Bri?' There was a challenge in Davey's words.

Bri shrugged. 'Come on, then.'

They raced into the building, their yells even louder as if for their own encouragement. Inside, Bri bumped into Billy, who had bumped into Davey.

'He ain't out the back, there's no way out.' Davey poked his head round a doorway next to him, the door itself hanging at an angle from one hinge, and wrinkled his nose in disdain. 'Phaw! Stinks in there.'

They heard movements from above, bricks falling, unknown objects slithering. Davey leapt for the stairs and cursed when a board cracked beneath his foot. His brother and friend, Bri, thought it hilarious. 'Wait till I get hold of him'' Davey said, giggling himself and carefully extricating his foot from the splintered timber. 'We're coming to get you, pratface!' he called out, whacking the hosepipe against the powdery wall. The others joined in the caterwauling and followed him up, choosing the steps carefully, both a little afraid of the damp, rotting house, but anxious not to show it. The shadows that could have been hiding anything from a dead body to a nest of rats hardly helped their mood.

Davey paused on the top step and stared down at the hole before him. 'Fuckin ell, alf the landin's caved in ere.' He eased himself around the opening and urged the others to follow him. 'Watch ow you go,' he advised them.

He peered into the first doorway and saw the room beyond had no floor. It was difficult to see anything at all in the next room, for the window was intact but covered in grime, making the interior dark, almost impenetrable. 'You in there, kid? I'm warnin yuh, don't make it arder for yourself.' Billy and Bri crowded in behind, the former picking up a lump of wood to throw into the darkest shadow. 'We know you're in there!' he shouted, hurling the wood. It bounced off the wall and clattered to the floor. For a moment there was silence, save for their own excited breathing, then a shower of dust and powdered plaster fell from the ceiling above.

'He's upstairs,' Bri whispered, and they all rushed for the next stairway, forgetting for a moment the poor condition of the floor beneath them. They mounted the stairs, tripping and falling over each other in their haste, laughing and punching, carried away with a sniggering hysteria created by their own fear and a sudden real hate for the boy they were chasing. Davey knew he was going to hurt the boy badly; he didn't know why, but it was a feeling he had no inclination to resist. Maybe it was because of his grazed knuckle; or maybe it was because there was something about the kid that rubbed him the wrong way. It didn't matter: the little git was going to get it.

The higher they went, the worse became the stench from the old house. 'Smells like a fuckin cat's died up ere!' Bri exclaimed.

Billy felt nauseous, the cloying odour clogging his nostrils, sinking into his stomach. He wanted to turn around and go back down, to leave the house, get away from the bomb-site. He didn't like it here anymore, didn't like the game they were playing. Billy was scared.

'All right, bastard, one last chance! If you come out now, we might let you off!' Davey grinned in the darkness, wondering if the kid was sucker enough to believe him.

A door, partially open and charred black as though it had been burnt at some time, faced them across the landing. A rustling sound from inside told them where their quarry was. A sharper sound that could have been a sob confirmed it. The boy was inside the room, shitting himself. Davey laughed and rushed at the door, raising his pointed shoe with the high Cuban heels to kick at the half-burnt door. It swung inwards, breaking free of its rusted hinges, and crashing to the floor. They crammed into the doorway and squinted their eyes to pierce the gloom. There were no sounds inside, just the awful smell. And then a tiny noise, a muffled whimper. They looked across into the far corner.

Something was huddled there in the shadows, a small form pressed up close against the wall. A whimpering sob again.

'Ah,' Davey said in mock-gentle tones. 'Does he want his mummy? Well mummy doesn't want him, do she? Cos he ain't go no real mummy. She got shot of him as soon as she saw him.' He sniggered, then whacked the rubber hose against his own leg. The sharp crack seemed to fill every corner of the decayed room. 'Let's get him.' There was a spitefulness in his voice that even his brother and his friend were nervous of. They

114

moved forward as one and the dark shape across the room seemed to huddle closer into itself.

Davey chuckled aloud and his two companions joined in, although it was more bravado on their part. He began to raise the hosepipe high over his head, its quivering end hanging loosely behind his back, ready to strike, ready to bring it down hard over the skinny kid's skull.

The crouching figure began to turn at their approach, the whimpering dying out but its trembling increasing.

The smirk on Davey's face wavered when dust began swirling around the room, particles shaken from the walls and ceiling as though brushed by an invisible wind. The whole room, like the figure in the corner, seemed to be trembling. Young Billy cried out as the section of floor beneath their feet sagged; he began to whine as timbers gave way; he began to screech as plaster and wood collapsed inwards. And the screaming and tearing of rotted materials was joined by the screams of the three boys, the two brothers and their friend, as they plunged down with the plaster and timber into the depths of the decayed house.

TEN

'LIKE I said, there's no one home.'

Kelso indicated the lightless windows of the peculiarly shaped building.

'It must be nice walking across a bridge to get to your own front door.' Ellie leaned over the wall and tried to see the bottom of the waterless moat surrounding the Martello Tower. 'Like having your own castle.'

'Or your own prison.'

They had left the car parked further down the muddy track which was thinly disguised as a road. On one side of the causeway, the shingle beach gently sloped to the shoreline; on the other side was a steep bank dropping down to another muddy road which ran from the boatyard back towards the harbour. Kelso had seen the bulldozer ahead parked near the centre of the higher track, massive and silent like the bones of some prehistoric metal monster, and hadn't liked the idea of trying to manoeuvre his car between it and the stacked pile of timber in the dark. As they had approached he explained that the machine was used to push back the tons of shingle that were continually being swept over the sea defences in stormy weather, and the timber itself used to build breakwaters. Ellie almost slipped in the mud and he grabbed her to prevent her from going down. She clung to his arm and had held on until they reached the tower.

'Let's go down and walk around the boatyard,' Kelso suggested. 'Who knows, maybe they've got a submarine down there.'

'That would be one way of getting stuff through undetected.'

Kelso laughed. 'It would, yes, except the mouth of the estuary is too shallow. Too many sandbanks, too; the local boatmen have to navigate their way in very carefully.'

They descended the wooden steps leading from the tower's footbridge down to the lower track and he turned to help Ellie from the bottom step. 'Ground's uneven,' he said as an excuse.

There was little sea breeze there, for the high embankment protected them; nevertheless, Ellie pressed close to him as though she were cold. They walked slowly, their attention on the river to their left and the greyish shapes of yachts and motor launches in the boatyard further ahead.

'It's so quiet here.'

'Not when those A-10s are skimming low overhead and bomb disposal are exploding mines left over from the war.'

'But now. It's hard to think there's any corruption going on in a place like this.'

'One thing I've learned over the years, Ellie, is that corruption exists in some form or other wherever you find people.'

'That's so cynical, Jim.'

'True, though. It varies in degree, but it's always around, like a dormant cancer waiting to be aroused.'

'I think you've been involved with criminals for too long. It's clouding your judgement.'

'Maybe so, Ellie. I'd like to be wrong.'

'How about a monastery?'

'What?'

'Corruption – in a monastery?'

'Some, I would think. As I said, it's a matter of degree.'

'How about the courts?'

Kelso laughed aloud.

'Sorry,' she apologised sheepishly. 'I asked for that.'

He stopped and faced her. She looked at him enquiringly when he gently gripped her arms. 'You could be right, Ellie. My view may have become distorted over the years. Too much dealing with scum on both sides of the law, too many things happening that . . . '

He broke off at the sound of an engine roaring into life above them. Two powerful lights flashed into the night, casting beams

118

that seemed to stretch into infinity. Then the lights were pointing downwards, blinding them both and, over the motor's roar, they heard the clanking of metal, the grating of gears.

Kelso had seen the broad expanse of metal perched high above them, the top of the yellow machine's cab just visible behind it, before the bulldozer tipped over the edge.

The bulldozer came at them fast, pushing mud, shingle and rotted timber that had been lying by the side of the earth road above. An empty oil drum bounced ahead of the machine and it was this that just caught Kelso's leg as he tried to pull Ellie aside. They both went down, knocked back into a shallow water-filled dip behind them, Kelso trying to keep his body rolling, but impeded by the girl. The noise was thunderous as the machine swept downwards, its speed hindered by the earth it was scooping from the embankment itself and the fact that its tracks were no longer being turned by the engine. Its own weight was carrying it towards the two figures below.

Kelso was on one knee and pulling at Ellie when he saw the bulldozer had completed its descent and was no more than two yards away, a huge mound of rubble and earth being pushed before it. He shouted a warning to the girl, pulled her upright, tried to throw both their bodies away from the advancing machine's path. But it was too late.

Their legs were swept from beneath them and the world turned upside down. They felt themselves sinking into something soft, then they were being kicked and stabbed by ungiving objects. Kelso felt something tear at his cheek, then he was rising, his grip on the girl lost, his body sliding over the slimy churning earth, over the top of the blade. He tried to stop himself, but there was nothing solid to cling to, nothing that wasn't moving, being twisted and heaved by the huge blade. He was sliding over the edge and knew he would fall into the gap between the blade and caterpillar tracks, to be crushed beneath them. He pushed a hand against the grille covering the machine's engine, but the forward motion was carrying him over the blade's edge, down into the gap. He felt himself slipping.

With a loud groan, the bulldozer slid to a halt and Kelso found himself poised above the deadly channel that no longer offered any threat. He hardly dared to move.

119

Ellie disentangled herself from the clumps of wood and wire, her breaths coming in short, sharp gasps. She felt slime clinging to her face and hands, and had to wipe her eyes with a sleeve to see again. She staggered free of the damp earth and rubble, crawling away on hands and knees, afraid that the machine might burst into activity once more. Finally collapsing onto one elbow, Ellie twisted her body to look back at the bulldozer. She was dimly aware of a car's engine starting up somewhere in the distance, but her attention was caught by the figure, lit up by the earth-mover's lights, lying sprawled across the machine's vertical blade.

'Jim!' Ellie stumbled back to the pile of earth and rubble, treading her way over it to reach Kelso. He turned as she reached him, his face in shadow against the glare of the headlights.

'I'm okay,' he gasped, as she pulled at his arm to drag him away from the metal blade. Together they staggered off the dislodged earth, each one supporting the other, not stopping until they were several yards away from the bulldozer.

They both fell to their knees and Kelso quickly raised a hand to Ellie's face. 'Are you all right? Are you hurt?'

She still had not regained her breath fully, but she managed to nod her head. Kelso wiped the dirt from his eyes and looked back towards the yellow machine that although now lifeless, still looked menacing. He cast his gaze along the ridge above them, looking for movement, but saw nothing.

'What . . . who . . . did it?' Ellie's voice was still breathless. 'Who . . . who tried to kill us?'

He pulled her close, aware of the hysteria that lay just behind her words.

'It's all right, Ellie,' he soothed. 'They've gone, we're safe.'

She clung to him and her breathing became more even. 'We'd better get on to Division, we'd better tell them what's happened.'

'No,' he said firmly.

Ellie pulled herself away from him. 'No? But we've got to, Jim. It's obvious our cover is blown. We've got to get out now while we're still in one piece.'

'No, Ellie, not just yet.'

She could only stare at him.

'Let's get back to the caravan.' He stood and tried to lift Ellie to her feet, but she pulled away from him again.

'You're crazy! We can't let them get away with this!'

Kelso knelt on one knee and spoke softly. 'We don't know why this happened, or if it's got anything at all to do with our investigation. It may have even been an accident.'

'You've got to be kidding! A bulldozer doesn't just start up on its own and try to crush the life out of people!'

He reached out a hand to calm her, but she brushed it aside. 'Listen to me, Ellie,' he persisted, 'I want to find out more before we have this place swamped with backup units. I want some concrete evidence that . . .'

'Isn't what just happened evidence enough?'

'No, it isn't. For all we know it could have been someone playing a nasty prank.'

'I don't believe this!'

'Or maybe it slipped down on its own.'

'You heard the engine, you saw the lights. Jim, what are you saying?'

She saw, rather than felt, his body slump. 'Ellie, I don't want anyone else involved – not just yet.' He spoke the words firmly. 'Please trust me.'

Ellie began to rise, and this time she let him help her. She was surprised to feel his hand shaking, but then, she was trembling herself. They both glanced around, feeling vulnerable in their exposed position. 'Let's get back to the car,' Kelso said, keeping hold of her arm. She noticed he was limping as they walked along the lower, muddy road. Her own body felt battered, but she was sure she had sustained no more than a few bruises. They had both been lucky: if soft earth had not hit them first, the heavy blade of the bulldozer would have surely crushed them.

'Are you hurt?' she asked, still puzzled by his attitude, but calmer now.

'It's just where the oil drum hit me, I think. It was a good thing it knocked us back, otherwise we'd have been under that bulldozer.'

'Smeared across the ground, you mean.'

'Delicately put.' He looked up at the rise above them, his body tense, and Ellie remembered the sound she had heard as she'd dragged herself clear.

'I think whoever it was has gone, Jim. I'm not certain now, but I thought I heard a car start up after we'd been hit. It drove away.'

He seemed relieved. 'You're sure? You're sure you heard it?' His fingers clenched her arm tightly.

'I'm not positive, but I'm pretty certain.'

Kelso breathed a deep sigh.

'You're not serious, are you – about not bringing a team in?' She tried to see his features, but the night was too dark, the dirt on his face making it even more difficult.

'I am. It's too soon. And I really think you should get out of this now.'

'Oh no, not again. We've been through all this– this doesn't change things. I'm still part of this operation and I say we bring in help.'

'All right, stay. But no one else – not yet. I've seen too many operations ruined by wollies stamping their bloody big feet all over the place.'

She pulled him around. 'It's this jinx thing, isn't it? You're afraid it's all going to go wrong again.'

'Leave it, Ellie, just leave it alone!'

'No!' she shouted back.

'Give me a couple more days, then. Let me dig up something better than guesses or suspicions.'

'So long as I stick with you.'

Reluctantly, he agreed, knowing it would be useless to argue. He wished, though, he could tell her of his real fears.

Kelso winced as she wiped away the dried blood from the gash in his cheek. Fortunately, the wound wasn't deep and his only other injury, apart from bruising, was a skinned shin. They had returned to the caravan, Kelso checking that it was empty before allowing the girl to enter. Both had showered to remove the caked mud and dirt from their faces and hands, their clothes discarded into a soiled bundle in a corner of the caravan's kitchen. Ellie had on a light-coloured dressing-gown she had

122

brought with her, her hair loose and wet around her face; Kelso, who did not possess such a garment, wore only jeans, a towel draped around his shoulders.

'Let me look at your leg,' she said and he tugged at his denims to reveal his scraped shin. Ellie pulled a face. 'I wish I had something to put on it – I'm afraid I wasn't prepared for any rough stuff. I'll get something in the town tomorrow.'

'It's no problem. Are you cut anywhere.'

She shook her head. 'I had a good look in the shower. I ache a bit and my neck feels stiff – otherwise I'm okay. Apart from my legs feeling like jelly, that is.'

'Could you use a drink?'

'I could.'

He moved off the kitchen stool and reached inside the cup-board overhead where his bottle of scotch was stored. 'D'you want some water with this?'

'I think I need it straight.'

Kelso placed two empty tumblers on the table and half-filled them. He raised his own glass towards her and she returned the gesture before taking a stiff swallow. Her body shivered, but she felt better. He opened the cigarette packet lying on the table and offered her one.

'For Christ's sake, Jim, haven't you noticed yet? I don't smoke.'

'Oh?' He looked surprised. 'Yeah.' He lit one for himself.

'Do you think we'll be safe here, tonight?'

Kelso smiled reassuringly, but she thought there was little confidence behind it. 'I think they've done their worst for one night.'

'So you no longer think it was some kind of bizarre accident?'

For a moment he seemed uncertain. 'You heard a car drive away. My guess is that someone was trying to frighten us – '

'They succeeded.'

'– or was trying to kill us. Either way, they probably think it worked: we're either scared, dead, or badly injured. They won't trouble us again until they know which and I doubt they'd like to cause a commotion on the caravan site – we've got one or two neighbours, you know.'

'That's a comfort.' The scotch, the frightening experience they had been through, and the alcohol consumed before, was combining to make her feel light-headed. 'I think I'm going to be sick,' she said.

Ellie made a lunge for the sink and her eyes blurred as the wonderful dinner she had had found its way back into the outside world. 'I'm sorry,' she apologised between the painful retching, 'I'm sorry.'

Kelso went over to her and rubbed her heaving back in sympathy. He said nothing as he pulled her damp hair back behind her neck, away from her face, and held it there until her body had ceased its spasmodic jerks. He reached for a paper towel as she straightened and handed it to her. She wiped her eyes, mouth, then blew her nose on it. 'I'm sorry,' she apologised yet again.

Kelso removed the cigarette from the corner of his mouth and kissed the top of her head. 'Don't worry about it; I feel a little queasy myself.'

Ellie leaned against him and felt his body momentarily stiffen. Then it relaxed and he was holding her, one hand gently rubbing her back as if to soothe her.

'We'd better turn in,' he said after a while.

She looked up at him and he deliberately ignored the question in her eyes. Ellie sagged against the kitchen sink as he went through into the lounge area and unfolded the settee/bed. He straightened the blankets, then switched off the light. Ellie splashed cold water onto her face before going through to her own bunk bed.

It was much later that movement in the room woke Kelso from a fitful sleep. The caravan was in total darkness and he silently cursed himself for not having left at least one light on. His body tensed and bad dreams fled back into their secret recesses to wait again for slumber's release. A noise, a shuffling sound, then a weight on the bed. Kelso fought back the paralysing dread and began to unfold his body, ready to strike before the intruder had a chance to.

The covers were lifted and a warm, naked body slid in next to him.

'Ellie.'

'Hush, Jim,' she whispered as she moved in close. He felt a hand slide around his waist.

'Ellie, please don't.' The words were spoken tightly, as

124

though he were forcing himself to say them. She could feel him trembling.

'I'm scared, Jim. I don't want to sleep alone.'

'No, you don't understand . . . '

'Can't you feel the atmosphere? It's so cold. Maybe I'm just frightened after what happened – I can't stop thinking about it – but I can't sleep alone tonight. Please don't make me.'

She felt his erection pressing against her stomach and pushed even closer, wanting his whole body to touch hers. Juices had already begun to flow within her and her flesh seemed to flare into a separate excitement wherever it made contact with his.

He moaned, and it might have been a final protest, but his arm reached behind her and its grip tightened. He moved against her, his body smothering hers, and she reacted with him, hands sliding down his back, reaching his buttocks, squeezing, pulling. She felt her breasts being touched, roughly at first, then the strokes becoming more gentle, more tender. He kissed her and the kiss, too, after the initial ferocity, became more gentle. Their lips were warm, moist, pressed together with restrained softness, until her tongue sought his, sliding between his teeth, yearning for its mate. Then his mouth was hard again, demanding and receiving an equal pressure, both of them aroused to an intensity that made them breathless.

His lips moved down to her neck, her shoulder, and then to her breasts. They lingered there and she felt a nipple drawn in, gently bitten, made wet by his tongue. She held his head down and groaned at the pleasure his mouth aroused in her. His hands found her thighs, caressed them, one hand searching inwards, touching her hair, fingers dipping between her legs, finding entry and becoming moist with her.

Ellie reached for him and his penis was hot, its hardness covered by soft skin that was eager to be grasped. He was big and it sent a new surge of excitement through her; she wanted to be filled by him, wanted to be penetrated and pinned to the bed so that she was helpless, powerless to move. Using both hands, she urged him into her, and he complied, lifting his body and moving across her. Her legs parted even further, her knees raised slightly, and she shivered as he felt her inner thighs, deliberately increasing her anticipation before touching the tip of his penis to her damp hidden lips. She guided him in, his own

125

hands now taking the weight of his body, creating a space between them so that entry could be more controlled, not wanting any tightness or pain to spoil the pleasure. Ellie sucked him in greedily, her deft fingers feeding in his full length, demanding all, devouring him until he was deep inside her and their pubic hair was matted together. She cried out and raised her legs around him, closing all her limbs over his body like night-time petals closing around their stamen.

They moved against each other, slowly and deliberately at first, relishing the sweet friction, Kelso withdrawing almost to his tip before plunging smoothly back into the vacuum he had just left, making her moan then sigh with each stroke. The movement became faster and Ellie could no longer prolong the agony; there would be time later for more leisurely lovemaking. She gripped him hard, her legs unfolding and pressing down into the bed beneath her, pushing against it for further thrust. Kelso felt the pressure of his own juices, the wild build-up, the incredible strain that had to be broken, the turbulence inside that had to be released. They both cried out as their bodies shuddered, once, twice, too many times to count, each spasmodic lunge a joy of its own, each one a separate exhilaration that led to the next, the intensity slowly dwindling until everything had gone, their movements weaker, their passion dissolving into a strength-sapping calmness.

His weight bore down on her and she relished it; she stroked his back, fingers running beneath the thick hair that hung over his neck. Ellie was about to speak when the windows of the caravan began to rattle.

Kelso pushed himself away from her and sat up in bed, his body a pale shape in the darkness. The rattling increased and, slowly at first, the walls began to vibrate. It was as though a fierce wind was hurling itself around the caravan, yet there was no sound of a gale, no whistling of air. Ellie raised herself on an elbow and grasped his arm. The vibration became a rocking motion.

'What is it, Jim? What's happening?' She clung to him now, but he seemed unaware of her.

Abruptly, it stopped.

And silence pressed against them.

Then Kelso began to moan, 'No, oh no, no . . .'

ELEVEN

THE FENCE brought them to a halt.

'That's it,' Kelso said, consulting the unfolded map. 'That's the beginning of the Eshley Hall estate.'

The five-foot-high wooden fence bridged the narrow waterway, a stout beam set into the banks supporting the upright struts.

'Does this fence enclose the whole estate?' Ellie asked.

'I think so. Down as far as the riverbank, anyway. It runs into a brick wall nearer the road.'

'So what do we do?'

'We climb over. I'll go first and have a quick scout around – I didn't notice any signs of guard dogs when I saw Slauden yesterday, but it won't hurt to make sure. Will you be all right here for a while?'

'Of course I will.' She instantly regretted snapping at him, but his distant behaviour after the strange happening the night before had begun to irritate her.

'Okay,' he said, dropping his shoulder-bag on to the grass. He grabbed the top of the fence and hauled himself up. Within seconds he had been swallowed up by the heavy foliage on the other side of the fence. Ellie squatted with her back against the wooden struts, using his bag to sit on. The grass was damp, the air misty dull. She pulled her collar tight and looked up at the sky; the clouds were grey and bulky, darkly ominous as though a storm were brewing.

Why was he acting so strangely? In their lovemaking she had

felt truly close to him, not just because of the sex act, for more than their bodies had fused together: it was as though something deep inside both of them had reached out, met, and blended. It couldn't have been just her own imagination – she knew he felt it, too. But after the caravan had stopped its peculiar shaking, he had turned away from her, a low moaning coming from him for a short while, which then faded into a moody silence. She had checked the windows but, as far as she could tell, there was no one lurking outside. Returning to the bed, Ellie had asked him what was wrong. Her own mind had reconciled itself to the fact that, although she had heard no sound, it must have been the wind that had rocked the trailer. There was no other explanation. Kelso would not answer her; he remained curled up in the bed, his knees drawn up, shoulders hunched inwards. She got in next to him and pulled the bedclothes up around them both, snuggling close to his back. Eventually, he had turned and put his arms around her, but still he refused to speak. Ellie had fallen asleep in his embrace and had found him gone from the bed the following morning.

He was in the kitchen, smoking a cigarette and staring down into a cup of half-drunk coffee. Although their conversation appeared normal enough, she sensed his aloofness, his withdrawal into his own inner thoughts. For some reason she, herself, could not understand, Ellie did not mention the previous night's events, or the distance that had sprung up between them. She felt hurt, but refused to show it. His aloofness had persisted during their long hike along the water-way; he seemed to be avoiding her gaze, only occasionally helping her when the terrain became rougher. In the end, her patience having run out, she was ready to confront him over his strange attitude when they had spotted the fence straddling the water. The moment gone, she could now only sit and inwardly fume. Yet there was a vulnerability about him that took the edge off her anger. She wanted to hold him, to draw out that underlying sadness that seemed to be at odds with the other side of him, that part of his nature that was friendly, relaxed – and passionate. Oh yes, he was passionate! He was like two separate people, one being amiable and amusing, the other sullen, morose. What the hell had happened to make him that way? Was this jinx complex so real that it could cause such a personality split? Maybe a good headshrink was what he needed, someone who could help him unload his guilt. Perhaps that was what it was really all about: he really believed he was responsible for the misfortunes of others. And could that be the reason for his behaviour towards her? Did he think the bad luck would rub off on her? Oh Christ, he really did need help.

'Hey!'

Ellie whirled at the whispered sound that came from behind and saw Kelso's face peering at her through the wooden slats.

'You scared me!'

'Sorry. It's all clear over here. D'you want me to help you over?'

'I can manage.' Ellie stood and tossed his bag over the fence. Kelso caught it and waited for her to climb over. He was surprised at her agility, for she was on top of the fence in two quick movements; but as she looked down at him, her balance became unsteady. He reached for her and caught her as she fell.

Kelso held on to her and Ellie secretly smiled: she had only pretended to be unsteady. She looked up at him and he hesitated before kissing her. His kiss was almost desperate, his reluctance to attain the previous night's closeness swept away by a demanding ferocity that left her lips, her cheeks, her neck, bruised and searing hot.

'Ellie . . . ' He seemed to be drawing away, but she clung to him, using her weight to slowly bring him down. They sank to their knees, then they were lying on the ground, foliage closing around them. She returned his kisses, her own desire aroused by his, the sweet memory of his naked body causing a hot flush that started around her chest but which moved down, tightening her abdomen, then seeping between her legs like a soft warm shadow that played on the skin's surface. Ellie pushed herself hard against him, one leg going over his thigh so that he filled the inner cavity that yearned for his pressure, and his fingers touched her cheek, her neck, his lips never leaving hers.

His hand slid between the buttons of her jacket and she quietly moaned as he caressed her breast, the silky material of her blouse no barrier but a sensual ally to his touch. Fingers that trembled only slightly found the buttons to her blouse and then his hand moulded itself around bare flesh, squeezing the nipple so that it rose to a tingling, vibrant peak.

She pulled her mouth away from him, gasping for air, her eyes half-closed, lips curled in a grimace that could have been pain or ecstasy. Daylight, dull thought it was, filtered through the leaves above her, creating a pattern of multi-shaded greens and greys. Her breathing became deeper, its pace increasing as his thigh pressed into her, vagina open and wet beneath the covering material, secretions pouring through as muscles contracted. And then – oh God, no! – then she could no longer control the flow, and she pulled him on top, hands like claws against his back, lifting her pelvis against him, her thighs wrapped around his leg. And she was coming, unable to stop, the rising orgasm too powerful to hold back. Kelso sensed what was happening and did not try to prevent it; he pushed even harder, his hand crushing her flesh, his thigh rigid but moving. She cried out, called his name, and then – unbelievably – the moment was there. The tendons in her neck became taut, her head pressed back into the soil beneath her, her back lifted itself from the ground, and she was climbing, floating, stretching, and small tears were forced from the corners of her eyes, and she was clutching at him, and her release was shattering, explosive, soft, and warm, and calm, and gently sinking. One tear trickled down into her hair and a softly shuddering breath passed between her lips.

'Oh, Jim, I'm sorry.'

He put a finger to her lips and she saw he was smiling.

'I couldn't . . . ' she began to say.

'It's all right, Ellie,' he interrupted. He kissed her and she responded with a warmth that overwhelmed any previous thoughts. 'I couldn't stop myself,' she managed to say at last.

Kelso chuckled. 'I told you. It's all right. It gave me pleasure, too, Ellie.'

'Do you want me to . . . ?'

He shook his head. 'It can wait, there's plenty of time.' He kissed her again and she could feel he had relaxed, his earlier tension dissipated.

'I thought you'd changed. I thought you didn't want me after last night.'

He sighed. 'It's not you, Ellie. I want you – I need you – badly. But I don't want anything to happen to you.' He looked troubled and she was afraid he would lapse back into his earlier

130

mood.

'Nothing *will* happen to me. Can't you see it's all in your own imagination?'

'I just wish that were true.'

'Can you ignore me then, Jim, pretend I don't exist? Pretend nothing has happened between us?'

She felt him tense as thought he was going to roll away from her, but she hung on. He buried his face in her hair and held her close for several moments. 'Maybe it will be different this time,' she heard him say. 'Maybe all my bad luck has just run out.'

But when he sat up and she could see his face, there was still doubt in his eyes.

They came across the deep but narrow gulley soon after they had resumed their trek along the waterway. It was partially covered by undergrowth and it was only by chance that Ellie spotted the opening, for she was on the opposite side of the waterway, studying the bank on Kelso's side.

'Jim, look!'

He followed her pointing finger, then knelt, clearing away some of the foliage to get a clearer view.

'It could be what we're looking for,' he told her. 'It leads off in the direction of the house.' In fact, Kelso was relieved, for he knew that if they had not found something soon, they would have journeyed beyond the house itself and their guess would have been proved wrong. 'Can you get across?' he asked the girl.

'Easy,' she replied, for the waterway had narrowed considerably by that point. She took a few paces back, then came running. Kelso reached for her as one foot thudded into the top of the bank on his side, and pulled her in before she could fall back into the water.

Together they studied the gulley and Kelso caught Ellie frowning. 'What's wrong?' he asked.

'It just occurred to me: no one would be allowed drainage into this kind of canal. It wasn't made for sewage.'

'Of course not.'

'So – if there is a drugs factory on the estate – they couldn't possibly risk using this canal.'

'Unless they had no choice.'

Ellie raised her eyebrows.

'This is the countryside, remember,' he explained. 'Eshley Hall is far enough outside the town for it not to be on main drainage. So they'd have to use a cesspit. Depending on its size, it would have to be emptied three, four, perhaps five times a year. Even if it were a septic tank, it would need emptying at least once a year. And that would be risky.'

'So they would have to make use of the canal.'

'That's my guess. They'd have to have something to flush away their waste, but I'd assume they'd use this drain sparingly, and only for harmless stuff that could be easily dispersed. The acid was a mistake.'

Ellie seemed happier. 'A big one. Let's hope you're right.'

They pushed their way through the undergrowth, following the gulley, both aware and excited by the fact that it had been carefully concealed. Eventually, the ground rose sharply and it was Kelso who uncovered the pipe protruding from a low point in the embankment.

'I'll bet this leads straight up to the house,' he told Ellie. He knelt and caught sight of something lying beneath nearby foliage. 'Look what we have here.'

Ellie shivered when she saw the dead vole. Its eyes were flat and glassy, its jaw stretched open wide as though it had protested its death. The body had not yet begun to decompose. Kelso prodded it with a stiff finger.

'I'd say it's been dead for a couple of days at least. No visible marks to show the cause, but it certainly wasn't old age.'

'Poisoned?'

They looked at each other and there was grim satisfaction on both faces. 'Could well be,' Kelso replied.

He quickly climbed the embankment, then slid down again. 'We're fairly near the house,' he told Ellie. 'I want you to take this thing back and get it opened up. Let's find out for sure what killed it.' He held up a hand when she began to protest. 'If the vole died from chemical poisoning – particularly if it's any chemical used in the making of drugs – then we'll have conclusive proof that our guess is correct. We'll have enough to instigate a search of Slauden's property.'

132

'But why can't we both take it back?'

'Because I want to snoop around a bit.'

'For what? This should be enough for now.' She pointed at the dead animal.

'I'd like to find out how they're getting the raw stuff in. This close to the coast, it *has* to come in by boat.'

'Then why can't I stay with you. You're just trying to get me out of the way again.'

'For Christ's sake, Ellie, I thought you were professional. The sooner we find out the cause of that vole's death, the sooner we'll know whether or not to move in.' His voice softened as he went on: 'Look, don't worry about me – I'm not going to take any risks. I just want to look around, then I'll get out.'

'You looked around the other day – at Slauden's invitation.'

'He kept me well away from this side of the estate. I'm sure if I'd wandered away from the sanctuary, someone would have been there to point me back in the right direction.' He reached inside the shoulder-bag and withdrew a clear plastic container he had intended to use for any chemical samples he might have found. Picking up the small, stiff body, he dropped it into the bag and sealed the top. Ellie took the package from him with obvious disgust.

'Here, keep it in my bag – I won't need it. Now get going, will you, Ellie? And keep this to yourself until you know what killed it. Then tell only me, okay?'

She moved closer to him. 'You won't take any chances?'

'No way.' He put a hand behind her neck and drew her lips to his. His kiss was tender. Ellie regarded him anxiously. 'Promise?'

'Ellie, I've tried for a long time not to feel this way about anyone, but now that I do, I don't intend to let anything spoil it. I'm treading carefully – for your sake and for mine – so will you scram and take a load off my mind?'

She touched his cheek and then was gone, the shoulder-bag clutched to her side.

Kelso swiftly climbed back up the gradient and lay flat near the top, just his head and shoulders showing where the ground levelled off. He could see the big, grey-stoned manor house through the trees no more than two hundred yards away.

Edging his body over the top, the detective crept forward, keeping low and moving silently through the undergrowth. Cover ran out just about seventy yards away from the building and Kelso kept himself hidden behind a stout oak. The ground sloped gently away to the main lawn area at the rear of the house. He wanted to get a closer look at the house, perhaps even get inside, but decided it would be better to wait for a while to make sure there was no one around. He was immediately thankful for making the right decision: a motor cruiser had come into view and it was heading for the boathouse at the end of the long garden. Kelso knew little about boats, but it looked to be the powerful, sea-going kind, about thirty feet in length and having an upper deck. He remembered having seen the cruiser moored in the harbour on several occasions. So this was one of Sir Anthony's little luxuries. Impressive.

He squinted his eyes to see if he could make out who the figures on the upper deck were, but the distance was too great. His binoculars were in the bag he had given Ellie and he silently cursed himself for not having retrieved them before she had left. He would just have to wait patiently until whoever was on the boat came up to the main building. He crouched low, back against the tree, head turned in the direction of the house, and waited. And waited.

Kelso glanced at his wristwatch. Over an hour had gone by since he had first heard the motor cruiser's approach. Were they still in the boathouse, perhaps working on the vessel? They had to be: no one had used the path up to the house. A heavy drop of rain fell from the leaves above him, splattered against the back of his hand. Terrific. Now he was in for a soaking. It could be that they had used the path running along the riverbank on the other side of the boathouse, the building itself cutting off his view. But that didn't make sense: the path only led into the bird sanctuary. Tiny pitter-patter sounds around him made him turn up the collar of his reefer jacket, raindrops beginning to work their way through the leafy layers above. What to do? Observation was one of the duties he liked least, even though it was something he should have become used to by now. He liked to be on the move, routing out or stirring things up rather than sitting and waiting. Especially when it was raining.

He also knew he did not have much time: Ellie was impatient

to bring in reinforcements, even though they had no firm evidence as yet. She believed the incident with the bulldozer the night before was meant as a warning or to get rid of them completely, and she may well have been right; but she knew nothing of his background, only of what others had told her. Ellie could never understand how unnatural happenings in his life had almost become commonplace to him. Maybe not 'commonplace', but he had learned to expect the unexpected. Still, he had to admit to himself, the bulldozer starting up on its own was a little too far-fetched. And Ellie had said she'd heard a car. Even so, this was one operation he did not want jinxed, not just because of his own reputation, but because she was involved. It had been a long time since he had allowed himself such feelings, and now he had become afraid once more. Afraid for her.

Kelso rose from his crouched position, keeping his back against the tree. He wiped a raindrop from his nose, then crept stealthily back into the thicker undergrowth, increasing his speed when he knew he was safely screened from anyone who might be observing from the house. He quickly made his way down towards the water's edge, thankful for the tall hedge that screened the area he was in from the sloping lawns. The hedge ended several yards away from the river and he became more cautious. The strange building, constructed in the same style as Eshley Hall itself, was about a hundred yards away and there was little cover between. He listened for a while, straining his ears to catch the sound of voices or movement inside the boathouse. He was too far away.

With one glance back at the house, Kelso ran forward, keeping his body bent almost double, and dropped down the riverbank. Fortunately, the bank was not too steep and, although one sneakered foot sank into the river, he was able to cling to the earth above the waterline. The bank was almost four feet high in parts and, by crouching, he was able to work himself along without being seen by anyone emerging from the boathouse or coming from the manor house itself. Here and there, where the bank level dipped or was impassable, he was forced to wade through the water, the mud threatening to suck off his soft shoes. He hardly felt the cold, for his concentration was intent on the building ahead; drizzling rain soaked and matted his hair, running down his face and falling from his unshaved chin.

The earth bank ran out, to be replaced by a straight concrete wall. Kelso cautiously raised his head to see how far he had come; the yawning opening to the boathouse was nearby, to his left, but he could not see the cruiser from that angle. He listened, but still heard no sounds coming from the interior. The building couldn't possibly be empty. Unless . . .

Kelso pulled himself over the edge, risking being seen from the house in the distance but having no other choice; he rolled over and came up in a crouching run, making for the side of the grey-stoned building. He smacked into the wall at the side, the palms of his hands cushioning the impact and noise; he stood there frozen, waiting for the sounds of running footsteps or alarmed voices. Nothing happened.

Surprisingly, the boathouse had no windows, which must have made the interior into a huge, black cavern. He eased himself around the corner and crept towards the waterway entrance, hoping no one would emerge as he drew nearer, listening at every step. Narrow walkways were at each side of the large square-shaped entrance, both edged with stiffened rubber to prevent the cruiser's hull being scraped, and serving as alternative access for anyone not wishing to use the door at the rear of the building. Kelso knelt so that his head would not be at eye level, then took a quick look inside, immediately drawing back. His second look was more lingering for, gloomy though the interior was, it was evident that the boathouse was empty. He was puzzled. There was no one on the boat – he would have heard some sound if they were below decks – and the back exit had not been used during the time he had watched. Even if they had emerged while he was making his way down towards the river he would have seen them walking back up to the house. There had to be another exit. And it could only be underground. Kelso wondered if it was a part of the estate's history, or newly built; and if newly built, for what reason?

He stepped inside, his wet sneakers squelching on the concrete.

The motor cruiser gently rocked with the current and it looked even bigger close up. Kelso slushed further into the shadowy interior, his eyes quickly becoming used to the gloom.

He scanned the walls but could find nothing that should not be in a boathouse – as far as he knew, at any rate. Pieces of machinery, an inflatable mounted on its side on one wall, a small crane-line affair, obviously used for lifting engines, a long workbench, a generator of some kind, and even a rack of fishing rods. A wall-phone was by the rear exit. He wondered what chaos would be caused if he picked it up and asked for room service.

Although the boathouse was cluttered with various equipment, there appeared to be a clear area towards the back. As Kelso approached, a rectangular black shape became more visible and suddenly he was smiling with grim satisfaction. The black shape was a hole in the concrete floor, and there were steps leading down. He peered into the depths, but could not make out too much. The hole was deep, the stairs stretching down to a distance that must have been well beyond the boathouse's rear wall. For one brief moment he wanted to turn back – the blackness below looked uninviting – but it would have been pointless at that stage. Yes, sir, I believe Sir Anthony Slauden is up to some skullduggery. Why, sir? Because he's got a hole in his boathouse. No, sir, that's not all, sir. He just may have had someone try and kill me and Miss Shepherd, sir. No, sir, I'm not sure he did. What else, sir? Well, I just don't like him. He's too perfect. No, sir, I wouldn't like to go back on the beat.

Kelso bent low and tried to see more, but it was useless. He descended a few steps then reached into a pocket for a match. The small flame flickered as a draught from somewhere disturbed it, but it gave off enough light for him to see what was below. There was a door, and from where he was perched, it looked as though it was made of metal. He climbed down a few more steps and the flame grew stronger as it moved below ground level. There seemed to be little gap between the door and its frame and Kelso could guess the reason why: that part of the country was prone to floods and if the river rose above the banks, then water would have cascaded down those steps and swamped whatever lay beyond the door. He felt pretty sure there would be flanges at the back which would seal the door tight.

So what was beyond? Sitting there like a half-drowned rat was no way to find out. Hot pain seared his thumb and finger and he dropped the match. Grey light from above quickly filtered through his temporary blindless and he fumbled for the matches once more. He struck one and breathed a sigh of relief, he hated dark, claustrophobic spaces. Always had.

Sticking two spare matches between his teeth for next time, he went down, the sound of his own breathing seeming to echo off the confining walls around him. He was near the bottom when the door swung open.

And when he turned to run back up the stairs, something was blocking out the light from above.

April, 1969

H<small>E HAD</small> been feeling bad all night. He always did when he'd had a row with the old man. And that was pretty frequent nowadays.

But Christ, it was *his* life! He had a right to choose for himself.

Giggles made him turn towards the small rostrum which served as a stage, where the group were packing away their gear, only the drum kit having a life of its own once the plugs had been pulled. Several girls stood around them, trying to chat up the musicians who kidded themselves that their regular gig in the Downbeat, a hall above a pub at Manor House, was just a stepping stone towards Shea Stadium. Even the fact that both the bass player and the drummer were into their thirties – the latter was already washing his hair three times a week to disguise its thinness – did not dampen their ambition. If the lead guitarist would start playing more like Eric Clapton than Hank Marvin, they knew they'd be made. If the lead singer stopped trying to be Buddy Holly their image might improve, too – *Heard It on the Grapevine* didn't exactly go with the Holly style.

'You coming, Jim?'

Two of his friends were making their way through the crowd shuffling towards the only exit. One was pulling on a shortie raincoat, while the other was tying a slim, tartan scarf around his neck. His wire-framed glasses and long flowing hair endeavoured to make him look like John Lennon, but the padded shoulders of his three-button jacket and his Harry Fenton shirt, spoilt the illusion.

'Where you off to?' Kelso asked, swaying slightly from the booze consumed throughout the evening in the downstairs bar.

'Up the Royal. There's nothing here.'

Max, the one who had just spoken, pulled up the collar of his raincoat, then adjusted his kipper tie. He had a second-hand Ford Anglia parked around the corner and the idea was to drive up to Tottenham where a larger assortment of girls would soon be leaving the big dance hall there; it was usually easy to pull some birds if you had a car and it was raining – none of them liked getting their Vidal Sassoons wet waiting for buses.

'No, I don't think so, not tonight. Think I've had enough.'

Max shrugged; he and his companion, Tony, were used to Kelso poodling off on his own. It usually meant he had a dolly lined up, but tonight they hadn't even seen him dance, let alone set up a lumber.

'Come on, Jim,' Tony urged. 'It's only eleven. You've just turned nineteen – you're a big boy now, for fuck's sake.' He, too, was swaying slightly from the drink. He liked to kid people that he was high on weed, but the truth was he'd never tried the stuff, and didn't even know where to get it. And the old bennies were becoming a bit pricey.

'You two go on. I've had it for tonight,' Kelso told them.

'Suit yourself, Jimbo, but I'm telling you now, we're going to score tonight.' Tony grinned, his eyes almost slits behind the glasses.

'Yeah, yeah, don't you always?' Kelso mocked. 'Just don't go baby-snatching.'

Tony looked offended and Max laughed. 'What else would fancy an ugly git like him?' Boppers and grannies, that's about his mark.'

'Don't forget the occasional sheep,' Tony replied without rancour.

'Yeah, even then you don't get a good-looking one.'

Tony feinted a left hook and Max raised his guard. Neither allowed their horseplay to become over-exuberant, for local heavies in the club did not respond kindly to silly sods from outside their manor. Kelso, Max and Tony were from Shoreditch, alien territory.

'See you later then, Jim.' Max waved a hand, later meaning anything from a couple of days to a week, and he and Tony jostled their way back through the crowd, careful not to nudge the wrong people.

Kelso sat on one of the chairs surrounding the dance floor, waiting for the crowd to diminish. A girl sitting opposite, sporting an old-fashioned beehive hairstyle and a nose that was doing its best to touch her chin, stared balefully at him. He gave his best impression of a smile, then turned away. Tony would love you, he thought. She crossed her legs, which weren't too bad, catching his attention again. There was a girl who would hang on to mini-skirts forever – it took a lot of attention away from her conk. He couldn't decide whether her expression, aimed directly across the room at him, was a smile or a sneer. Whichever, it wasn't too enhancing.

The girl was joined by three others, who had been chatting to the band. She said something and they all looked slyly over at him. Oh shit, he thought. She thinks I sat opposite on purpose; she thinks I'm trying to pull it. No chance. He stood and felt all four pairs of eyes on him as he made towards the door. One of them giggled and his ears became hot.

Once outside the club, he whipped off his tie, rolled it up, and stuck it in his jacket pocket. He felt a little light-headed and the fresh air wasn't helping to keep down the pints of beer he'd consumed. He hiccuped.

The bus was waiting at the traffic lights, the large road junction busy at that time of night. Kelso saw the amber signal light up and he quickly weaved through the clutter of young people who, despite the thin drizzle, were reluctant to end the evening, the pavement outside the club both their debating platform and sexual showcase.

Kelso just made the bus as it was moving off. He hung onto the hand-bar, his chest heaving with the sudden exertion and more hiccups. He saw the beehive girl emerging from the club with her three friends, and her nose pointed at him like a zap-gun. He climbed the stairs to the upper deck, not having the nerve to blow her a kiss, nor wanting to shrivel up under her gaze. The air was thick with smoke upstairs, a condition he contributed to by lighting up himself. The cloudy inhalation helped his hiccups. Pulling at his shirt collar so that the pointed tips rested on top of his jacket lapels, he relaxed into a seat and looked down at the bright shopfronts as the bus bullied its way through the late-night traffic. His thoughts returned to the old man.

He liked his dad – his stepfather, to be precise – and their disagreements were few. But the same old topic had arisen between them once more and, as usual, both their tempers had flared. He always regretted the upsets, knew it wasn't good for the old man, but he couldn't fulfil another man's ambitions, not even when that man had taken him in as a kid and brought him up as if he were his natural son. Edward Kelso had been a policeman – a good one too, by all accounts – and although he'd never got beyond the rank of sergeant in the uniformed branch, he loved the service almost as much as he loved his wife and the little orphan he'd made his son.

Angina had forced his career to a premature halt, but he still kept in close contact with the Force, still swapped gossip on the latest blags with his old cronies. He could have stayed on, working at a more relaxed pace behind the scenes, but that wasn't his style: he liked to be up front, right there in the action. And Nellie didn't want him to risk even the desk job anyway. His early-retirement pension from the Force was fair, and she had taken night-time work in the local children's hospital to make things manageable. He hated her working nights, though – said the streets weren't safe for her to be coming home that late. He usually went to meet her and they'd walk home from the hospital, her arm linked through his, like a courting couple out for an evening stroll. Some nights he did not feel well enough to go out, but those occasions were rare, and he would sit and worry until Nellie walked through the front door. Then one night – and, it seemed, almost inevitably because of the old man's fears – she failed to come home.

Jim Kelso had always known Nellie was not his real mother; secrecy regarding his background had never been allowed in the Kelso household. They had brought him from the orphanage when he was barely six years old, for they were childless themselves and saw him as the fruition of their own marriage. Just as his stepfather now saw him as the possible fruition of his own foreshortened career.

Nellie, that lovely little lady who had a will of iron but a soul

142

that was soft and yielding, and who for young Jimmy Kelso, was a mother, friend and mentor, had been hit by a drunken driver, the man claiming he hadn't seen her in the dark. She had smashed through the windscreen, her broken body ending up crumpled in the back seat, one leg dangling through the shattered rear window. Perhaps he hadn't seen her, but then his car should never have mounted the kerb in the first place, something he had at first denied only to be shown photographic evidence of skid marks on the pavement. Kelso hoped the bastard was still in jail, but knew it wasn't likely.

His stepfather had withered before his eyes after that. He had always been a big man, even through his ill-health; after the accident – 'bloody murder' Kelso Senior preferred to call it – he had seemed to shrink within himself. His bitterness and anger grew as his physique somehow became smaller. The Law should have more powers, he never tired of telling his stepson, more powers to stop people behaving like animals, the strength in numbers to prevent any man from hurting another, the right to lock someone up even if they only *thought* he was about to commit a crime. What was once to him a matter of public duty had, over the years, become an obsession and the young Kelso had grown tired of the constant harping. He had his own wounds to lick, his own grief to get over. He had lost two mothers: one had abandoned him for God-only-knew what reason, the other – the mother who really mattered – had been taken away in a manner both brutal and senseless. It was hard to bear, difficult to accept. And an awareness had been growing in him, an unease that had always been with him because of certain things that had happened during his life, things that seemed to have no logical explanation. Things that frightened him. Things that told him – although he constantly rejected the notion – that he was different.

The dispute tonight between him and his stepfather was the usual one, and it concerned his future. Jim Kelso had no desire to join the Police Force – short hair, uniforms, discipline, were not his bag. Law and Order was not that important to him. He'd stayed on at school to take GCE exams for his stepfather's sake, scraping through six of them, but he had the right to shape his own future. He wouldn't be the instrument of someone else's ambition, nor their revenge. Dad had to understand that. The job in the supermarket was only temporary, something to bring money into the house until he had found a more worthwhile occupation, something that he could become involved with, that would sustain his interest. At the moment, though, it was difficult to find a commitment to anything; and *that* Kelso Senior found hard to understand.

If he wanted a commitment, then what was wrong with helping to prevent the erosion of standards in the society they were living in? Couldn't he see what was happening around them? Murders, rapes, robberies – all were on the increase. Lousy, stinking hippies, refusing to work, openly flaunting their pot smoking. *And when was the last time he'd had a haircut?* Degenerate shows in the West End like *Hair*, with people running around with no clothes on. It had taken the Law years to pin something on those murderous villains, the Kray brothers. They were on trial now, guilty beyond doubt, but would they hang for their gangland killings? *Not bloody likely!* Scum like that couldn't be erased anymore. Not even that bastard in the States who'd gunned down Robert Kennedy could be put down like the mad dog he was! It was sickening, the whole bloody world was going into decline and he, his own son, couldn't find any commitment!

The young Kelso had immediately regretted his angry reply, words that shook the old man visibly. He had said he didn't care about the world's morals, didn't care if they blew themselves into oblivion, or murdered, raped, robbed, screwed, smoked, drank themselves to death! It wasn't *his* problem. And his stepfather's pent-up frustrations were not his problem, either!

For just one brief instant, the retired policeman had seemed to grow back into his old size again, and had towered over his stepson, grabbing the boy's lapels, his body shaking with rage, face becoming mottled red with anger. Jim Kelso had been afraid – not for himself, but because he feared the old man's heart would not take the strain. He flinched when the hand came up to strike him. The blow never landed. Instead, the old man's eyes had become distant behind a watery layer and his hands had dropped away. He had become shrunken and old once more.

Kelso had wanted to apologise, had wanted to hold onto his

stepfather and to show him he cared. Had wanted to make him feel a man again. Instead, he'd turned away and left the house, for affection between them had become an embarrassment over the past few years. He had tried to get reeling drunk that night, but neither his mood nor his pocket allowed it. Now he just wanted to get home and somehow make amends.

Kelso stubbed out the final half-inch of cigarette under his foot and grabbed the handrail of the seat in front. He descended the stairs and waited on the platform for the bus to glide to a halt. The rain had stopped and the streets had a shiny freshness to them, lights from shop windows reflected in shimmering patterns.

Cutting down a sidestreet, Kelso tucked his hands into his trouser pockets, hunching his shoulders and staring down at the pavement in front of him. He was still a little unsteady, but the night air no longer threatened to disturb the contents of his stomach. Four pints was all he had been able to afford and much of that had been passed through into the club's john; it felt like the fumes were trapped in the top of his head, though. The next street was his and, as always, he experienced a tiny wave of comfort on seeing his own house. It had always come to him, whether he'd been out for ten minutes or ten days, and he guessed the early years in the orphanage had left an indelible mark on him, an insecurity he was sure he'd never lose. Even though he hardly remembered those parentless years, he had never really shed the fear of them. His home symbolised more than just stability; it represented a refuge from emotionless authority, care without feeling. His adopted parents had given him not just love, but a sense of being his own self, an individual who had family support, prejudiced in his favour, something the State could never provide. Home was both his retreat and stronghold, his buffer and springboard. Dad was still his rock.

He knew there was something wrong even before he'd crossed the street to the front door.

Something cold from within pushed at the lining of his stomach. His right hand was already trembling and he had to steady it with his left to insert the key into its socket.

The hall light was on, the door to the front room ajar. 'Dad?' he called out, and there was no reply.

The small, television lamp was on in the front room, the television itself blank and lifeless. A cup, empty save for stale tealeaves, stood on the magazine table next to his stepfather's armchair; biscuit crumbs littered its saucer. He called out again, but still there was no answer. In bed? Dad would never leave him to wash up his dirty cup.

Kelso walked to the foot of the stairs. 'You up there, Dad?'

He went up, two at a time.

And stopped on the small landing.

An unreasonable dread made him want to stay there: he did not want to look into any of the rooms.

The bathroom door was closed.

'Oh, no, Dad,' he said softly to himself. Recently his stepfather had fallen into the habit of dropping off to sleep in the bath, only pounding on the door rousing him. The young Kelso always made a point of checking on him every ten minutes or so now.

He knocked on the bathroom door. 'Dad? You in there?'

The door was unlocked, a precaution the ex-policeman always took because of his heart condition. Kelso turned the handle and pushed the door open. Blood drained from his face.

He couldn't be sure, but he thought something moved in the periphery of his vision, a flickering shadow or perhaps a steam cloud from the bath itself. Or it might have been his own distorted reflection in the misted mirror on the wall to his right.

He couldn't be sure because his attention was rivetted on the naked figure lying over the edge of the bath, obscene because the buttocks were raised high in the air. Edward Kelso's heavy torso spilled onto the floor like white dough, soft and shapeless. His face was turned towards the door and it was yellowy-blue, the lips dark in colour. His eyes were only half-closed and his mouth was open as though he had screamed in agony before dying.

One hand was clawed, caught up on a rung of the chair that always stood beside the bath. The chair on which the old man always placed his glyceryl trinitrate tables, the pills that were always kept within easy reach lest an angina attack should prove to be the real thing, the real killer.

He had never reached them. The tube was against the wall several feet away, probably swept off the chair by his fumbling

146

hand.

Yet the tube stood upright. As though it had been carefully placed beyond reach.

TWELVE

KELSO SPAT the matches from his mouth and dropped the small flame he was holding. Behind him, the stiff, metal door was slowly opening, throwing a subdued light onto the stairway; above him, whoever was blocking the grey daylight was descending the stairs. He spun around as a flashlight suddenly blinded him, closing his eyes tight against the white pain.

The door below was open wide and the figure that stood there seemed vaguely familiar.

'Don't let him get out!' a voice shouted.

There were others coming through the doorway now and Kelso realised his only chance to get away was up. He turned, shielding his eyes against the flashlight, and grabbed at the foot which was on a level with his head. He yanked hard and the foot came away from the step; the tumbling man yelled in surprise as his body bounced down the stairs. A frantic hand grabbed at Kelso's clothing and he almost fell with the man, but the clawed fingers had not gained a good grip; he threw himself against the wall and the body went by. Kelso bounded up the stairs, reaching for either side of the opening above with both hands to pull himself through. He thought he had made it, when something tugged at his foot, causing him to sprawl flat, half out of the opening. He tried to rise, but there was a firm grip on his leg; twisting over, he saw the head and shoulders of the man who had frightened Trewick in the pub appear from the dark hole. Leather jacket. Missing finger. Whether it was a grin or a sneer on the man's face, he couldn't be sure, but his striking

149

foot wiped away whatever expression it had been. The broad-shouldered man cried out as his nose exploded into a gusher of blood, yet his grip relaxed only momentarily; Kelso had to lash out with his foot twice more before he was free. By then, another figure was emerging from the stairwell.

Kelso was on his feet and running when the other man caught up with him. They went down in a heap, their scrambling bodies rolling against the side of the cruiser so that it drifted a few inches away from the dock on that side.

'Bastard!' the man holding Kelso shouted, as the detective squirmed and lashed out with both fists. A backhander slapped Kelso's head hard against the concrete; ignoring the pain, he retaliated immediately by jabbing stiffened fingers into a point just below his attacker's jawline. The man fell away from him and he used his feet once more to kick himself clear. He was on one knee when Leather Jacket, his chest and lower face covered in blood, came running at him. Kelso managed to turn his head as a booted foot came towards it; the blow glanced across his cheekbone, sending him tottering backwards against the hull of the cruiser and Leather Jacket moved in, the rings on three fingers of his left hand forming a decorative knuckle-duster.

Kelso ducked the clenched fist and went in fast and low, his head thudding into his opponent's stomach. The broad-shouldered man staggered into the shelving on the wall behind, upsetting lubricant containers and tins of paint.

Someone else had jumped from the stairwell now, closely followed by the man who had fallen to the bottom. The one who had stopped Kelso from leaving the boathouse was rising to his feet, a hand clutched to his neck. A tool-rack was nearby and Kelso saw him pluck a heavy-looking wrench from a socket; he thumped the head against the flat of his other hand and looked meaningfully at the detective. He began to move in closer.

Kelso looked around the cavernous building. Two men to his right, one limping from his tumble down the stairs, Leather Jacket gasping for breath against the shelves behind him, and the one with the wrench blocking the only way out.

'Get the bastard!' he heard Leather Jacket wheeze and the three men closed in.

Kelso sprinted towards the cruiser and grabbed the handrail, swinging himself up onto the prow. He slipped, his sneakers still wet from his journey along the riverbank, and felt rough hands pulling at his shoulders. He was hauled from the boat, and allowed to crash down onto the concrete flooring. Fists rained down on him and pain shot through his body as wildly aimed boots sank into his flesh. He tried to roll himself into a ball, but they lifted him to his feet and propelled him back towards the boat which, once again, shifted in the water.

'Hold him there, just fuckin hold him there!' Leather Jacket came lurching away from the shelves, his eyes full of malice above a red mask.

Kelso's arms were pushed backwards against the side of the cruiser and the wrench poked him hard in the stomach. Leather Jacket pushed the wrench-wielding man aside and stood in front of the detective.

'Right, you little bastard. You got this comin!'

He grabbed Kelso's hair and pulled his head up; he smashed his fist into the detective's face, once, twice, once more for good measure. The rings cut into Kelso's skin, grazing both cheekbones and closing one eye. He prevented his nose from being broken by shifting his head fractionally as each punch landed; by the third blow, his senses would not even allow that. He slumped, but his body was held upright.

His attacker stepped back. 'Gimme the wrench!' he shouted at the man behind.

'Hold it, Bannen, you'd better . . . '

'Gimme the fuckin wrench!' He snatched the tool and advanced on Kelso once more. He lifted the limp man's head, again using a grip on his hair. 'I can't kill you yet, cunt, but I can give you something to be gettin on with.'

He brought the wrench up hard between the detective's legs.

Kelso screamed as fire exploded in his groin. The two men at his side could hardly hold him as he doubled up, a stream of saliva spurting from his lips. They let him sink to his knees and his forehead almost touched the concrete floor in his agony. His low moan turned into a sharp gasp as, yet again, his head was yanked upwards. His one good eye was blurred as he looked into the sneering face only inches away. 'When we've done with you mate,' the man called Bannen said softly, 'I'm going to cut off your ears. Then your nose.' He roughly

151

tweaked Kelso's nose between thumb and finger. 'Then, cocker, I'm going to split your eyeballs with a razor blade.'

He stood upright and his swiftly raised knee brought Kelso a painless blackness that he welcomed.

The darkness persisted even when he knew he was awake again; it was the pain that informed him of his returned consciousness. The left side of his face felt strangely frozen yet throbbing and, when he tried to blink, it felt as though the eyelids on that side had been sewn together. His right eye seemed to be still moist from pain-induced tears. He raised a hand to his face, and the effort was slow, forced. He touched the area around his left eye and it felt like someone had packed quick-drying putty over his skin; he winced as his finger probed deeper, deliberately causing himself the hurt because it was better than the numbness. His mouth and throat were clogged with bile and he knew that he must have been sick during his consciousless state. He was lucky he hadn't choked to death on his own vomit.

Kelso spat out what he could of the remaining sickness and fumbled for a handkerchief in his pocket. A shuddering groan escaped him as the ache between his legs became a sharp dagger pressing into his testicles. He lay inert for several long minutes, afraid that movement would cause the stabbing sensation again.

Gradually, a thin band of light came into focus and he realised it was shining from beneath a door. He tried to remember what had happened and his thoughts were hazy, too jumbled to make sense of. Then it came back to him in a rush: finding the drain, the dead animal; the crawl along the riverbank to the boathouse; inside the boathouse, the discreet stairwell, the metal door. He remembered only vaguely the beating he had taken, but Leather Jacket's ugly face only inches away from his was sharp and clear.

How long had he been unconscious? It could have been minutes, it could have been hours. For all he knew, it might well have been days. Kelso tried to raise himself, taking it steady, each inch an aching misery. Feeling a rough wall behind him, he leaned against it, his right temple becoming damp from the brickwork. Where was he? Somewhere in the tunnel running from the boathouse? Maybe beneath Eshley Hall itself. He eased his back round against the wall and slowly drew up his legs. His groin was still tender, but he knew he had not suffered a rupture; the pain would have been much more intense. Kelso licked his lips to smoothe away dried blood.

Thank God Ellie hadn't been with him – he dreaded to think what they might have done to her. She would have sense enough to get the estate raided when she found he hadn't returned to the caravan. Perhaps he should have listened to her in the first place and had the place turned over as soon as they had known something was wrong. He touched a hand to his injured face again. Shit, what a mess! At least he was the only one involved this time.

Kelso tried to stand, but found he was still too weak. Instead, he crawled towards the narrow band of light, puddles on the floor making his knees and hands wet. Although dried blood clogged his nostrils, he was aware of the damp, musty smell of the room; he was definitely beneath ground level and, at one time or another, water from the river had seeped into this room.

He reached the door and its wood texture felt old and sodden. There was no handle on that side, only a keyless lock. He was on his knees, head pressed against its surface, when he heard footsteps outside. A key rattled in the lock and the door was pushed open, knocking him backwards onto the floor. Two heavyset figures peered in at him.

'He's awake,' one said as they came into the cell-like room. Rough hands lifted him to his feet and the two men cursed as his legs gave way.

'You'll bloody stand up, mate, if you know what's good for you,' one said.

Kelso did his best to steady himself and they gripped him tightly, holding him upright. He was propelled forward into a gloomy corridor, its walls shiny damp, its floor uneven and puddle-filled.

'What . . . what is this place?' Kelso managed to ask.

'Shut your mouth,' was the reply.

They half-carried, half-dragged him along the corridor and eventually, after what seemed to be several minutes, they reached a wide, metal door. Kelso wondered if it was the same

153

door which lead back up to the boathouse. He soon realised it wasn't.

The contrast between the dingy passageway and what lay beyond was startling: the metal door – again there were deep flanges to seal it tight when closed – opened out into a huge, low-ceilinged basement area. The walls, floor and ceiling were smooth concrete, the walls themselves covered in a patchy, chalky substance which Kelso guessed was lime; there were no windows, but fluorescent lights made the room unnaturally bright. Two long workbenches dominated the centre area and running between them was a long, open gutter. The worktops were filled with laboratory glassware and equipment; Kelso recognised several rotary evaporators, which he knew were used in the manufacturing of LSD.

The heavy door slammed shut behind him and while it was being locked, he leaned back against the wall, pretending to be more dazed than he actually felt. One of the men held him there as his companion busied himself with bolts and lock. Vision from Kelso's swollen eye was limited, but by turning his head from side to side as though still disorientated, he was able to study the room's contents in more detail. There were many containers on the shelving which lined the walls – bottles, cartons and, at the far end, large drums with the word METHANOL stencilled in white on them. The two men moved him on and he managed to sneak a closer look at the chemicals on the shelves: calcium lactate, hydrazine hydrate, and the substance most necessary for LSD processing, ergotomine tartrate. There were also large containers of starch on the floor beneath the shelves. His senses were beginning to sharpen, revived by the discovery.

They passed gauze trays, obviously used for drying, and two big grey-metalled units which he assumed were watertanks. Twisting his head to the right, he saw on the workbenches machines that he knew were infra-red spectrometers, instruments used for measuring chemical quantities, as well as plastic moulds which puzzled him at first until he saw the hundreds of tiny perforations on their surface. Such moulds were used to shape LSD microdots. He became even more alert when they approached a door at the end of the room, for the shelves at that end were filled with containers clearly labelled

154

TETRAHYDROCANNABINOL. THC – a derivative of cannabis!

This was no small-scale enterprise but a well-stocked and highly organised laboratory, almost a drug manufacturing industry. He wondered what else came off the production line.

The door before him was opened and he was pushed through, this time finding himself in what looked like a conventional cellar, a single lightbulb making a dismal attempt to combat the gloom. Grimy brickwork pillars cast dark shadows into the corners of the cellar and wine racks filled with dusty bottles stood against the walls. A sliding noise made him turn and he saw the door they had just come through was now screened by more wine racks; a long chest was wheeled back to cover the movable rack.

'Okay, up the stairs.' The man who had just concealed the doorway, a short, axe-faced individual, pushed him towards a rickety set of steps. Kelso just caught hold of the bannister, but could not prevent himself from going down on one knee.

'Take it easy, you prat,' he heard the other man say. 'We don't wanna carry him up.'

Kelso was yanked upright and forced to mount the stairs, each step creaking beneath him. His legs felt stiff from bruising, but he managed to get to the top with the aid of the two men. It was almost with relief that he staggered out into the wide hallway of what surely was Eshley Hall itself. It came as somewhat of a shock to see it was dark outside; he *had* been unconscious for hours rather than minutes. The sound of rain beating against the windowpanes, increasing then decreasing in intensity as the wind lent its force, came to his ears. He was almost tempted to make a break for the double-doors at the far end of the hall, but realised he would never make it; he just didn't have the strength yet. Once more he waited while the door behind was locked and he deliberately let his chin sag down onto his chest to further the impression that he was still in a bad state. He forgot the pose when the door opposite opened and Slauden's personal secretary, Henson, stared out at him.

'Bring him in,' Henson snapped.

The first face Kelso saw when he was pushed into the room was that of Sir Anthony Slauden himself. The dapper little man was seated in a deep-brown wing armchair, its high back making him look even smaller; in his hand he held a brandy glass, flames from the roaring log fire reflecting in the amber liquid. He was casually, but still immaculately, attired in grey slacks and a fawn polo-neck sweater; soft, elegantly styled shoes and a tweed jacket with leather elbow patches completed the relaxed image. Slauden frowned when he saw Kelso.

'My God, what have you done to him, Bannen?' he asked angrily.

Leather Jacket was standing by a drinks cabinet. There was no apology in his voice when he replied: 'He put up a bit of a fight.' He lightly touched the side of his nose, which was red and swollen, as if indicating the evidence.

Slauden showed little sympathy for his own man. 'I've told you before, Bannen, I want none of this insane violence. Is that clear?'

Kelso was surprised at the big man's meek response.

Slauden studied the detective for several moments before saying, 'Bring him over here.' He indicated a long settee opposite his own chair and Kelso was led towards it. It felt good to sink into the soft cushions.

'You look as if you could use a stiff drink, Kelly.'

Kelso wondered if Slauden was mocking him.

'Pour him a brandy, Julian,' Slauden ordered, and it was obvious that the personal secretary was not happy with the idea. Nevertheless, he walked briskly to the drinks cabinet and poured a brandy. Kelso found it difficult to keep his hand steady as he took the glass. The first sip hurt his cracked lips, but the hot liquid felt good as it rushed down his throat. For the first time, he noticed a thin, bespectacled man nervously watching him from the other side of the room. The man was sitting at a small, antique writing desk, papers spread out before him. He kept jiggling the PRESS button of a biro against his jaw, his agitation at the sight of Kelso obvious.

The detective's attention was drawn back to Slauden as the little man crossed his legs, tugging at the trouser crease of one knee so that it would not lose its sharpness. 'I don't much approve of alcohol, young man, but a small nip of brandy is another matter,' he said.

Kelso, revived even more by the drink, leaned back into the settee and replied flatly: 'Apparently you approve of drugs, though.'

Slauden smiled. 'Not in the least – hate the damned stuff, as a matter of fact.'

Kelso's uninjured eye widened. 'How the hell can you say that when you've got a bloody drugs factory downstairs?'

'I also have a company that produces animal feedstuff – that doesn't mean I eat it.'

Julian enjoyed the joke; the thin man with the spectacles seemed uncertain that it was one.

Kelso shook his head. 'It doesn't make sense. Why would someone like you, with your wealth and reputation, be involved with the dope trade?'

The smile disappeared. 'For one very simple reason, Kelly, but I don't feel it necessary to answer questions from your kind.'

'My kind?'

'Nasty little scum. A cheap crook. Isn't that what you are – you and your friend Trewick?'

Kelso could only stare.

'Come now, Kelly, you didn't really think I believed you were a damned bird-watcher, did you?' Slauden laughed. 'I know you were only snooping around yesterday looking for your partner in crime.'

Kelso did not know whether to feel relieved, or even more apprehensive: did their error put him in a better or worse situation?

'It was perfectly clear, Kelly, that you had only a rudimentary knowledge of birdlife. Perhaps you could have been forgiven for not knowing that the storm petrel does not, in fact, breed here, but when I tested you further, I'm afraid you failed rather dismally. Rather stupidly, actually.'

'I don't know what you're talking about, Slauden.'

'Of course not. Nor did you yesterday. I informed you that I had a goosander nesting in the reeds by the river; anyone with a good knowledge of the subject would be well aware that the goosander nests in trees.'

'I'd forgotten.'

Again, Slauden laughed, but this time disdainfully. 'What we have to find out from you, *Mr* Kelly, is just how much damage you and Trewick have done to my organisation with your petty pilfering. If, indeed, it was petty.'

'I still don't know what you're talking about.'

Slauden's knuckles showed white around the stem of the glass. 'I really do hope we won't find it necessary to resort to extreme measures. We'll all be very busy after tomorrow and will have little time for foolish games.' He drained the brandy and held out the empty glass; Henson took it from him and placed it on a small leather-topped occasional table. Slauden sat stiffly in his chair, eyes that were almost black fixed on the detective.

'What's happened to Andy?' Kelso asked, more in desperation than out of curiosity.

'Sir Anthony told you not to ask questions,' Bannen said, approaching menacingly.

'Wait, I want no more of that,' Slauden snapped. He watched Kelso thoughtfully for a few minutes, steepled fingers against his lower lip; then he seemed to come to a decision. 'Unfortunately your friend, Trewick, came to some grief. We knew he was stealing from us, you see, but we didn't know to what extent and just who was helping him dispose of the merchandise. Then you came on the scene – you were seen together on separate occasions. His disappearance caused you some concern judging by your attempts to locate him. I wonder if your anxiety was for Trewick or because your source of supply might dry up?'

Kelso swallowed more brandy and said nothing.

'We weren't very sure of your involvement until I invited you here to Eshley Hall. The mistakes you made left little doubt.'

'So you tried to frighten me off last night.'

'No, not at all. I tried to have you killed.'

'Jesus Christ, just because you thought I was stealing drugs from you?'

'My – shall we say "clandestine" – business earns me profits of several million a year; do you imagine I'd let anything or anyone jeopardise that?' Slauden's tiny, well-manicured hands gripped the side of the chair before he controlled his rising anger and relaxed them once more. 'Trewick paid the price of his folly. His rewards for helping to bring the merchandise into the country apparently were not enough for him – he had to create his own market using goods that did not belong to him. His greed could have ruined everything.'

'He brought the drugs in?'

'Come now, Kelly, let's not play these stupid games. I'm sure you're well aware of how the merchandise was smuggled into the country. What I need to know is just how big *your* particular network is. How many others are involved? Or was it just you and Trewick – and, of course, this girl you live with?'

'Didn't Andy tell you?'

'I'm afraid I never had the chance to ask him: Bannen was a little too enthusiastic when his two thugs, here, delivered Trewick to him.'

The two men by the door looked uncomfortable as Bannen began to protest.

Slauden wearily held up a hand. 'Yes, I know, Bannen: he broke his neck falling down the stairs when you brought him back. No doubt Kelly fell down those same stairs.' He turned his attention back to the detective. 'Like you, Trewick was an amateur, a bungler. We would never have known about his thefts had he not made a serious error. With the vast quantities my laboratory processes, under the guidance of our learned chemist, Dr Vernon Collingbury – ' Kelso glanced towards the man sitting at the writing desk and at whom Slauden had briefly pointed ' – his pilfering would have gone on undetected for years, but he used a singularly foolhardy method to get the stolen drugs out – although perhaps the only one because of the thorough searches everyone, without exception, undergoes on leaving the basement area.'

'How did he manage it?'

'You don't know? I'm sure he must have boasted to you.'

Kelso decided to gamble – at least this way he was gathering information and gaining time. If they discovered he was with the Drugs Squad, they would probably get rid of him immediately. They'd have little choice. 'Andy wouldn't tell me how he got hold of the stuff.'

'He's lying,' Henson said.

'Why should I lie about that?' Kelso countered. 'It won't help me any.'

'No, it won't help you at all,' said Slauden. 'Your friend and colleague used a simple idea. He stole very small amounts each time – LSD crystals mainly, because they were easier to handle. A plastic bag containing the drugs was dropped into the labora-

159

tory's drainage system. As you probably realise from the glimpse you had when you were brought up here, our processing requires thousands of gallons of water during distillation to keep the equipment cool and the only way we can shed such amounts is by draining into the local canals or the river. The river is too risky because of traffic – our drainage pipe might be seen.

'We, along with everyone else in the area, were puzzled by the peculiar incident concerning the family living at the edge of town. In such a close, and perhaps, unworldly, community, such occurrences are not common. We became quite alarmed when we realised that the Preece family lived nearby the particular canal in which we disposed of our waste and, because we have always been extremely careful never to flush any harmful substances into the system, we suspected either an accident or that someone was deliberately using the drain for their own surreptitious purposes. The temptation had always been there for those who worked on the processing, but each individual knows the dire consequences of such a misdemeanour. The pipe and drain were examined and a small grille, just big enough to prevent any package of a certain size from passing through, was found across the channel outside the house. Whoever had been stealing merely dropped his package into the waste system, then collected it from the outside at a convenient moment. Unfortunately, on one occasion, the container burst – perhaps it was chewed open by an animal or pecked by a bird – and the contents flushed into the waterway leading towards the town. It was a chance in a million that the Preece family used water containing a tiny amount of diluted LSD crystals, but a chance that could have exposed everything.'

Kelso finished his brandy, and thought of the vole he and Ellie had found: Trewick's little packages might well have had their contents spilled more than once – the animal had not been dead that long.

Slauden continued speaking and Kelso began to suspect that the drugs dealer's frankness was merely a skilful ploy to encourage him to open up and reveal his own part in Trewick's treachery. His only ace was that Slauden seemed to be underestimating his intelligence, treating him like a small-time crook. Some ace. He also wondered if he were not grandstanding for his own hirelings, a little man impressing his minions with his own cleverness. 'We were still not certain of just who was stealing from us, but Andy Trewick was high on our suspicion list. He associated with the Americans on the NATO base, you see – a natural outlet for soft drugs. Also, his social activities were centred around Norwich and Ipswich, where there is a big demand for cannabis and marijuana. The last factor which made him highly suspect was that he was naïve enough to imagine he could get away with it; nobody else in my employ would be so stupid.'

'Amen to that,' Bannen commented, his wide grin accentuating the redness of his swollen nose.

'Trewick was watched very carefully for some time until two events caused us even more concern. One was your arrival in Adleton. Your occasional "chats" with our wayward fisherman seemed innocent enough – we soon learned that you were supposed to be a conservationist – but your anxiety over his disappearance, even though your enquiries seemed casual, confirmed the connection. It was then we had to consider whether Trewick's activities were just confined to the surrounding area, or had branched into a wider field, where the demand – and the price – is always high. We concluded that you were helping to push our property into the London market. And that, my greedy friend, would have proved extremely harmful to us. It also implied that we may have been wrong in estimating just how much was being taken from our laboratory. Dr Collingbury still insists the amount was minimal, but then at present-day street value, a single LSD microdot is worth more than £5, one pound of cannabis is worth between £600 and £700, and a pure cocaine can fetch well over £13,000 per pound. Mix the coke with mild powder or lactose and your profit margin is phenomenal. So you see, quantity is relative to price. And, of course, a new source of supply in the city always creates interest, and speculation from outsiders – be it from the police or others involved in the drugs trade – is something we do not encourage.'

'Look, you've got this all wrong . . . '

'Allow me to finish. I said that there were two events which increased our concern. The second was the most alarming of all.' Slauden reached into the fireplace and picked up a short log lying among others in the hearth. Kelso could feel his own muscles beginning to tauten as he watched him place the log in the fire. Another followed and the flames lapped hungrily at the damp wood. Finally, satisfied that the fire was replenished, Slauden wiped his hands with a handkerchief and settled back in the armchair. 'I learned the other day,' he went on as though he had not interrupted himself, 'from inside sources, that a pilot from the NATO base had deliberately crashed his aircraft into the sea after having injected himself with LSD. I think you can well imagine the stir such an incident caused among the military and the Ministry of Defence. What if the plane had been armed with nuclear missiles? What if the deranged pilot had chosen to attack a strategic target? And what if the whole episode was part of some sinister plot by a foreign power to undermine confidence in the NATO Forces defence structure in Europe? Just imagine, if you can, the furore – suppressed though it was – that broke out.' He gave a short laugh. 'Do you know the enemy whom many US military chiefs of staff fear most? The enemy inside. The left-wing infiltrators who supply their susceptible troops with drugs. It's become a major headache since Vietnam, and the generals are still unsure how to combat it. Reds are no longer under the bed – now they're making it. They know the moral fibre of the fighting man has been weakened by too much soft living and influenced by too much liberal thinking in the media. Pleasure and apathy are the trends, and the soldier, sailor or airman is no different from his civilian counterpart: he wants his share.

'You may have noticed, Kelly, that in England alone, the frequency of military aircraft crashes has increased considerably over recent years. Much of the blame has been attributed to dangerous low-flying training exercises – the only way enemy radar can be foxed; but have you wondered if the cause of the "accidents" was not more sinister? Perhaps you haven't, but those in authority certainly have. And that's why the results of the autopsy on the pilot who crashed a few days ago threw them into such panic. It made matters very uncomfortable for us here, knowing the base would be overturned in trying to locate the drug's source, and we knew that Trewick's dangerous activities would have to be brought to a swift halt.'

162

Kelso was angry despite his fear. 'But you had no definite proof it was him.'

'His running away was proof enough. He knew we were on to him.'

'And you killed him for that?'

'His death was premature, but yes, we would have disposed of him anyway as soon as we had learned what we needed to know.'

'So when I talk, you'll "dispose" of me.'

'Not necessarily. It may be that you can be absorbed into my organisation. If you can prove to me that your outlets are worthwhile, then perhaps you can be of use.'

Kelso did not believe him for one moment, but he was trapped by his own cover, a guise that had developed into something more. He shook his head and said doubtfully, 'I don't know.'

'Then let me take you into my confidence and tell you more of my organisation. Perhaps I'll manage to convince you of my sincerity by showing you how you could fit in.'

'I don't think he should be told anything more,' Henson commented.

'Me, neither,' Bannen put in. 'Let's get rid of him now; you know we can make him disappear off the face of the earth without leaving so much as a fingernail.'

Slauden's eyes blazed. 'I don't believe I need *your* opinion, Bannen. That goes for you, too, Julian. Allow me to handle this in my own way.'

Kelso wanted to make a break for it there and then. He knew ultimately there was no way he could win, no matter how he lied, or whoever listened. He glanced towards the door, but the two men who had brought him up from the basement stood before it, looking bored yet nonetheless menacing. The chemist still sat at the writing desk by the window and looked frightened by the whole situation. Bannen stood beside Slauden's chair, ready to pounce on Kelso at the slightest provocation, while Henson sat nonchalantly on the arm of the settee.

Kelso knew it was no use: even if he had not been in such a battered state, it would have been impossible to tackle all of them. A burning log on the fire crackled and he stared hopelessly into the flames. His attention was drawn back to the small man opposite.

'Our set-up is simply this: we deal in the importation of raw material and the exportation of the fully processed product.' Slauden smiled. 'By "raw material" I do, of course, refer to various basic drugs. Cocaine comes from Peru, cannabis from Pakistan, India and the Middle East. Opium comes mainly from Turkey. My own legitimate chemical company provides certain precursers and compounds used in processing or synthesis, although we bring in ergotomine tartrate, the base used in the synthesis of pure LSD, from a company in Laupheim. Ironically, the government, itself, encourages the production of milk powder in my own mill across the river – providing it's suitable only for animal consumption – whenever the country suffers yet another "milk mountain". All negotiations are carried out in the Algarve area of Portugal, which I'm sorry to say, is fast becoming known as the mecca of such transactions; it's from there that all materials are brought into this country.'

'You've got boats from Portugal coming up-river?' Kelso's curiosity was overcoming his apprehension.

'That would be rather stupid. It could be done, of course, but it would be too risky. Even the once-relatively safe method of smuggling items in aboard light aircraft has become too obvious for safety. No, Kelly, the boats come nowhere near our own shoreline. Surely Trewick told you *that*?'

'I've already told you: he was cagey. He wouldn't let me know too much.'

'And you couldn't work out that the goods were exchanged at sea?'

'Trewick's fishing boat!'

Slauden looked at Kelso in surprise. 'Tom Adcock's boat, actually; your friend was only a deckhand. Do you really mean to say you didn't know?'

'Andy kept everything to himself,' Kelso replied, 'He said it was best I didn't know too much.'

'I see.' The detective caught the look that passed between Slauden and his personal secretary. 'Then no doubt you are anxious to learn just how the goods were brought in under the watchful gaze of the coastguard and police patrols. It's all very

164

simple, really; an idea taken from the Germans in the last world war. They used to secretly bring down submarines through the fjords of Norway into the open sea by towing them beneath harmless-looking trawlers. We have merely adapted their idea: the drugs are sealed in watertight, weighted containers, attached to Adcock's drifter somewhere in the North Sea, then towed back into Adleton's harbour. When the time is right, and always at night, my men – we have some excellent underwater divers – detach the container and hook it onto my own motor cruiser, which is conveniently anchored nearby. From there, the container is brought up-river to my boathouse and its contents unloaded. The underground passageway – built, by the way, by the original owners of Eshley Hall, who were smugglers like myself – provides a discreet and useful link to my laboratory. The empty container is returned for the next run and exchanged for another, which holds the new merchandise. Rather clever, don't you agree?'

'It's beautiful,' Kelso was forced to admit, even though the revelation confirmed his fear that there was no way they would let him go free. Slauden was feeding him the information in the sure knowledge that it would get no further.

'Once we have the, uh, raw materials, as it were, safely in the laboratory, processing and packaging takes place. Our LSD tabletting, for instance: we take great care in producing as many variations of shapes and colours and content as possible, so that they cannot be traced back to one particular source. How many variations do we have now, Dr Collingbury?'

For the first time, the bespectacled man spoke and his voice was as nervous as his demeanour. 'I, er, er, nearly sixty now. I think.'

'Yes, nearly sixty. We also produce LSD in liquid or crystal form, as you well know. From crude morphine blocks we produce heroin of the highest quality, and naturally, it's safer than the extremely nasty "Chinese" which has flooded the market in recent years. Of course, ours is far more expensive, but then "Chinese" contains many impurities – highly toxic poisons, in fact, such as strychnine. It's hardly surprising brown powder often comes cheaper than cannabis. Two other synthetic drugs we produce with similar effects to the opium alkaloids are Pethidine and Methadone, and even ready-mixed pure cocaine and heroin is packaged here.'

'It's some operation,' Kelso commented flatly.

'Quite so.'

'And you manufacture THC. Isn't that as dangerous as "Chinese"?'

'Hardly. The risk is only from overdose and that is entirely up to the individual. We merely cater for every need and, if cannabis is too mild for certain people, we are happy to provide something stronger.'

'Terrific,' Kelso muttered under his breath.

Slauden's voice became tight. 'We deal only in quality merchandise here, Kelly. I'm sure you realised that when you sampled what you stole from us.'

'You should get the Queen's Award for Industry.'

The little man's smile was strange. 'In a way you are right. My organisation is both efficient and productive. The standards I set are high.'

'Do you mind telling me how you distribute the drugs?'

'Why not? I've told you everything else.'

'*That* might not be wise, Sir Anthony,' Henson quickly said.

'Nonsense. At the end of this conversation, Kelly will either be with us, or against us. The latter has only one consequence. He cannot harm us in any way.' Henson looked uncertain, but Slauden continued: 'The drugs are taken across river to my mill, which not only produces animal feedstuffs, but specialises in transforming certain raw materials that other mills cannot utilise because of lack of equipment. It gives us more delivery outlets, d'you see? We supply to other mills all over the country.'

'And the drugs go with the deliveries?'

'Can you think of a more innocent guise. Who would imagine that among twenty tons of animal feed there would be perhaps half-a-million pounds' worth of drugs. The appropriate sacks are dropped off at certain points along the route, of course, many at ports from where they can be shipped abroad. Obviously we work on a cell system after the delivery point, so that if one group is discovered, then we, the nucleus, cannot be traced. Occasionally, I export direct from here, using coasters from Amsterdam and Rotterdam that bring in dicalcium phosphates or fertilisers. Unfortunately, such legitimate shipments are not frequent and the 250-ton vessels coming upriver attract attention, so their use is limited. However, dispersement of our product has never been a serious problem.'

Kelso was shocked. Slauden's operation was simple, productive, and effective. He had a perfect personal cover and an ideal business front. No wonder the reprisal against Trewick had been so severe. He wondered how many other 'misguided' employees had suffered the same fate.

'Now perhaps you can see how you could personally benefit from joining my organisation. I promise you, the rewards are great. But first you must give me some information about your own network.'

Kelso cleared his throat, thinking fast. 'I worked alone with Andy Trewick. It was no big deal, just a steady supply to friends of mine in London. Students, photographers, advertising people – like I said, nothing big.'

'And the service men from the NATO base.'

'No, that was Andy's side of things. I only dealt with the London end.'

'And the girl?'

'Ellie? She's just my girlfriend; she's got nothing to do with all this.'

'He's lying again.' The words were soft, unaccusing, and came from Henson, who was casually examining his fingernails.

'I'm not. Why the hell should I lie to you?'

'To save your fuckin skin,' Bannen snarled. 'He's not in this alone. If he's peddlin in town, he's got a lot more back-up. Let me get it out of him my way.'

Kelso tensed, but Slauden shook his head. 'I had hoped, Kelly, that by taking you into my confidence in such detail you might be equally frank with me. Please try a little harder.'

'I've told you the truth. There's nothing more to tell.'

'I hope I haven't wasted my time, Kelly.'

'That's all there is to it.'

Bannen moved away from the chair and towards Kelso. 'Come on, you fuckin toe-rag, what other villains are workin with you?'

'Bannen, he may not be working with other villains at all.' Henson was looking across at Slauden, who gave the slightest nod of his head.

'What are you talkin about?' Bannen spat out. 'There's

bound to be others involved. Gawd knows how much Trewick creamed off.'

Henson switched his gaze to Kelso. 'Oh, there may be others involved, but perhaps not the sort you're thinking of. It could be that our friend here is working for the police.'

Bannen was stunned. And so was Kelso.

'You're crazy!' Kelso protested.

Henson smiled.

'I think we'll find out soon enough.' Slauden leaned forward in his chair. 'Dr Collingbury, you know what's needed.'

The bespectacled man left the room and Slauden said, 'We may well be crazy, Kelly – if, indeed, that *is* your real name – but I'm afraid we can't take the chance with you. We're expecting our next shipment tomorrow, which means we will be frantically busy over the next few weeks; we will have no time to play games with you. Frankly, you're a disappointment to me, neither convincing nor interesting. But there is a way of finding out the truth without resorting to Bannen's brutal methods.'

'For Christ's sake, I *am* telling you the truth!'

Slauden appeared not to have heard. 'There is another kind of violence, you know; a violence far worse than the physically bruising kind.'

Dr Collingbury re-entered the room clutching a small, black case.

'I refer to,' Slauden continued, 'violence of the mind.'

The black case was placed on a sideboard and opened. 'Sir Anthony, is this really necessary?' the chemist asked nervously.

Henson rose from the settee and went over to the sideboard. 'Yes, it is,' he answered for his employer. Brushing the thin man aside, he busied himself with the contents of the case.

'The absorption of lysergic acid into the system can usually be a most euphoric experience,' Slauden said. 'Or, under certain conditions and at too large a dosage, it can be a mind-shattering nightmare. The conditions you will be thrown into and the amount you will receive will send you into extreme shock. It will be an experience I don't think you will wish to repeat. We have to know about you, Kelly, so why not tell us now and avoid this unpleasantness. It really would be the best thing to do.'

Kelso said nothing.

168

Slauden sighed, then snapped, '600 microgrammes, Julian.'

Kelso knew the standard dose was 100 microgrammes.

Henson turned to face them, holding a syringe filled with clear liquid. 'Roll up his sleeve, Bannen,' he ordered as he came towards them.

Bannen was only three feet away when Kelso reached into the fire and drew out a burning log. The detective ignored the pain from the hot timber and swung the firebrand towards the advancing man's face. Bannen tried to duck, but wasn't fast enough; the burning end of the log struck his cheek, leaving red hot cinders clinging to his skin. He screamed and tried to beat them away with his hand, but Kelso struck again, using the log as a short spear. It struck Bannen just below his already swollen nose and he fell backwards, hands clutched to his face.

Kelso faced the others, the weapon weaving before him, almost challenging them to come to him. Henson began to back away, while the two men at the door seemed hesitant. It was Slauden, himself, who moved fast, leaping from his chair and slicing the edge of his hand hard into Kelso's upper arm, numbing the muscles there. The burning log fell from the detective's hand.

The two men by the door moved in. Dr Collingbury who had involuntarily backed into their path, was thrown aside as they lunged at Kelso. He struck one squarely on the forehead, but the blow had little effect. He went down with both men on top and they used their combined weight to pin him to the floor. He knew it was useless to struggle, that he was still too weak from his previous beating, but he fought them anyway, and once more they pounded his body to beat him into submission. He briefly glimpsed Bannen, his face red and blistered, trying to reach him through the tangle of bodies.

'No!' Slauden roared. 'Julian – the injection, quickly!'

Kelso felt his arm wrenched from his coatsleeve, then his shirt ripped at the shoulder. He struggled against them, but his arm was forced to bend so that the veins stood out clearly. The syringe came plunging down and he felt the needle prick his skin. Henson was grinning as he depressed the plunger and Kelso spat in his face.

Dr Collingbury, still on his knees near the door, moaned quietly as he watched what was happening. He turned his head sharply towards the window as the rain beat against the glass with a frantic intensity. The heavy curtains were closed, but they could not muffle the spattering sound and, for one frightening moment, the bespectacled man felt certain the glass would shatter under the fierce onslaught.

April, 1976

SHE SWORE under her breath when she saw there was no light shining from the window. Oh Christ, don't let him be out, not tonight, not when I've plucked up the courage to come back! I want him to be there, I need him to be there.

The girl swayed slightly and a middle-aged man passing by almost stopped to ask if she were all right. But the faintest whiff of whisky made him decide not to. Little slut. She was no more than twenty and just look at her! If it wasn't drink with these kids nowadays, it was drugs. She had no business standing there like that, blocking the pavement, looking as though she could hardly keep her feet. He was close enough to see her features lit by the streetlight, and he shook his head more in sadness than disgust. She was pretty, *bloody* pretty. What a waste! He hurried by, muttering to himself, but the girl hardly noticed him.

For a while, Sandy was unsure of what to do, then she smiled. She still had a key – Jim had never asked for it back. Of course he hadn't; he wanted her to come back to him. He loved her still, even after the things she had done. If he didn't he would have made sure she returned the key.

Sandy crossed the road and a car tooted its horn as it passed dangerously close. Kelso's flat was on the top floor of a terraced house in Maida Vale, a flat they had shared on and off for six months. The 'off' times were not always her fault.

She fumbled in her bag for the keyring, found it, and held it close to her face to find the key that opened the front door. It

171

was larger than the rest and the one to the flat upstairs was next to it. For a brief but unsettling moment Sandy wondered if he had changed the upstairs lock; but no, Jim would never do that to her. Despite his angry words, despite his sullen moods, he would always welcome her back. He always forgave her in the end. This time would be no different, even though they hadn't seen each other for nearly three weeks.

She inserted the key in the lock and pushed the door open. The hall light was on and she could hear music coming from a ground floor apartment. She closed the door and made for the stairs, almost tripping on the first step and putting a hand to her mouth to suppress a giggle. What a surprise he would have! What a lovely birthday surprise! She knew that *he* needed her too and felt sure her absence – the longest she had been away from him – would have made him realise the fact. Okay, she was a neurotic bitch at times, but then, even *he* had his moments. She'd always forgiven him those.

Sandy climbed the stairs and the higher she got, the more her anxiety increased. She stopped halfway up the last flight and sat there, her back against the wall. Her fingers unconsciously went to her mouth and she bit at the ragged ends of her finger-nails. It was a habit that vexed him, but she couldn't help it; she had told him it was no worse than his chain-smoking and that had sent him into one of his moody silences again. Oh God, what a pair. What a bloody silly, fucked-up couple to be living together. His neurosis might not have been as obvious as hers, but that was only because he locked it inside, hid it away so that no one else even suspected it was there. She was aware, though, because they were lovers – *good* lovers – and their secrets were shared. If only they could have helped each other.

The girl looked up at the door on the landing above and blinked her eyes to focus on it. She shouldn't have drunk so much tonight – he hated her drinking – but it had given her the courage to face him again. She was ashamed of what she had done. She was always ashamed. After. She shook her head. Sometimes she was even ashamed before, but it never stopped her. Sandy tasted blood in her mouth and quickly withdrew her fingers; she didn't want to make him angry any more.

The time-switch controlling the lights snapped off and she found herself sitting in darkness. She didn't like the dark, but

172

needed just a few more moments to regain her composure. Perhaps he was in, maybe watching TV, maybe in bed, exhausted. His police work kept him up at all hours – another bone of contention between them – and sometimes it was as much as he could do to undress himself before falling into the sack. *That,* of course, had never much pleased her, because bed, to her, meant something other than just sleeping.

Jim had once told her he had never wanted to join the Police Force and when she had asked *why the hell had he, then?* he had become silent, unwilling to talk any more. It had taken many more weeks and many more intimacies between them for her to find out the reason and, even then, the revelation was given grudgingly. He had said that it had been his father's – an ex-policeman himself – last request just before he died of a heart attack. Jim had joined the police a month after his father's death. She knew he had no regrets now, and that he had become dedicated to his work; but often he seemed disturbed, perhaps too concerned by the corruption and filth he had to deal with. Maybe more than that was bothering him, but he had always been reluctant to give too much away, even to her.

Be fair, Sandy! Too much concern has always been given to your hang-ups to allow time for Jim's! She twisted the strap of her bag, pulling the twisted leather tight as though it were a garotte. He'd been patient, tried to understand, tried to help. But she couldn't stop herself and finally he had come to realise it. She loved him and their sex was incredible. Incredible but not enough. One man had never been enough. He had forgiven her the first time, but not the next. And the third time had been the limit. Why couldn't he understand she loved him despite what she did, that physical love-making had nothing to do with her emotions. It was just a need, a craving. Like alcohol. Oh Sandy, what a screwed-up, vicious bitch you are!

She was shaking again. Earlier, alone in the house of a friend who had taken her in, she had started to shake. Three tumblers of whisky had controlled it, four had given her the resolve to return to Jim. Another now would calm her. Why the hell couldn't she take valium like other women?

Sandy lurched to her feet and made it to the top of the stairs. She switched on the landing light once more and had difficulty in getting the key into the lock. Finally the door opened and she stumbled inside.

'Jim?' Sandy waited in the narrow hallway, listening for his reply.

He really was out, probably busy trying to catch the bloody Irish who were systematically blowing up bits of London. In a way it was a relief not to find him there; she had relapsed, wasn't quite ready for the confrontation. She would beg, plead, promise. No more screwing with others, no more drinking. Well, maybe cut down on the drinking.

She giggled, this time letting the sound go free, for there was no one to hear. She needed another drink to promise to cut down on the drinking.

Sandy found the whisky bottle half full. She poured a small measure into a glass – just a finger full – and jerked it into the back of her throat. She felt better instantly and poured herself another. The lamp she had switched on bathed the room in a warm glow and she settled into the small sofa on which they had made love so many times. The room was untidy, but not dirty, and she wondered how he had got on without her. Pretty well, she imagined. Jim was never that good at looking after himself, but he got by. He always would.

The whisky was slowly sipped, for now the trembling had stopped, she could allow herself to relish the taste. She really would change this time, Sandy promised herself. Their living together had been traumatic – again, not entirely her fault – but no way did she want to lose him. *And there was no way the bastard could dump her!*

She clenched the glass tightly and drained its contents. It wasn't just her; *he* had a lot of things to answer for! His moods, the way he would suddenly make her keep quiet as though he was listening for something, the times he hid things from her. Oh yes, he'd always denied hiding things from her! But things didn't just get up and walk away of their own accord! And twice she had come home to find her clothes scattered all around the room! How was that for a neurosis? She had picked them up and put them away again, saying nothing when he returned from duty. And he had said nothing. They *both* said nothing. Christ, what a pair.

There were other, little things that had annoyed her, but they really weren't worth arguing over. Jim never even remembered having done them, so what was the point?

The only worthwhile point was that she loved him, and wanted to be with him. Not just for a few more months, but forever. If marriage came into it, that would be fine; if not, but they could still live together, then that was fine, too. Sandy looked at her wristwatch. After eleven. Oh come on, Jim, come home now. I need you here.

She shivered and realised how cold it had become. More whisky would make her feel warmer. Again she made it a small measure, not wanting to be *too* drunk when he returned. A giggle escaped her once more when she had an idea, a lovely surprise for him that would shake the weariness of late-night working from his bones. She placed the glass on the coffee table just in front of the sofa and pulled at her high-heeled boots. Sandy rolled back against the cushions as the first boot came off and was smiling broadly when the second hit the floor. After pulling off her coat, she took another sip of her drink.

Her flared jeans came next, tugging them down over her hips and sliding them from her long, slim legs. She tossed them into the middle of the floor, halfway towards the hallway. Next came her tights, but these she carried out into the hall where she dropped them near the front door. Then down the hall towards the bedroom, lifting her sweater over her head as she went. She paused at the bedroom door to drop the sweater and hesitated before turning the handle.

She frowned. It was that smell again, the foul stench she had complained to the landlord about a couple of times before. She was sure there was a dead mouse or some other creature stuck somewhere in the pipes. The landlord had scoffed at the idea and done nothing about it, had said if it was true, then the body would soon be corrupted to nothing but bones and the smell would disappear. But it was stronger than ever now.

A whoozy feeling came over her and she began to regret having drunk so much. She wanted to be awake when Jim came home. He would see the trail of clothes and know whose they were – he'd better bloody know! He'd follow the trail into the bedroom and then he would be there beside her, forgiving her, loving her, pinning her to the bed with his love rod!

Sandy reached behind and unhooked her bra, leaving it dangling from the doorhandle as she entered the room. Rising excitement and the coldness of the room made her nipples spring forward from the softness of her breasts and she grinned lasciviously when she saw his bed – *their* bed – in the light from the outside streetlamp. Sandy stopped when she noticed the mound beneath the bedclothes.

He had been there all the time, the bastard! Dead to the world. She giggled. Her cold hands would soon wake him up.

Sandy padded round to the other side of the bed where there was space to slide in. She looked down lovingly at him for several moments, watching the covers rise and fall with his deep breathing. The light was not far from the bedroom window and in the past they had both delighted in the milky whiteness it gave their bodies when they had made love on top of the bedclothes. Her figure cast a shadow over his shape as she quietly moved forward.

She was still smiling when she lifted the bedclothes and slid in beside him.

She lay on one elbow, tensing herself for the moment, enjoying it to the full.

Then she whisked the bedclothes away.

And the figure turned towards her.

She didn't scream. She couldn't. Her throat was paralysed. It was only when the thing in the bed moved towards her that the scream managed to break free.

Kelso was exhausted but still merry from the birthday drinks he had consumed. He was crossing the road and searching through his pockets for the front door key when he heard the cry. He looked up just in time to see his bedroom window shatter and the white body come hurtling down.

THIRTEEN

ELLIE TURNED off from the main A-road, switching the Escort's headlights to full beam to penetrate the blackness ahead. She accelerated and groaned inwardly at the engine's sluggish reaction: if the police could not afford to furnish their undercover officers with more recent models, then they could at least spend a bit more time and care on their maintenance. The drive up from London in Kelso's car had made her weary.

She glanced at her wristwatch, angling its face towards the dashboard lights to see. Almost 1.30. Jim would be anxious. Still, it had been worth waiting for the tests on the vole. Ellie had taken the tiny rotting corpse straight to the government forensic laboratory in Stamford Street, Waterloo, before reporting to her senior officer in Fetter Lane, for she had not wanted to delay the analysis for a moment longer than necessary. She was aware that the process could take days, perhaps weeks, if she went through the usual procedures, and she deliberately sought out an old acquaintance, an analyst who had dated her a couple of times in the past. Ellie had found him a little boring and had brought their budding relationship to a swift but tactful conclusion. Now she was glad she had used tact.

Foxcroft, the analyst, had been doubtful and suspicious: it would take some time to discover the information she needed unless she gave him some firm indication of what to look for, and why wasn't she using the normal channels anyway? It had taken considerable charm and a veiled promise that their relationship might be allowed to blossom once more if he did her this one favour. Foxcroft had nearly fallen through the floor when she told him she would need the analysis later that evening. She had been forced to tell him that she suspected the animal had died of LSD poisoning and his protests had calmed. The vole looked as though it had been dead for just two, maybe three, days so he should be able to find some traces still in the kidney or liver. A urine test would have been easiest, but obviously it was too late for that. He still wasn't sure if he could carry out the analysis in such a short time, but he would do his best – it really was a *hell* of a rush. Ellie kissed his cheek for encouragement and said she would return later that night.

Out of loyalty to Kelso, and against her own better judgement, Ellie had refrained from telling her senior officer of their findings and suspicions; she had not even mentioned that she had brought the dead vole in for tests. She felt guilty about her own deviousness, but she had made a promise, one which she intended to keep. Her excuse for returning to London was that she had wanted to find out how the overall investigation was progressing, which was something that could not be discussed over the telephone, and her senior officer, Gifford, thought it a reasonable course of action. He informed her that much of the pressure had been taken off the operation when it was learned that the US pilot had suffered a family tragedy the year before – his wife and two young sons had been killed in a road accident – and the plane crash had been deliberate suicide. A letter stating his suicide intention had turned up at his parents' address in California dated on the same day he had taken up the A-10 for the last time. How regular medical and psychological tests that all pilots were obliged to undergo had not revealed his condition, nobody knew or was ready to accept responsibility for; the mind could deliberately delay a severe shock for its own protection, but the pressure would always build to a breaking point, and no one could predict just when that point would be reached. Although the pilot had suffered acute grief at the sudden loss of his family, he had appeared to recuperate steadily over the months that followed. How much of a part drugs had played in his recovery no one could be sure, but it was generally agreed among the medics on the base that drugs – probably of the softer variety at first – had helped to

178

overcome the mental anguish. Heads were going to roll, that was for sure, and the USAF commanding officer would eventually find himself working at a desk closer to Washington, but at least the authorities had some relief in the knowledge that the pilot's lunacy was not part of some devious Russian plot. However, it did not explain how such drugs had become available to the pilot, so the investigation still had top priority, although the urgency had diminished. So far, Gifford told Ellie with some frustration, no inside drugs ring had been uncovered. There were a couple of leads, but these only involved service men picking up marijuana while on leave in London. Such offences meant instant court martial, so, obviously, no one was willing to give out information voluntarily.

When the senior officer remarked that she, herself, might only be allowed a minimum of time on her area of investigation unless there were some positive results, Ellie nearly blurted out what she and Kelso had turned up so far. Instead, she assured Gifford that she felt they were close to something but, as yet, were only following up loose theories. Fortunately, her superior had sufficient confidence in her investigative abilities not to press the issue. But, he told her firmly, the minute anything concrete turned up, he wanted to know. He didn't want the Drugs Squad moving in without them.

From the Customs and Excise headquarters, Ellie went to her flat just off Wigmore Street, and after cooking herself a meal, packed some more clothes for her stay in Adleton. She happily hummed to herself when she tucked away some of her more flimsy underwear. It shouldn't be happening, she mock-scolded herself. He was a professional, she was a professional, and they were involved in a serious, and probably dangerous, investigation. Making love was a distraction that shouldn't have been indulged in. She stared at herself in the dressing-table mirror. *Falling in love* was a distraction that shouldn't have been indulged in.

She sat on the bed, wary of her own emotions, feeling both happy yet afraid. But why should there be any fear? What was it about him that caused such a reaction? For some reason, Ellie began to weep, but the tears were not the kind that wracked the body, that came in short, anguished gasps, but tears that seeped singularly from the corners of the eyes and fell slowly down her cheeks. Ellie rested her head against a pillow and soon she was asleep.

She returned to the government laboratory later that evening, having stopped to make a small purchase on the way. The analyst had not yet begun his autopsy on the vole and he insisted that she leave him alone to work in peace. They agreed to meet later in the bar of the nearby National Theatre and Ellie strolled along the Embankment for a while, her collar turned up and hands tucked into her pockets against the dampness of the air. It was bitterly cold for April, the kind of weather that was depressing because winter had overstayed its time and warm sunshine was hard to remember. She wanted desperately to make contact with Kelso, but there was no way it could be done. She looked north across the river and saw the rainclouds resting low on the horizon. There was something ominous in their heavy blackness, a pressing darkness that made her shiver inwardly.

The bar in the National Theatre was almost empty by the time Foxcroft arrived, the various intermissions of each play performed in the huge, grey-slabbed theatre complex long since over. He had a curious look on his face when Ellie bought him a gin and tonic at the bar, but he refrained from asking any questions until they were seated at one of the white round tables which littered the vast lounge area.

He *had* found traces of LSD in the vole and was curious to know just how the creature had come into contact with the drug. Classified information, she told him. He looked disgruntled. Again, why had there been no formal documentation with her request? No time, she explained, and she was working purely on a hunch. She had squeezed his hand and left him there with a dissatisfied and slightly miffed expression on his face. Her promise to return the favour some time failed to elevate his mood.

The drive back to Suffolk was both tedious and frustrating. Heavy rainfall lashed at the windscreen as soon as she was through the outskirts of London, and oncoming headlights did their best to dazzle her off the road.

It was only as she had approached the minor roads leading towards the coastal town that the rain eased off, and now, as she reached the first few houses of Adleton, her apprehension inexplicably began to grow. She had slowed down earlier as the car passed the narrow road which led down to Eshley Hall, an eerie feeling drawing her gaze in the direction of the manor house. She had forced herself to ignore the peculiar sensation, pressing her foot down hard on the accelerator pedal to speed on by, but the unease had persisted.

She was determined now to convince Kelso to call in the troops; the dead vole was definite proof that there was LSD coming out of Eshley Hall and an authorised raid would confirm it. It was much too dangerous for them to continue on their own; the incident with the bulldozer proved that. Jinx or not, Jim was going to listen to reason this time.

The Escort was descending the hill leading down to the town centre and Ellie gently applied the brakes. At the T-junction at the bottom of the hill, she turned left and drove towards the caravan site. It was hard to believe there were other people on earth, the streets were so quiet, no lights shining in the houses on either side of the road. Still, it could hardly be described as a lively town even in daylight hours, so what could she expect in the middle of the night – or early hours of the morning to be more precise?

The car bumped over the rough track inside the site and the caravans stood like cardboard cutouts in the glare of its headlights. Steering through the ranks towards Kelso's trailer, Ellie kept a wary eye out for any lurking figures; she saw none, but that didn't mean there weren't any there. She brought the Escort to a halt beside the right caravan and switched off the lights, instantly regretting her hastiness in doing so, for the quarter-moon was hidden behind rolling clouds, and the night outside was a dense black. For a moment, she considered tooting the horn to get Kelso to come to the door, but then grew angry at herself for acting like a nervous schoolgirl. She grabbed the shoulder-bag and her hold-all filled with fresh clothing and stepped out of the car. It wasn't so dark once her eyes had become adjusted, but nevertheless, she hurried over to the caravan's door.

She cursed herself for not having taken out the spare doorkey Kelso had given her while still in the car but, knowing his habit of leaving the door unlocked anyway, she reached for the handle. Idiot! He'd done it again. The door was open.

181

Ellie pushed it wide and called out his name as she mounted the steps. Even though she could not see, Ellie knew that the hands that reached out for her in the darkness did not belong to Kelso.

They had taken him across the river, bound, gagged, completely wrapped up in coarse material. He knew they had dragged him back along the underground passageway and onto the boat; he knew he had lain below on a narrow bench or bunk while they journeyed across, moving upstream towards the old mill. But reality had rapidly slipped away.

Kelso was aware of what was happening, but the awareness was becoming too acute, too unreal. His skin began to glow where the rough material touched it and, although he knew they had covered him in sacking, the cloth felt like huge boulders joined together. And he could see through the cracks, could almost slide through them, could almost absorb the rocks into his own pores. The unreality had become the true reality.

Yet his senses had remained on a conscious level, he had not forgotten his plight, had not forgotten that the men around him meant him harm.

When they had taken him from the boat, carrying him as if he were nothing more than a loose bundle, raindrops, each one a separate cascading waterfall, had drenched the sacking material, falling between the chasms to soak his skin and enter him so he himself had become a reservoir, a lake that contained living creatures, his own cells joining with the micro-organisms which danced in the raindrops. He almost panicked, for his breathing seemed restricted, too shallow.

Then he was inside the huge cavern that was the mill and they had pulled the sacking from him so that he felt he was falling into the very vastness of the building itself, into a universe of rusted red steel girders and cobwebs that hung from the rafters like dusty lace drapes. There were three men around him, the same two who had brought him up from the cellar earlier, and Henson, whose face loomed before him like a huge inflated balloon, every vein, every pore, visible even in the gloom of the

182

poorly lit building. The balloon came even closer and Kelso nearly panicked, feeling he would be swamped by it, suffocated in its softness. The eyes, brilliantly blue, no longer belonged to Henson's face. They swam out on their own and they were full of crystals that dazzled Kelso like diamonds sparkling in a shaft of light. But still part of his consciousness remained on the level of normal human concepts.

'You're lucky,'' a voice boomed out, filling his head and bouncing from wall to wall inside his skull. Henson's distorted mouth was moving and he was afraid of the huge chasm that opened and closed. The words were not in synchronisation with the blood-red lips, though; sometimes they lagged behind, sometimes they were said before they were physically formed. 'If Bannen had brought you here, he would have killed you, orders or not. You've hurt him twice too often. It's lucky his burns need treatment.'

Kelso's hands were still tied behind his back and he tried to scream through the gag that the ropes were cutting into him, that they were becoming tighter, searing his flesh, melting away the bones in the wrists. The three men paid him no heed. He was pulled across the floor, white dust rising like a snow blizzard, each particle clear and beautifully shaped.

They moved through into another part of the building, Henson switching on lights as they went, and the structure around them seemed to change shape. The girders were no longer straight, but bent inwards as though trying to reach one another; even more disturbing, they were no longer solid – they seemed to be made of a pliable substance, not plastic, but liquid. Kelso began to panic, sure that the building was collapsing around them, but the three men did not seem to be aware of what was happening. The ceiling was lower in this part of the building and he could see the rotted wood above them, and he tried to sink to his knees, certain that the ceiling was slowly descending on them.

'He's fuckin gone with it already,' a voice boomed.

'It's hardly surprising with the dose he's had. He'll be in a lot worse state soon.' It could have been Henson's voice replying, but sounds were becoming indistinct, for every part of the building was making its own noise and the sagging floorboards above them were loudest of all. Even the dust particles seemed to *click* as they struck each other.

'Look, Kelly.' Fingers sank into his face and became part of him. His head was swung towards a tower-like construction that narrowed into a funnel towards ground level. A metal shaft led away from its base through the wall of the building. 'That's a pulveriser. That's where everything is mixed into a fine powder.' Henson picked up white dust from the floor and threw it into Kelso's face. The particles were suspended in space, a galaxy of fiery stars. He closed his eyes and the stars shattered around him.

'That's where Trewick finished up!' the voice bellowed. 'He was ground to dust, Kelly. Into animal feed. Not a bone of him left. You're going to go the same way unless you come clean with us!'

'He can't hear you! He's too far gone – he doesn't know what you're talking about!'

But Kelso did, and he was even more afraid. His mouth was dry, his throat parched.

They dragged him on, through a doorway, past a steep concrete stairway that disappeared into the darkness above, and towards an area of solid concrete. They stopped before a wooden trap-door in the stone.

'That's what the workers here call The Pit, Kelly! It leads to the conveyor-belt that carries the grain from the bins above us to the outside! If anything goes wrong with the belt, someone has to go down there to sort it out. Only trouble is, no one wants to go down there!'

Their laughter beat at his mind, bludgeoning his senses.

'You know why, Kelly? Because it's bloody dark down there, even in the daytime. And it's full of rats! Have you seen the kind of rats that run loose in feed mills, Kelly? They're big because they're well-fed! There's no way that we can keep them down, not in a place like this!' Again the laughter, but there was also fear in the sound. 'They'll be keeping you company tonight. If you're lucky, they won't eat you! But they might try!'

The trap-door was lifted and Kelso stared into the black world that was from another dimension. He tried to scream again, but the sound was muffled. His hands were suddenly loose and the knife that had freed him prodded his back.

'Down you go!' a voice shouted.

He saw the rungs leading down and he backed away from them because they were not solid and he would sink through them.

'Down, Kelly. You're lucky Sir Anthony wants you alive, otherwise we'd have left your hands tied. You'd have had no protection at all!'

He tore the gag from his mouth and began to plead, his mind, through fear, focusing in on what was happening. They grabbed him and threw him down.

One hand held onto the lip of the opening, but the fingers were viciously kicked away. He fell, the few feet feeling like miles, and landed on the concrete floor. The trap-door was slammed shut above him and he clapped his hands against his ears to block out the thunder. A deep rumbling sound followed as something heavy slid over the hatch for added weight.

A squeaking sound told him he was not entirely alone in the darkness.

'Let me out!' he screamed, reaching out for the ladder he knew was somewhere in front of him. His hand closed around a metal rung and he pulled himself towards it, reaching up for the next, then the next. His head hit the trap-door as soon as he stepped onto the first rung and the pain flashed through his brain like sheet lightning, stopping not only there within his mind, but spreading throughout his body, flowing out again through his extremities. Reason told him that the pit he was in was not deep, yet he could not shake off the feeling that he was in some vast arena. He reached up once more and beat against the wood, screaming for them to let him out. He could hear scuttling noises all around.

He had no idea of how long he stood there, pleading and trying to force the trap-door upwards, for time had suddenly lost all meaning. It was *now,* and he was *now,* and his screams were *now,* and the darkness was . . . no longer darkness.

Lights were exploding around him, beautiful lights that appeared as blinding white suns that showered into violent shades of red, blue and purple. Kelso sank to his knees and hid his eyes from them, but there was no escape for they were inside his own head. The lights dazzled him and he became no longer afraid of them, for they released his thoughts, somehow freeing his spirit. He wanted to see them, wanted to experience them.

He wanted to *be* them. And he was. His body began to glow; his nerve ends began to tingle. Electric currents were running through him and a part of him that came from his mind ran with the currents, exploring his own body, one moment inside his fingertips, the next following the flow of blood inside his heart. He felt close to orgasm, each separate part of him an organ for pleasure, his enlarged penis no longer the sole instrument for such pleasure and release. But even that feeling was transcended as everything around him took on a brilliantly light blue hue; he was in the sky and there were no confines around him. The concrete grey slabs from where grain was fed through became gigantic buildings, none of their edges parallel, but each one related to an adjoining line, bending to meet each other and bristling with vitality, a life that was not of the material kind but the same as his own, for he had become part of that incredible landscape and the landscape had become a part of him. Then he was no longer just a part – he *was* everything around him.

Tears glistened in his eyes and he saw everything through a multi-faceted diamond; nothing was singular, nothing stood alone. He felt close to something that was subliminal, something that was real, could be perceived, yet still could not be touched. Something in a dimension that was so close to the one that he, himself, existed in, only a thin tissue, an incorporeal substance separating them. He glided into the ethereal barrier, knowing he only had to rent the tissue with a finger nail to pass through . . .

. . . and everything began to change . . .

Blackness threw itself at him and creatures scuttled across the void, creatures with long pointed heads and bristling fur; and the euphoria vanished to be replaced once more by the excruciating fear.

And there was the smell.

Not the smell of the dust around him, nor even the smell of the crushed powder. It wasn't the smell of rat spoors and it wasn't the smell of spiders in their webs.

It was the stench of corruption.

The odour that had assailed him so many times in the past. And suddenly, he was reliving those moments. Images flashed through his mind, parts of his life that he had tried to dismiss, tried to block out for the sake of his own sanity. Some memories were stronger than others, lingering before him as though they were taunts, tormenting and causing him to cry out with their clarity.

The smell became even stronger and he began to retch. Even though his body convulsed, his muscles tensing then jerking loose, his limbs twisting uncontrollably, the memories flooded through.

He was gazing down at Sandy lying crushed and broken on the pavement.

Years between sped by, incidents that he could never explain appeared briefly, then dissolved into other incidents.

He was staring at his father's naked body draped over the side of the bath, the old man's face contorted in an expression of horror and pain.

More years flew by. More incidents.

He was cowering in the bombed-out house and the three boys were coming up the stairs after him. He was turning and they were no longer there. The terrible screams over the tearing, crashing sound as they had plummeted down into the floor below, one to be killed, one to be forever paralysed, the other, the youngest, never to remember what had happened that day.

More time streaked by, always going back, and all clearly seen.

He was in the orphanage, sitting on a bed, talking to someone – a friend, but it wasn't clear who the friend was. The door, already open, swung wide and the old man had charged in, had shaken him, cursed him. And the terrible sound only moments later when the old man had tripped and fallen down the stairs. The odd look on his face, the odd angle of his neck, when all the children had rushed out to see what had caused the noise.

Years becoming slow, like a train approaching a station.

And then . . . oh God . . . and then . . . he was tiny. He couldn't move. His head was filled with a steady thumping noise that was somehow comforting. And everything was black. But not just black. It was red too. Blood red. And it was becoming bright, too bright. And something was pushing him out, out into a blinding vastness that frightened him. And he slid from the womb easily, even though there was no one else to help, only the trembling exhausted hands of his mother. He could hear her sobs, her cries of agony, and the rough sheets he lay on were covered in blood. And he lay between his mother's thighs, and there was something else emerging, something that made his mother scream, something he could not see with his eyes, for he had no vision, but something he knew was with him, was part of him. And soon it was lying beside him, its limbs moving feebly as were his own. And he was pushing at it, not knowing why, a baby only just formed that was repulsed by something that had entered the world with him. And everything was black, black, BLACK!

As Kelso crouched there in the darkness of the pit, his body wracked by his own sobs, his mind tortured by his own memories, the smell became intense, suffocating. A cloying sickness that covered him like black oil.

And something touched him. A hand scaly and brittle – and cold – closed around his and held it tightly.

FOURTEEN

ELLIE WAS surprised to see, through the cabin windows, that the cruiser had turned off from the river and was heading into the marshes. She felt sure that the boat would become bogged down in reeds and mud, but soon realised that whoever was steering knew a way through. The roof and upper storey of the old mill rose up from the heavy morning mist, its lower portion vignetting into a swirling grey. Even at that distance, she could see the building was in a dilapidated state: the red brickwork was stained and badly patched and the tiled roofing had collapsed inwards at several points.

Was that where they were taking her? To Slauden's mill? Was it there that they were holding Kelso? She looked across at the thug sitting on the opposite bench seat in the motor cruiser's compact cabin and caught him coolly appraising her body. He grinned when their eyes met, and deliberately scanned her figure again, his gaze slow and lingering.

Ellie turned sideways on the cushioned bench and drew her legs up, hugging her knees to her chin, grateful that she was wearing jeans. The night had been a long one, full of fears, full of anxiety over the safety of Kelso. They refused to tell her what they had done with him, only taunting her with the threat that she would receive the same treatment if she didn't answer their questions. A tall, grey-suited man had conducted the interrogation and Ellie assumed he was Sir Anthony Slauden's personal secretary, Julian Henson. She had seen nothing at all of Slauden himself.

Ellie had fought wildly when they had grabbed her at the caravan site, but a painful bruise on her right cheek and a tenderness around her rib-cage had been the only reward for her resistance. Although they had thrown a blanket over her head, she felt it reasonable to assume from the length of the following car journey and by the view from the room they had locked her in later, that they had taken her to Eshley Hall. Henson's questioning had been soft at first, implying rather than stating that he knew both she and Kelso were involved in drug pushing and that their source was Andy Trewick; he wanted to know who else was involved and where the stolen drugs were distributed. She had feigned ignorance and gradually his tolerance towards her began to wear.

Her boyfriend had already admitted stealing the drugs with Trewick, she was told, and to save Kelly's skin she had better add a few details of her own. Ellie had managed an astonished laugh, but it wasn't convincing. The two thugs – not Suffolk folk these two, more like Whitechapel – were all for slapping her around a little, but Henson would not hear of it. Sir Anthony would be displeased. God bless Sir Anthony. The interrogation had continued, but Ellie had refused to be worn down: she didn't know what they were talking about, and knew nothing about drugs. Who the hell was Trewick, anyway?

Eventually they had left her alone for a short time, giving her a chance to explore the small, bare room that was her prison. Naturally the door was locked and there would have been no point in climbing out of the tiny window, even if she could have opened it, for she was at the top of the manor house in what must have been the servants' quarters at one time. Either that, or an attic. The sky was slowly dawning grey outside and she could see the wide river below, dark and brooding. Even as she watched, a mist swirled in from the direction of the sea and covered the river's surface in a smothering shroud.

The sound of the door being unlocked had made her turn and Henson marched in, swinging the door wide so that it rebounded off its hinges. It gave her some satisfaction to see he looked as weary as she felt, but that little ray of pleasure swiftly dissipated when he snapped at her: 'We know you're both working for the police, so you may as well tell us everything!'

For a moment – just for the briefest second – she almost fell for the bluff; then quickly dismissed the doubt. Firstly, *she* wasn't with the police, and secondly, if they really thought she and Kelso were, then why all the questions about drug pushing?

When Ellie informed Henson that he was mad, she thought he would hit her, despite Sir Anthony's displeasure. Instead, she was dragged down the stairs and through the grounds of the estate into the boathouse. The trip up and across the broad river had been short; now she could see they were travelling along a narrow waterway leading through the marsh, long reeds brushing against the motor cruiser's windows as the boat passed. A small jetty came into view.

Henson swung down into the cabin and his expression was grim.

'Perhaps some time with your boyfriend will convince you to tell the truth,' he said.

'What have you done with him?' There was a heavy weight in Ellie's stomach.

'You'll find out soon enough. Bring her up!'

The man opposite Ellie stood and jerked her to her feet. There was no point in resisting as he shoved her towards the hatch. It was cold on deck, but good to be in the open once more. A hand roughly pushed her onto the jetty and she almost slipped on the damp boards.

Henson led the way and Ellie followed, the other two men walking on either side and slightly behind. One held her just above the elbow to prevent her from making a break.

'It really is a pity, Miss Shepherd,' Henson said over his shoulder. 'You could both save yourselves so much inconvenience. I promise you, you won't like where you will be kept over the weekend. Fortunately, the mill staff – those who are not employed in our other activities, that is – will not be back until Monday. By then, I think, you will have had enough?'

'What the hell's happening here? We've done nothing wrong.' Ellie reached forward and pulled at his shoulder. 'Look, I don't know what this is all about and what you're all up to. What's more, I don't care. Just let us both go and I give you my word we'll say nothing.'

Henson shrugged his shoulder free. 'Don't be so bloody ridiculous,' he told her.

Ellie shuddered when they entered the courtyard of the mill, for its very bleakness seemed to reflect the dread she felt inside. At the far end a building straddled the yard, an archway cut through its ground floor giving access for lorries to the main road outside. Barn-like structures loomed over the courtyard on either side, their walls covered in moss, only a patch of faded red brickwork occasionally showing through. Metal drums, red, green and black, were scattered untidily around the edges of the open space and sodden loading platforms, the type used with fork-lift trucks, were stacked at various points. The yard's tarmac was cracked and puddle-filled, only tufts of grass and weeds breaking through to relieve the overall drabness.

Ellie cringed back when she saw the black opening they were heading for and the hand holding her arm forced her onwards. 'Don't keep your lover boy waitin, darlin; I should think he needs a bit of comfortin by now.' The other man sniggered at his companion's humour.

The shadows of the vast building's interior seemed to spring down and absorb her into its dispiriting gloom. The floor was covered in a fine powdery dust, the product of the mill itself, and the smell of molasses and starch pervaded the air. Sections of the walls, obviously white-washed at sometime in the distant past, were streaked black and growths of fungi could be seen where the crumbling brickwork had not been covered. Sacks of feedstuff were piled high and odd pieces of machinery skulked in the darkness as if waiting for prey.

They led her through a maze of openings and package-lined lanes, the building itself a complex of vast storage rooms and processing areas, until they reached a door. Henson unlocked it and pushed her through; she found herself in a square chamber, a metal staircase rising at one end and disappearing into the upper floors.

'No, not up there,' Henson said, noticing her looking up at the stairs. 'The stairs lead to the grain bins; you're going some-where else, Miss Shepherd, a place that will make you feel as though you've been entombed in a crypt. I think you'll have plenty to say to us once you've spent some time down there – particularly when you see the state of Kelly.' There was no emotion in his voice when he added. 'I hope he's still alive – you'd find it difficult to keep the creatures down there away from dead meat.'

He walked over to a crate standing in the middle of the concrete floor. One of the other men pushed past Ellie and helped him move the crate to one side. She saw it had been covering a trap-door.

Henson reached down for the inset handle and pulled upwards, leaving a gaping black hole in the concrete. 'Down you go,' he told Ellie.

'You're kidding! I'm not going down there!'

Henson sighed. 'We're not giving you a choice, Miss Shepherd – unless you want to tell us certain things.'

'Can't you get it into your thick skulls – I've got nothing to tell you!'

He jerked his head and Ellie was shoved towards the hole. 'You can climb down or be thrown down. That's your only choice now.'

She sat nervously on the edge of the opening, placing one foot on a rung below. A not-too-gentle tap of a shoe against her spine encouraged her further. Before her head and shoulders disappeared from view, she gave Henson one last pleading look and for a moment, from the look in his eyes, she thought he might change his mind. Instead, he closed the trap-door and she had to duck down quickly before it struck her.

'Bastard,' she said.

She clung to the ladder, too scared to move, waiting for her vision to adjust. But even after a full minute there was still only total darkness.

A scuttling to her right made her stiffen, and a high-pitched squealing made her panic.

She banged her fist against the trap-door. 'Let me out, you bastards! For God's sake, let me out!'

A grating noise from above told her that the crate had been moved back into position. She thought she heard footsteps walking away.

Ellie stayed on the ladder for a long time before she cautiously moved a foot down towards the floor. More shifting sounds made her freeze.

When she ventured a foot down again, she was surprised how soon it touched floor level. She stood at the bottom of the ladder, slightly crouched, still trying to pierce the blackness around her, nerving herself against the small scrambling sounds that she heard. Ellie reached into her coat pocket and her fingers closed around something she had bought only the previous day. Although she had been searched when captured, only her shoulder-bag and its contents had been taken away. She tore open the small box and flicked on the lighter. Her thumb found the control dial and the flame rose higher; the light was still poor, but gave her some comfort.

Something moved and she just caught sight of a small bristling body scurrying into the shadows. Two others followed and she had to resist the urge to scream. Keeping her arm outstretched, Ellie moved the light from left to right, trying to distinguish shapes in the darkness. The flame singed a spider's web and she quickly withdrew her arm.

Pipes and concrete columns cluttered the confined space and a horizontal square-shaped shaft appeared from the shadows to sink into what must have been an outside wall. Ellie guessed its purpose, for Henson had said the stairs above led to the grain bins; the shaft would house the conveyor-belt which carried the emptied grain outside to be poured onto waiting transport. Ellie moved forward, hoping the lighter fuel would last for some time, when something lying against the wall behind the ladder caught her eye. She hadn't noticed it before because she had been too busy trying to penetrate the far depths of the underground chamber; but now it gained her attention.

It looked like a bundle of rags or sacking at first; as she moved the light closer she realised it was something more.

'Jim?' Her voice was almost a whisper. 'Jim? It's me, Ellie.' Her voice became louder, concern outweighing fear. They had said they were taking her to him, and they had implied he would be in a bad way.

Still crouching, Ellie made her way towards the still form, but she hesitated when she was only a few feet away, suddenly even more afraid than before. She could not understand why, but something made her loathe to touch the body lying there – if, indeed, it were a body. The scuttling sounds had stopped and there was no more squealing. Ellie felt a thousand tiny eyes were watching her in the darkness.

She tried to speak, to say his name, but her throat was too dry.

The form, which had been so still, moved and Ellie found

194

herself backing away. She held herself in check, aware that the very atmosphere of the cellar was heightening her fear, goading her into hysteria.

'. . . Jim? . . . ' she finally managed to say, and the figure moved again as though a shiver had run through it.

Ellie almost dropped the lighter when something scrabbled across her foot. The rat quickly disappeared.

She drew in a deep breath before forcing herself to go back towards the huddled shape. Her footsteps were slow as if she were deliberately delaying the moment when she would reach the wall. But soon there was nothing else to do but reach down and touch.

She held the light forward, spoke his name once more, and allowed her trembling fingers to grasp the bundle lying there.

The figure began to turn.

Then she was in his arms, holding him, softly calling his name, the flame from the lighter extinguished. And Kelso was holding her, scarcely believing what was happening, sure that he would never have seen Ellie again. His clutching fingers were weak, his thoughts jumbled and uncomprehending, but he could feel that she was real, could feel her tears that wet his own face.

'Oh, Jim, what have they done to you?' Ellie cried, for she had seen his battered face before the light had gone. And worse than the physical punishment that was evident was the terror in his eyes.

'Ellie?' His voice was thick, his words slurred. 'Is it really you?'

She held on to him, squeezing him tight as if to make him feel she really was there. 'What did they do, Jim? What did they do to you?'

Kelso felt her lips against his skin and his mind slowly began to clear, the physical contact bringing his scattered thoughts back to reality. 'Injection.' He ran his tongue over his lips, trying to wet them so he could speak. 'They injected . . . me . . . with . . . LSD.'

She pulled away, but could not see his face in the darkness. 'Oh those bastards!' she said, pulling him close once more.

'It's all right, Ellie.' He shook her gently. 'I'm . . . I'm okay. Now.'

It was several minutes before either could speak again, Kelso because his mental faculties had not yet fully returned, Ellie because she was too overcome with emotion. It had been a long night.

Eventually, Ellie loosened her embrace and lightly ran her fingers over Kelso's face. 'How much did they pump into you, Jim?'

She felt him shake his head in the darkness and when he spoke, his voice sounded distant. 'I don't know . . . I can't seem to . . . I can't remember, Ellie. Everything's hazy.'

'It must have been quite a dose if they intended you to freak-out. I'm just surprised that you're conscious.'

His hand gripped her arm tightly. 'Something . . . something happened.'

'I'll bet it did.'

'N-no . . . something happened here . . . ' His body stiffened and he seemed to be listening. Slithering noises made Ellie shift her position so that her back was against the wall.

'It's only rats, Jim,' she reassured him, the thought of the bristling creatures lurking in the darkness sending a shudder through her body.

'No . . . it's not the rats. Something . . . something, else.' He lapsed into silence and the girl pulled his head down onto her shoulder.

'Don't try to talk for a while,' she told him. 'Just let your senses find their own way back. Give it a little time.'

His breathing, at first shallow, and harsh, began to slow. He murmured something incomprehensible, then she realised he had fallen into a deep sleep. Ellie let him rest, knowing the mental ordeal he had been through would have left his mind in a shattered state. Despite her own fears, exhaustion took its toll and she, too, fell into a troubled slumber.

The hand that brushed her cheek awoke her with a start.

'Ellie, is it really you?' It was Kelso's voice and it was his hand.

'Jim, how long have we been asleep?'

'Asleep?' He sounded more alert now.

'Are you feeling okay?'

'I'm . . . my head's still a bit fuzzy. Christ, Ellie, what's happened?'

'They drugged you. Put you down into this hell-hole.'

'Yeah, I remember that. But how did you get here?'

She quickly told him the events of the previous night and, as she talked, Ellie sensed his mind was quickly clearing, bringing him back to reality. She was surprised at just how fast he was recovering. When she had finished, he said: 'What a bloody mess. I should have listened to you and called in help.'

'No, we did the right thing considering what little evidence we had. Anyway, now we have proof.'

'Terrific. Will you ask Slauden to give himself up, or shall I?'

'Let's just try to get out of this place. They may try an even stronger dose . . . '

His body stiffened once more. 'Jim, what is it?'

There was a tremor in his voice when he replied. 'Last night. Christ, last night!' Kelso tried to get to his feet and she held onto him, trying to calm his panic. His legs were still weak and he collapsed next to her.

'It was only a bad trip, Jim. Just a nightmare.'

He was shivering now. 'No, Ellie, it was something more,' he said after a while. 'I went through more than just hallucinations last night. I remembered things, things in my past I've tried to cut out. I remembered being a kid, Ellie. A baby. Oh God, I remember being born.'

Kelso began to weep quietly and Ellie could only kneel before him and cradle his head in her arms.

'The acid must have made you regress – it sometimes happens. But you're all right now, Jim. Try not to think about it anymore.'

His head came up slowly. 'I know why I'm a Jonah, Ellie. I know why these terrible things have happened to people around me. And I wasn't alone down here last night. Something was with me . . . ' His voice trailed off into a low moan.

She shook him gently. Then harder when there was no response. 'I don't understand, Jim. Please help me to.' Ellie wanted to push back the darkness, to see his face, to pull him back from the abyss of despair that he was falling into. In

197

desperation, she reached into her pocket and drew out the lighter. He jumped when she flicked it on and his eyes half-opened against the glare.

Ellie tried to force a smile. 'I bought it yesterday. It's for you, Jim, a present.'

He looked at her uncomprehendingly.

'Don't you know what day it is?' Her cheerfulness was a pose, but she had to shake him out of his mood. 'I read it in your file. It's your birthday, Jim.'

Ellie cried out at the look of stark horror that suddenly appeared on Kelso's battered face.

FIFTEEN

THE DEPRESSION was moving in a south-easterly direction and deepening as it travelled. Its origin had been in the cold waters around the south of Iceland and now it had reached the Atlantic where the tips of the undulating waves were skimmed off by a sudden breeze that had sprung up from nowhere. Within minutes, the breeze had become a wind and, by the time the depression's centre had neared the Hebrides, the wind had become a gale.

By noon, urged on by the wind-drift, the depression had reached its greatest intensity and had swung south into the North Sea. The wind's ferocity had reached Force 10 with individual gusts reaching a velocity of 120mph, and it followed in the wake of the depression, circling counter-clockwise and striking the east coast with the strength of a tornado.

The depression began to fill as it moved southwards at a speed of almost 30mph and the waters began to pile up before it. Fishing fleets were forced to flee back to shelter, those not fast enough and those who had refused to heed the first warnings, swamped or swept along by the rushing sea. Other commercial ships tried gamely to resist the surge, but these, too, were forced to flee to the nearest ports where, even in the most sheltered harbours, docking proved hazardous. The Edinburgh-Reykjavik ferry sank. There were no survivors. Thousands of acres of trees in the eastern part of Scotland were flattened by the winds that travelled inland. A North Sea oil rig's leg buckled under the strain of pounding waves but, miraculously, the platform did not topple into the sea as had a sister rig, the *Alex Keilland,* only a few years before. Those on board, many of whom had been injured when the structure had tilted, had to decide whether to take to the life rafts or remain on the perilously angled rig. They were aware that Sea King helicopters would never reach the crippled platform in such conditions, yet most chose to stay with the rig: the sea looked the more dangerous of the alternatives. The banked-up waters sped along the coastline, sweeping inland where the sea defences were weak or the lay of the land was low, devastating coastal towns and ports, destroying property and lives with merciless fury.

The rise in the sea-level increased as the north wind relentlessly pushed it onwards, for movement was blocked further south by the narrowing of the North Sea basin between East Anglia and Holland, and the bottleneck of the Straits of Dover. The water rapidly accumulated and began to pile up as it moved southwards towards the vulnerable coastal towns.

SIXTEEN

Sector Officer George Gavin slammed down the phone and stared out into the stormy blackness beyond the windows of the coastguard lookout tower. It would be on them at any moment. Bloody fools! As in '53, the warning had come too late! The build-up to the flood had begun in the early hours of the morning, but only when the rising waters had steam-rollered their way down half the coast of eastern England had the alarms gone out.

He checked his watch and swore softly. A few minutes past eight. There was an unnatural darkness outside as though the winter night had suddenly returned. The town would be unprepared, memories of the last disastrous flood dim in the minds of the older inhabitants, and merely interesting stories to the younger folk. George had been sector officer for that area of coastline even then, and had felt helpless against the sea's vicious onslaught: now that same sense of uselessness had returned. The local Constabulary, whom he had just spoken to on the telephone, had already been alerted to the danger and units had been dispersed to the nearest seaside towns. But there was no time for evacuation, only a chance to warn people to get themselves above ground level. If only more time, more money, had been spent on building sea defences . . . The flood barriers and walls that had been erected after the '53 flood would have some effect in reducing the catastrophe, but the Waverly Committee, appointed by the government to indicate a margin of safety for sea defences with regard to risk and costs had made the 1953 flood the standard for all other floods. A higher surge had never been taken into account.

It was George's duty to stay in the lookout tower situated at the southern end of the town's sea parade until circumstances dictated otherwise, but this time his loyalties were more immediate. Mary, his wife, was no longer the robust woman she had been in the fifties: tonight she would be propped up with cushions on the sofa in their front room, watching television. She rarely complained of the arthritis that almost crippled her limbs, but the pain was evident in the lines that had eaten into her face, aging her once strong features with a severity that had nothing to do with passing years. George knew he had to get to their small house just a few hundred yards across from the deserted car park behind the lookout tower. There were no other warnings he could give and even less duties he could perform to help the general situation. Mary's safety was his prime concern.

The wind smashed into him as he stepped from the cocooned shelter of the tower, almost throwing him down the metal steps. He clung to the handrail for several long seconds, shocked by the ferocity of the gale and struggling to regain the breath that had been knocked from him. Rain lashed at his face, forcing him to shield his eyes with one hand. He became even more frightened when the wind buffeted his thin frame, trying to force him away from the railing, and quickly used both hands once more to grip the metal. God, he hadn't realised the wind was so strong even though he had seen the waves whipped mercilessly white by it from inside his lookout post! The reports from further up the coast had not prepared him for its intensity. Perhaps it had gained such a momentum only in the past hour. He began to descend the steps, clinging to the rail and moving cautiously. Had it not been for Mary he would have crept back into his shelter and prayed for the rest of the night.

By the time he reached ground level, his cap was gone and his eyes stung with salt water pelting in from the sea. He was reluctant to let go of the rail, knowing that he would be fully exposed to the elements once he left the shelter of the building. Closing his mind against the danger, he stepped out onto the parade, his body crouched low against the tearing wind. Both hands shielded his eyes now and, when he looked along the edge

202

of the sea wall towards the north from where the worst of the storm was approaching, a numbness ran through him.

He knew there was no chance for him, not even if he ducked back into the shelter of the building, 'Oh, Mary, Mary,' he said, as the solid wall of black water hurtled along the seafront towards him.

The caravan park on the northern fringe of the town was the first area to be hit by the massive wave. It had easily broken through the defences further along the coast, gale force winds driving the sea swell forward with a force that was impossible to stop.

On site No 11, Joseph Frazetta was running the buzzing vibrator over the nipples of the girl lying beneath him in the bunk bed. They had arrived earlier that afternoon and this was only their third bout of lovemaking. Joseph, who was forty-two and had his own small printing company in Colchester, reckoned the caravan – or 'Mobile Home' as his wife, Doreen, preferred to call it – was the best buy he had ever made. Ideal for the family and summer holidays, great for renting out to friends when he wasn't using it, and terrific for bringing girlfriends to when he was 'officially' away on business. Mandy, the girlfriend who happened to be under him at that moment, was not too ecstatic, though.

The storm outside had bothered her for the past hour. She was sure the wind had shifted the caravan's position a couple of times. And she was sure, despite Joey's reassurances, that it was about to be blown over at any moment. Even the delicious tingle from the humming machine could not push the anxieties from her mind.

'Come on, babe, relax,' Joey urged as he moved the tip of the vibrator down her rib cage.

'How can I bloody relax with that commotion outside?' Mandy complained.

'It's nothing. These shacks are solid enough.' He nuzzled her neck. 'The worst'll be over soon, you'll see.'

'Oh yeah? What worst? Your dick or that storm?'

He chuckled. 'You didn't complain the first time, darling.'

'No, nor the second. Give us a bloody break, though, Joey. We haven't even had dinner yet.'

'Plenty of time for that, babe,' he soothed. 'Can't go out when the weather's like this.'

Joey ran the vibrator over his own nipples and moaned at the sensation.

'Who'd you bloody buy that for anyway?' Mandy asked, the whine in her voice beginning to irritate her lover a little. 'You're enjoying it more than me.'

'Mustn't be selfish, Mandy.' He passed the instrument lightly over her lips, then down her neck between her breasts. Despite her concern, she shuddered when the tip ran over her stomach and into her pubic hair.

'Ooh, that's nice, Joe.'

'Course it is, babe. I told you you'd like it.' He taunted her by bypassing the place she wanted to be touched and instead brought the skin on her smooth thigh alive. She pulled at his wrist and guilded the pulsating plastic towards the tender opening that had become moist once more. The first sensation was like a pleasurable electric shock and the second, as the mechanical penis entered, sent shivers of excitement radiating outwards.

'Ooh, that's good.'

'Yeah, me next, darling.'

She groaned, but he hardly heard over the howling outside. 'Just a bit more with this, Joe. Then you can have me.'

'No, not you, babe. Me. And the vibo.'

'What? How . . . ?' She sighed. 'Sometimes I wonder about you, Joey.'

'We all like our little pleasures, doll.' He was grinning from ear to ear and his eyes closed with pleasure as her writhing increased. They snapped open when he felt the caravan lurch sideways.

At first, Mandy thought that the sensation had come from within herself such was the pleasure she had been feeling, but as the room around her began to turn she knew something dreadful was happening.

Then it was as if a giant hand had smacked against the side of the caravan. They tumbled from the bunk bed and everything was plunged into darkness.

'Joe!' Mandy screamed, but a crashing, splintering sound drowned the cry. She felt air rush into the room; either the windows had smashed or the walls had cracked. She felt wet. She was lying in water. Rushing water.

She tried to get to her feet, but the room was spinning, objects falling.

'Joey, where are you?'

Bedclothes tangled her naked legs and as she reached out to free herself, her hands came in contact with her lover's body. She pulled at him and felt him stir. 'Joey, what's happening?'

He couldn't answer, there was too much dizziness inside his head. He must have struck something as he fell from the bed. But what the fuck *was* happening? Water was lapping around his bare arse.

He managed to crawl onto the bunk bed and he lay there, teeth sinking into a pillow. Mandy managed somehow to scramble up onto his back and she clung to him. Clung to him until the caravan smashed against a tree and overturned and what was up was now down. And what was a wall became the floor. And what was the floor was just a torrent of foaming water.

There were not many fishermen on the beach that evening, for the bad weather during the day had precluded any reasonable catch. The shore anglers had not even bothered to leave the comfort of their homes let alone attempt casting lines into the angry sea, and those whose livelihood depended on what their small boats brought in from deeper waters had long since abandoned their day's toil. They had returned early and winched their vessels up onto the shingle beach, cursing the weather and their trade which was already dying. One or two worked on in the wooden huts that stood in a disordered row before the low seawall, mending torn nets, a task that had to be completed before the next day's fishing. They stopped and listened when the howling wind took on a new sound. It was a low rumble and, as it quickly developed into an approaching roar, they realised the noise had nothing to do with the wind. The shadows of their bodies, cast by the lamps they worked by, grew to giant proportions and curved around the walls and ceilings as the fishermen rose from their benches and hurried to the doors. They looked towards the north, from where the thundering noise was coming, squinting their eyes against the pelting rain. The disbelief on their faces quickly turned into expressions of despair.

There was only one person foolhardy enough to be walking the beach that evening, but he was a man that not even dire circumstances could bend. Twenty years as a High Court judge had hardened him against the iniquities of human nature; nothing could shock him any more, and not much could stir pity in him for his fellow man, be they perpetrators or victims. His senses, his emotions, had become jaded by years of judgement. He had learned in his first few years as a judge to hear only dimly the complications of each case – and *every* case became complicated by the sparring of prosecution and defence counsels – and to keep the facts clear and simple in his own mind. He had long ago abandoned grey areas, for he believed they could only thwart justice. Even now, in his retirement, he refused to believe prejudice had ever played any part in his decisions, nor had he ever been swayed by the smooth arguments of counsel. He was certain his judgements had always been correct, even though more than one had been overruled in subsequent courts of appeal. That, he told himself, was only legal tomfoolery. He had invariably decided upon the guilt or innocence of the person in the dock within the first few days of trial and, once his mind was made up, little could alter that decision. He sometimes smiled inwardly at the barristers – particularly the young, up-and-coming 'bright boys' who somehow, often uncannily, guessed that the verdict was prematurely clear in the judge's mind long before the end of the case – as they made frantic and ingenious attempts to persuade him otherwise. He knew that some of them considered his eventual elevation to the Court of Appeal to be a means of putting him where he could do the least harm; but that was merely malice on their parts, for many had felt humiliated in his court. No, he had never regretted any judgement he had made, for there were never *strong* doubts in his mind. Smaller doubts that tried to nag away at his resolution were easily swept aside by the knowledge that he was never wrong. He was always right. That was why he was a fool. And only a fool would have walked along the shoreline on such a night.

Even his Welsh Terrier, the judge's sole companion in his retirement and who had never once in its twelve years' life-span doubted his master's decision, was not *that* foolish. The dog had fled the beach minutes before and was now whimpering on the door step on their home near the centre of their town.

The judge called out against the wind, but the terrier was nowhere to be seen. Dratted animal, he thought. Hadn't missed an evening's walk along the beach for the past two years, come wind, rain or snow. It certainly looked fierce out there, but damn it all, winter was over! The cutting wind and driving rain denied his assertion.

Where was that rogue? Cowering behind a fisherman's hut, no doubt. Frightened of a little bit of bad weather. Thinking the old man was wrong to bring him out on such a foul night. Stupid, stupid dog. The old man was never . . .

His muttering stopped abruptly and he looked into the distance. A strange rumbling sound was approaching, but it was difficult to trace its source in the darkness and with the rain dashing against his eyes. It may have just been the trembling of his old, podgy legs, but he was sure the shingle he stood on was undulating with some movement beneath the surface.

Then he saw the massive wave appearing from the gloom like a thick black wall, its top fringed with a churning whiteness that threatened to roll down and smash against the beach at any moment. Huts and fishing boats were absorbed into the dark wall without resistance, while others were swept before it, some pulverised so that only fragments of hurtling wood remained.

The judge could have run, but it would have done him no good. He could have screamed for help, but that, also, would have done him no good. Standing up to face the onslaught was a poor alternative. He sank to his knees and rolled himself into a ball. He had never been so terrified in all his life. Somewhere along the line, he had acquired the notion that his position in law had given him some kind of invulnerability against adversity, that his infallibility in judgements extended to decisions outside the courtroom. Now, as the water pounded over him and he was swept along with the torrent, he knew that he had been wrong to walk along the beach that night. About that, he was right.

The hotel overlooked the seafront and the dining-room was not crowded on that blustery April night. The headwaiter, or *maitre d'* as he preferred to be called, strove to look elegant in his black jacket and sharply creased trousers, but the tiny bow-tie clinging to his neck like a shrivelled bat and his slightly frayed shirtcuffs thwarted his best efforts. The long jacket served to conceal the shine in the seat of his trousers but could not, of course, conceal the shine in the bottom of his jacket. His squat nose, which looked peculiarly overwrought, did not sit too happily with his finely trimmed, pencil-line moustache, and his neatly plucked eyebrows were somehow in contrast with the heavy, purplish bags beneath his eyes. The effect was of someone who had modelled the superficial parts of his body – his hair was brilliantined flat at the top with crinkly grey pieces carefully cultivated to sweep over his ears to meet at the back of his neck – to match every magazine ad's idea of the perfect restaurant *maidre d'*. Only the loose heaviness of his features let him down. And the feebly disguised shoddiness of his attire. Not to mention the occasional lapse of good professional manners when a waiter made one mistake too many. Or a diner was over-demanding.

He quickly scanned the room to make sure everything was in order, his attention drawn mainly to the long centre table where the freemasons were having their monthly get-together. There were several important businessmen from the surrounding area among them, as well as one or two councillors, and the headwaiter always made sure their every need was catered for. There were many better hotels and restaurants to work in in that part of Suffolk and recommendation by word-of-mouth was important in such a community. The only other diners were a young couple, probably in their late twenties, and an older couple, probably in their early forties. Second honeymoon or just a dirty weekend? The older pair looked more in love than the younger two. Perhaps they were the ones not married. A man sat alone in the corner of the room, slowly munching his food with all the self-consciousness of someone without a dining partner. He would have business somewhere in the area. Not a sales rep though; there were cheaper hotels in the locale that they used.

The windows rattled against their frames, startling him from his thoughts. My God, the weather was a bitch tonight! He doubted there would be any customers from outside the hotel that evening and there were not many guests staying anyway. He felt pleased: he could pay more attention to the freemasons. In an hour or so they would retire to the conference room upstairs which they had booked until 12pm, and there they would go into their silly 'secret' rituals. They weren't aware of the giggles they provoked in various members of the hotel staff eavesdropping at the door.

Ah, they had finished their first course. He snapped his fingers and frowned when John, the young Australian waiter, did not instantly appear at his side. No doubt flirting with Helen, the part-time waitress. Little slut! And so was she.

He walked towards the swing-doors leading to the kitchen and quickly stepped aside as John came crashing through, a big grin on his face. The beam vanished as he stopped before the *maitre d'*.

'Really, John, sometimes I despair of you.'

John subdued his grin into a boyish smile, the kind he knew his superior was fond of. 'Sorry, Mr Balascombe,' he apologised sheepishly. 'Just giving Chef a hand.'

'Your duty it out here, John. A good waiter spends as little time as possible in the kitchen.'

'Yes, Mr Balascombe.' You old poufta.

'See to the centre table; they're ready for the next course.'

'Right, Mr Balascombe.' Dirty old buggerer.

John swept towards the crowded centre table whose occupants thought his smirk was a subservient smile directed at themselves.

The headwaiter sighed inwardly. The boy wouldn't last through the summer. He was trouble. Like the Italian last year, who imagined private favours earned special privileges in the dining-room. Not so, though; nothing would interfere with the smooth running of his professional domain. He had once dreamed he was *maitre d'* on the *Titanic* and had gone to each table as the ship sank, enquiring if everything was in order. *Tartare* not spicy enough, sir? Perhaps a touch more Worcestershire. A little dressing on your green salad, madame? French, or perhaps vinaigrette? The game soup is too watery, sir? Perhaps it's just the sea spilling over into the dish.

He glided authoritatively towards the freemasons' table, casting a well-practised eye towards the other diners; it wouldn't do to have any grumbles within range of his more important clients. He would make sure Helen gave the two couples and the solitary man all the attention they required.

He smiled benevolently at the ageing gannets and several turned to look up at him with wide-open mouths. Sorry, I have no worms. Perhaps I can find some juicy cockroaches in the kitchen. He said, 'I'm sorry about this awful weather, gentlemen,' as if he were its creator. They good-humouredly informed him that it wasn't his fault, although one or two implied they would hold him responsible next time.

His eyes and smile glazed slightly when he saw John allow the dregs of a soup spoon to drip onto the head of the man he was leaning over. Fortunately the thick mat of hair obviously had no roots in the aged scalp it covered, so the diner was unaware of the accident. The headwaiter felt his knees go weak when he saw John reaching into his pocket for a handkerchief and he desperately tried to catch the waiter's eye. It was like a bad dream. Everything slowed down. John produced a grubby wadge of grey material, a crumpled-up ball that resembled a small, washed-out brain, and carefully, every-so carefully, guided it towards the green blob of pea soup that refused to be absorbed in the man's Crown Topper.

Mr Balascombe resisted the urge to faint. Had his thinking cells not become paralysed he may have offered a silent prayer; had his mouth not locked open, he may have offered a strangled but discreet discouragement. Instead it was left to the harsh forces of nature to save the situation.

All heads turned towards the windows that looked out onto the seafront as they heard the deep rumbling noise.

The first boat crashed through the far window of the dining-room, sweeping in with the torrent of water, its mast snapped in two by the brickwork at the top of the frame. It smashed onto the table where the young couple sat, crushing them so that drowning had nothing to do with their deaths. The second boat was larger and became wedged in the centre window of the dining-room. Every ground-floor window on the east side was broken as the huge wave hit the hotel front and sea-water poured into the building.

The headwaiter screeched as the torrent raised the big centre table high into the air, cutlery and dishes sliding its length to be cleansed of foodscraps as they had never been cleansed before. Mr Balascombe fell backwards, other bodies piling into him and the entire contents of the dining-room were swept towards the far wall. Objects struck him, stunning him, and he could not be sure if they were tables, chairs, or human limbs. Sea-water rushed up his nose and into his throat and he spluttered for breath; he twisted his body in a vain attempt to take up a swimming position. As he burst through the kitchen doors and caught a crazy, swirling image of the transfixed kitchen staff, a small part of his mind was relieved that John had been prevented from using the handkerchief. It's an ill wind, he thought as he went through the window on the other side of the kitchen.

He was heading out of town when his car's headlights picked out the solid black wall racing towards him. He wasn't puzzled by the sight, only frightened. He stood on his brakes and locked the wheels with the handbrake, spinning the steering-wheel to his right so that the BMW went into a tight skid and turned in the direction from which it had just come. His foot was already on the accelerator pedal before the car had completed the turn and he had to fight the steering-wheel to gain control. First, Second, Third, and he was roaring back into the rain-lashed streets, his foot down hard, body hunched forward for better vision through the speckled windscreen, the wipers working frantically to keep it clear. His reactions had always been good – sometimes he thought that maybe they were too good, for he had the tendency to leap before looking. Tonight, though, he and his car would have already been under several feet of water had it not been for prompt action. He was scared, yet a wave of excitement ran through him, a heightening of senses that had become rare since marriage, a son, and business commitments. Fear was a great motivator – perhaps the greatest – and a great adrenalin-pusher. He had known that in his racing days where speed had been both foe and ally; no such sensations existed for him in the plodding commercial world of buying and selling autosport goods. The two shops he owned provided him with an income, but could not provide stimulation. They were no adrenalin-pushers. The wave behind him was.

Mercifully, the road along the seafront was empty of people and moving vehicles, not many encouraged to venture out on such a night. He used the centre of the road, aware that it narrowed considerably further ahead so that turning right would be a comparatively slow process. And he had to turn right to reach higher ground, which meant he would have to make the manoeuvre now, before he reached the narrower confines.

He glanced into his rear-view mirror, and saw nothing but blackness behind. A small green lawn, at its centre a stone monument in the shape of a cross, was lit up by his headlights and he swung to the left, intending to sweep in a wide arc to enter a small sidestreet on his right. He would have made it had he not tried to avoid the dog that suddenly streaked across his path.

Reacting rather than thinking, he turned the wheel even further to the left, then tried to straighten it when he saw the low sea-wall rushing towards him. He avoided the dog, but hit the wall.

Sparks flew from the car's bodywork as metal and concrete screeched against each other. Instead of taking his foot from the accelerator pedal, he kept his foot down, hoping to tear himself away from the wall rather than be twisted into it. He ignored the grinding, scraping sound and the shower of sparks flying past his passenger window, and pulled against the tug of the steering-wheel, using his strength and skill to ease the BMW away from the wall without stopping.

Too late he saw the stone steps that jutted outwards from the wall and his front, left-hand tyre had hit them before he could wrench the wheel around. The impact send him bouncing upwards, his head striking the car's sunroof. The BMW spun round, once, twice, rear right-hand corner canoning off the wall, spinning so that the front hit again at an angle, rebounding and speeding backwards, leaving rubber smeared against the wet road.

The seat-belt, after the initial wrench upwards, had firmly locked him into the driver's seat. He was stunned, but still aware of what was approaching his windscreen, for the car was now facing the rushing wave. Feebly, he reached for the ignition key and turned it, pressing a leaden foot down on the clutch. He pushed the gear-lever into First and gripped the steering-wheel, twisting it towards his left. The engine whined pathetically as the car crawled forward a few inches before bumping to a halt. The smell of burning was strong.

There was nothing outside now, just the lights bouncing off the black churning wall only a few feet away. Then no light at all. The wall was around him and the car was moving once more. The wall broke through the windscreen before he had a chance to scream.

The wave swept through the town, pounding against and tearing through buildings, pouring into sidestreets and cascading down into basements. Debris and bodies were carried with it and other waves followed the first, supplementing each other, driven on by the volume behind, the fierce wind lashing at the crests so that they spewed white. It was too late for the townsfolk to close their shutters, too late to pile up sandbags before their front doors and, for many, too late to climb upstairs or onto their rooftops, for the flood had hit too fast, too suddenly. It raced into the high street, a churning, bubbling deluge now, seeking out every low opening, picking up anything not welded or concreted into the ground, a watery mass of destruction.

The usherette sat upright in her seat and craned her neck round, peering through heavy-lensed spectacles into the flickering gloom of the cinema. On screen, the walls of the old house were dripping blood and the madman with the axe stalked the dark corridors searching for his prey. A severed hand from his first victim was tucked into his belt.

Someone snickered again, a suppressed sound that spread like an infectious disease along one particular row of teenagers at the back of the tiny theatre. Hilary Burnchard, the usherette, stood with her back against the entrance/exit door for several moments to let the troublemakers know she would not stand for any nonsense. There were other patrons – not many tonight, granted – who had paid good money to see the film and who didn't want it spoilt by hooligans who couldn't or wouldn't behave. She knew the ringleaders all right, for in such a small town, reputations and names were all too familiar.

The madman with the axe had stopped outside a door and was testing the handle. It was locked. Now he was crouching to look through the keyhole, an insane grin on his hairy features.

Hilary averted her eyes; she hated this bit. She had seen the film four times already that week and had still not got used to the horror and gore. She wondered what the film world was coming to: whatever happened to those nice musicals they used to make?

Several girls in the audience shrieked when the thin, foot-long spike came through the keyhole and pierced the madman's bulbous eye. Blood spurted along the glistening spike and the actor's scream drowned out the guffaws of the disorderly row of teenagers.

Hilary's lips tightened into a straight line when one of the boys, clutching his eye, jumped to his feet and moaned, 'I only wanted to see if the bathroom was free!'

She walked across the aisle just below the screen, her step slow but steady, unaware that the cut-out silhouette of her head was moving across the face of the writhing man and was about to be snapped off by his gnashing teeth. She wondered what had caused the increased howls of laughter from the back row.

The little cinema was in the high street and occupied the same building as an estate agent and a solicitor's office, the latter two being on the first floor above the theatre. It did not take many

214

bodies to fill the rows of seats, but somehow it was always half-empty. An open book with a pencil stub attached by string usually stood just outside the foyer in the afternoon for people to sign their names should they want to see that night's showing: quite often, the manager decided not to open if there were not fresh names in the book and the particular film was experiencing a dismal run. His staff – projectionist, usherette and cashier – were employed on the basis that they worked only when there were enough customers. Hilary did not always enjoy the job, particularly when there was a horror or dirty movie on, but the money, a pittance though it was, came in handy to supplement her husband's income as a handyman-cum-gardener. She especially did not enjoy the job when there was a rowdy bunch present.

She strolled up the slight incline towards the back of the cinema as the giant door behind her slowly began to open. The row of teenagers nervously eyed both her and the screen as she approached, one or two of them finding it difficult to stifle their giggles. The door made a loud creaking noise as it opened wider and the madman was silent as he watched with one, wide, good eye.

The cinema had become quiet once more: no rustling of sweet papers, no shifting uncomfortably in seats, no suppressed giggles. A shadow moved in the doorway. Someone – or *something* – was about to emerge.

Even Hilary, who had seen the film four times before and knew what was going to happen, stared anxiously at the screen, the teenage irritation forgotten for the moment. And it was she who shrieked when the exit door burst open and the manager stood there waving his arms and shouting.

The audience caught a few garbled words that sounded liked 'blood' or 'flood' just before water gushed through and began to fill the auditorium.

It took severe conditions to keep the regulars away and Ron, the barman, knew that tonight's weather was not the worst they'd experienced. It was gusty, all right, but most of his customers were used to that, being seamen. It would take a monsoon to keep his lot away. Maybe not even that.

'Come on, Ron, let's be havin you!'

He turned and waved towards the group of men at the far end of the bar, then continued counting the change into the hand of the customer he was serving. He walked down the bar towards the impatient group, retrieving his half-smoked cigarette from an ashtray as he went. As usual, the air was thick with smoke. Once, Ron had tried to give up smoking, but soon had realised he was inhaling so much lung pollution from the pub's atmosphere that it would make little difference.

'What'll it be, gents. Four more of "Old"?'

'That'll do us.'

Ron placed the cigarette in an ashtray at that end of the bar and picked up a drained glass. As he pulled the first pint, he asked, 'Anything out there tonight?'

The group knew what he was referring to, for they were fishermen. 'They'd have to be bloody mad,' one of them, a thick-set man whose eyes glowered angrily beneath bushy white eyebrows, replied. His face had the craggy, weathered look of someone who spent much of his life on the open sea which, indeed, he had. He was the owner of the drifter now moored securely in the town's natural harbour and the men around him were his crew. None were blood kin, for he had been cursed with daughters who had long since fled his bitter grumblings and the confines of the small town. His grumbling was more bitter than ever that night, for conditions had lost him a day's work and his crew still expected to be paid.

Ron placed the pint of ale before him and he sucked at it noisily without waiting for the others.

'Didn't see old Tom Adcock's boat in,' one of his crew members said.

'Nah, nothin stops im goin out,' his skipper growled. 'Take a bloody hurricane. Some of the catches he comes back with sometimes, I don't know why he bothers.'

'Well, I bet he's steamin back now, catch or no catch,' the barman said. 'He's got more sense than to risk losin his boat.'

'Aah, I'm not so sure about Tom anymore,' the skipper retorted. 'Keeps sayin he's gonna pack it in soon, retire somewhere where you can't smell salt in the air.' He grudgingly

216

joined in the laughter around him. 'Funny notions, old Tom.'

'Won't get much for his boat nowadays, so where'll he get the money to retire on?' one of the men said reaching for the next pint.

Ron shook his head, his usual affable grin on his face. 'Can't see him leavin the sea, anyway. Reckon he'd rather go down with his boat than rot in his rockin chair.'

The others nodded in agreement and the skipper placed the exact money for the drinks on the bartop as the last pint was drawn. Ron slid the loose change and pound note off the bar and into the palm of his hand, then walked back towards the cash till. He rang up the order and placed the coins and note into their appropriate compartments, thinking for the thousandth time how lucky the governor was to have such an honest barman. The Mister and Missus enjoyed their social life and more often than not left Ron in complete charge of the pub, knowing they could trust him. Tonight they were seeing a show in Ipswich; tomorrow it was a licensed victuallers' dinner and social. Not bad for some, he thought, without rancour.

A cold blast ruffled the hair on the back of his neck as the double-doors were flung open and a man and woman almost staggered in. The man had some difficulty closing the doors behind him. The couple were well wrapped up in raincoats, scarves and hats and they dripped puddles as they made their way to the bar.

Ron's grin broadened. 'Just out for a stroll then?' he enquired.

The couple scowled back at him. 'Bloody weather!' the man said, shaking water off his hat.

'Doesn't keep him indoors, though,' his wife said tartly.

'No, nor you, woman,' came the reply.

'What'll it be, Eric?' Ron asked amiably. 'Guinness and a shandy for Mag?'

'No, I'll have a gin and tonic – warm meself up. Give her her shandy.

'Right you are.'

Ron had just pushed a small glass under the gin optic when he noticed that bottles on the shelf were vibrating slightly. He frowned and turned back to the bar to point out the strange occurrence to his customers. But they were looking up at the ceiling. The decorative chamber pots hanging up there were stirring, clanking against each other as though invisible fingers were jerking their strings.

Ron's mouth dropped open.

His customers were switching their gaze from the ceiling to each other in bewilderment and it was the woman he was serving who realised what was about to happen. She began to shout a warning but the rumbling noise was warning enough.

The windows and doors burst open as the sea flooded in.

Pandemonium broke loose as customers were swept off their feet and furniture became floating debris.

The surge hit the bar counter and smacked upwards towards the ceiling, dislodging chamber pots, bringing them down like shrapnel on the heads of the struggling customers below.

Ron fell backwards as more water poured over the bar. He crashed into the shelves behind him and bottles showered down. Then he was choking on sea-water. Then he was swallowing it.

'The buoys! They've gone! We're losing them, Skipper!'

Tom Adcock's groan was loud, a wail against the stormy sea. He shook off the despair. 'It don't matter! It's ourselves we got to worry about!'

The wind lashed rain against the windows of the small deck cabin and he could barely see two yards in front. His three-man crew were crammed into the cabin and clutching at anything solid to prevent themselves from being tossed against the walls. The man who had just checked on their illicit and now lost cargo wiped the salt water from his face with a shaky hand. Just a few minutes outside, with no protection against the elements, had badly frightened him. 'We'll never make the estuary! There's no way we can get into it.'

Adcock's face was grim. 'We've no choice! We can't outrun the storm!'

The bows of the *Rosie* lifted high into the air, rising over the mountainous wave and plunging down the other side with sickening speed. Water smashed onto the sturdy little fishing boat and the splintering of wood threw fresh panic into the crew.

'We're goin to break up!' someone shouted.

'Just shut your bloody traps!' Adcock told them, his voice raised so that it could be heard over the pounding waves and howling wind. 'The *'Rosie'*'ll get us home! She's never let us down yet!'

The drifter was rising again and Adcock saw what he had been looking for. Or, at least, thought he saw, for visibility was appalling. 'Get over here, Ned!' he ordered. 'D'you see em? Dead ahead!'

'I see em, Tom! Lights! We're at the coast!'

'Do we send up a flare, Skipper?' another crew member asked as he peered out into the storm, trying to see what the others had seen.

'No! We don't need no lifeboat! Lot of bloody good they'd be in this sea!' Adcock quickly checked his instruments and tried to recognise the formation of lights as the vessel dipped and heaved. 'I see the lighthouse, boys! We're almost there!'

'Can we get in, though?' Ned demanded to know.

'We'll get in all right! I promise you that!'

He fought with the wheel while the men around him silently prayed. They prayed and he cursed. They should have left it. The reports had said weather conditions would be bad that day. Bad? That was a laugh! Only greed had sent him to pick up the shipment. It was a big load this time: two containers worth millions to that bastid Slauden! Not that his own share wasn't worth the risk. Was it, though? Was anything worth losing your life before its natural time? Andy knew the answer to that. Stupid bastid!

He could see the lights of the town now and he envied the people tucked up safe and warm in their cosy little houses. Bet the boys were in the pub wondering how the *Rosie* was faring. Well set one up for me, lads! I'll be there soon!

'Tom, mebbe we ought to sent up a flare.'

'No need, Ned, no need. We'll be safe and dry within the half-hour! Old *Rosie*'s got plenny to say about the matter!' Adcock gave out a gruff laugh, more to encourage his crew than as an expression of his own relief. 'Nearly there, darlin,' he said softly to the boat, gripping the wheel tightly to prevent it from spinning. 'Just keep goin for me, girl, just keep goin.'

A hand clutched at his arm. 'Skipper! Can you see that!'

He squinted his eyes to follow the direction of his deckie's trembling finger and his face creased in puzzlement. 'What the hell are you talkin about, boy! There's nothing to see but bloody waves!'

'Wait till we come up again, Skipper! I'm sure I saw something!'

Adcock steadied himself as the drifter rocked violently. Then they were rising again and as they crested a wave he saw something that he could scarcely believe. It was only its imminent nearness that made it visible.

Adcock's eyes were still wide and staring ahead as the boat plummeted downwards once more.

'What was it, Skipper?' the deckhand crouched on the floor of the cabin shouted. 'What's to see?'

But there was no need to reply, for the mountainous wave that was making its way down the eastern coastline was almost upon them, rearing up out of the night like a rushing wall of blackness, a wall that crushed everything in its path.

'Ooooh, Jesus, help us!' someone screamed as the forty-foot wave blanked out everything before them.

Then the black wall swallowed the boat like a whale swallows plankton.

The flood passed through the town, breaking, destroying, drowning. People and animals were sucked into the swirling waters. Walls were smashed, cars overturned, fragile buildings demolished. The houses and hotels along the seafront were worst hit, many of the occupants plucked from their homes and swept out to sea. The town's lifeboat, perched proudly on its concrete mounts, was wrenched free and thrown against nearby buildings. The stone memorial, dedicated to those from the town who had lost their lives in the treacherous seas over the decades, was toppled and smashed into unrecognisable pieces. Not one fisherman's hut remained along the shoreline. Not one house facing the sea remained unscathed. Even the coastguards' lookout tower was dragged from its perch and swept away. Stones from the shingle beach hurtled through the water like bullets, embedding themselves in walls, breaking through windows to kill or maim those inside. The boatyard at the far end of town became a racing flotilla of broken timber.

Those lucky enough to survive the first massive onslaught climbed to their upstairs rooms, battered, frightened but grateful to be alive. Others, those who lived in bungalows, broke through ceilings to reach lofts. Some climbed onto their rooftops where they were exposed to the full intensity of the howling storms. Men swam through the floating debris, risking the fast-flowing currents to search for lost loved-ones, wives, children, parents.

The lower regions of the town were devastated and the people knew – those who were still capable of knowing – that the worst was not yet over, that the night would be agonisingly long and cold, that exposure might claim them even if the waters did not.

The floodwaters reached the estuary and filled it, surging upriver and swamping the surrounding marshes, pushing onwards, the force still behind it, urging it on to destroy, to pound, to smother.

SEVENTEEN

DR VERNON Collingbury cast anxious eyes towards the night sky, his vision immediately blurred by driving raindrops on his spectacles. He ducked back into the shelter of the boathouse.

He had accompanied Sir Anthony to the motor cruiser in the vain hope that he could dissuade the man from his current course of action. When he had become associated with Sir Anthony, many years before, it was on the assurance that the enterprise, illegal though it was, would be confined to drug processing and distribution alone: no other criminal offences would be committed, nor permitted. He had been a fool to believe it. A gullible, naïve fool.

Yet there had been no violence until recently. Or had there? What did *he* know of Sir Anthony's other activities. What did *he* know of what went on outside the processing laboratory. His job was to direct the team of technicians, skilled men who were hired several times a year, chemists who were brought secretly to Eshley Hall to process the raw material. None of them ever knew the location, for they were brought collectively from a pre-arranged meeting-point; they travelled in the back of a truck which offered no views of the outside world. They did not even know whom they were employed by. Four men, handpicked by him for Sir Anthony. Two were university drop-outs – he had taught them himself and knew their capabilities – and the other two were men with whom he had worked in the past. Men who could be trusted as long as the money was right. And there was no quarrel about that.

Greed – the great seducer. Money – the great reconciler. Kelly, the unfortunate man who had been so severely beaten and then drugged, had asked Sir Anthony why he had indulged in drugs dealing, but had received no answer. But he, Sir Anthony's bought chemist knew, for both he and his employer shared the same motive. Sir Anthony had admitted it at the beginning of their association, for he felt no shame and saw no reason why he, Dr Collingbury, should. It was all for money. No political motive, no burning ambition for revenge on a society that had changed so radically since the last world war and with which he could – paradoxically though it might have seemed – feel only disgust. Nor was it any great ideal, a fervent belief that the taking of drugs lead to mind-expansion, and through it, enlightenment. No, the motive was purely and simply money. Sir Anthony subsidised his other, failing, business interests with the profits from his highly lucrative private industry. Perhaps somewhere in his own mind he justified his illicit business by blaming others, the politicians and trade unionists who had slowly stifled the country's economic growth, forcing such as he to either move their operations to more sympathetic countries, or to indulge in other, less public activities in order to survive. He may have had those thoughts, but Dr Collingbury doubted it. Sir Anthony was corrupt. But then, little more so than those who had engineered his knighthood.

Dr Collingbury readily agreed to organise the underground laboratory, eager for the wealth that had eluded him throughout his long, tiresome career. The country held more regard for footballers and pop stars than men of learning. But now, murder had entered the scene. He should have known that with men like Bannen and his thugs working for the same employer, violence was always near to hand. But murder was even less palatable.

He was sure that Kelly was to be killed; Sir Anthony could not possibly let the man live. And now he had heard them talking of a girl, someone they had brought to the house in the early hours of the morning. Who was she, and what would they do to her? Sir Anthony had ignored his questions and entreaties as they had made their way along the tunnel to the boathouse. All he was interested in was whether or not the laboratory was fully prepared for the incoming shipment.

They had walked to the end of the boathouse and stood there in a group, shoulders hunched against the biting gale, concerned over the safety of the *Rosie* and the valuable cargo it would be bringing back. The motor cruiser had been made ready and Sir Anthony had stepped aboard with one last comment to Dr Collingbury, which had been shouted over the noise of the wind and the revving engine: 'You just worry about the work you do for me, Vernon; let me worry about anything else!'

Did 'anything else' include murder? Wasn't the young deckhand's enough? How many more would there be now that the pattern was set?

As he stood there with the wind sweeping through the boathouse and buffeting his thin frame, Dr Vernon Collingbury considered going to the police. And rejected the idea almost immediately.

'Let's get out of this fuckin weather!'

The shout startled him and he turned to see one of Bannen's henchmen standing behind him. Sir Anthony had taken only Henson, Bannen and another man with him over to the mill, leaving this one behind to make sure the tunnel doors were securely closed; the river sometimes had a nasty habit in these conditions of overflowing and flooding the underground tunnel leading to the laboratory.

He nodded his agreement; he must have been standing there for at least ten minutes after the boat's departure and his clothing was soaked through. Well, his conscience had been wrestled with and it had been the loser. It accepted the defeat.

'What's that noise?' the man behind him said. Dr Collingbury listened and his eyes grew wide as the sound grew louder.

The man pushed past him and craned his neck around the boathouse entrance. Even in the poor glow from the building's overhead light his face looked pale as he drew back.

'What is it?' Dr Collingbury shook him to get some response, but he was roughly pushed aside as the man ran for the steps at the rear of the boathouse.

The chemist watched the scuttling figure in bewilderment, then looked around the edge of the entrance himself. His vision was still distorted by the raindrops on his glasses, but there was no mistaking the deep rumble as the tidal wave sped upriver towards him.

He spun round, almost slipping on the wet concrete as he ran towards the tunnel. The wave was well over the banks of the river and even in his panic he knew it would have been fatal to make for the house through the sloping grounds. 'Don't close it!' he screamed as he saw the man below at the flood door.

The man glanced up at him and hesitated for a second, then continued to push at the heavy metal door from the inside of the tunnel.

'No! No, please!' Dr Collingbury fell rather than jumped the last few steps and a shoulder and arm went through the decreasing gap between door and frame.

The man on the other side began to kick at him, for he knew from his brief glimpse of the approaching wave that the tunnel would be completely flooded unless the barrier was shut tight. He was also aware that the flood door at the other end of the tunnel was wide open. If he had not been so fear-stricken, he would have known that it would have been quicker and easier to pull the chemist through. Too late he realised his mistake and tried to pull the fallen man into the tunnel.

Dr Collingbury screamed once again as water cascaded down the short staircase and swept the flood-door back against the wall. He felt himself propelled along the tunnel and caught quick, confused glimpses of the other man's thrashing body. His head struck against the stone wall of the corridor and he was numbed with pain. He spluttered and tried to draw in breath, but the raging waters around him would allow no respite. He was tumbling, turning over and over in a mad, pounding rush, his limbs brushing against the ceiling then the floor as the river filled the tunnel.

His drowning was unpleasant, but it did not last very long.

EIGHTEEN

THEY HUDDLED together in the darkness, both feeling the
pressure of the mill above them, pressing down, seeming to be
squeezing the ceiling towards the floor. Kelso's panic appeared
to be under control although occasionally his whole body would
stiffen at a sudden sound in the pit. He would flick on the
lighter, its flame dwindled to almost a pinpoint, and hold it
before them, sweeping it from left to right, trying to pierce the
oppressive gloom. Only when he was satisfied that the noises
were those of scuttling vermin, or the building itself groaning
against its own weight, would he extinguish the flame and settle
back against her. His body continued to tremble for minutes
afterwards, though.

They had spent hours earlier searching the underground
chamber, looking for openings, weaknesses in the walls and
ceiling. At first, Kelso had scrabbled away at loose brickwork in
a wild, futile frenzy, his fingers becoming red with his own
blood as he tried to force his way through. He stopped only
when she pulled at his hands and told him it was useless. She,
too, had felt the claustrophobic panic but, unlike Kelso, had not
given in to it. But then, Ellie had not been through the same
nightmare as he.

Eventually she had crept away, passing him the lighter which
had become hot with constant use; she was too weary to
continue searching and had become afraid of him. He had
seemed possessed, ignoring her entreaties, concerned only with
finding a way out. Ellie had rested her back against the ladder

beneath the trap-door and quietly wept; his fear had made him a stranger to her. In the few, vital days she had known him, Ellie had almost become accustomed to his sudden moods, but there had always remained some small link between them, some underlying emotion that neither one could deny. Now that link was broken; she did not know this fear-stricken desperate man at all.

And then, abruptly, he had stopped.

She heard him softly call her name as though he had just realised he was not alone. Ellie had answered. Then he was with her, holding her, brushing away the tears from her face with the back of his hand. She held on to him, but she was still a little afraid.

'I'm so sorry, Ellie,' he had murmured.

She was silent for a moment, then allowed her head to sink to his chest. 'Won't you tell me what happened to you, Jim? You said you knew . . .'

'I'm still confused. It's so incredible I'm not sure it wasn't all just an hallucination.'

'What was, Jim? Please tell me.'

'Not now. It's better that we spend our time trying to find a way out.'

Somehow she knew he was holding back because he did not want to frighten her any more than was necessary; the situation they were in was frightening enough.

'There is no way out, Jim. We're as good as sealed up inside a vault down here,'.

'Or a crypt.'

'Go ahead and cheer me up.'

'I'm sorry.'

'Don't keep saying you're sorry; just open up to me. Remember I'm *with* you.'

He kissed her forehead and she responded by pulling his head down so that their lips met.

'Don't love me, Ellie,' he whispered. 'Don't love me.'

'It's too late not to,' she replied.

After a while, they continued their search, this time Kelso's efforts less frantic, more studied but no less determined. Eventually, when the lighter's flame had diminished considerably, they gave up.

'The rats,' Ellie had said when they settled back against the wall behind the ladder. 'How the hell do they get into this place?'

'Along the piping. Whatever holes there are, Ellie, they're no good to us. They'd be too small even if we could find them.'

'So what do we do?'

'We wait.'

'For Slauden's henchmen to come back and pump you full of drugs again?'

'Your turn to cheer me up? Once that trap-door's open, we may have a chance.'

'Oh really?' she said skeptically.

He felt around in the dark for a few seconds and then pressed something into her hand. It was heavy and rough-edged, part of a broken brick. 'What's this for?' she asked.

'Put it in your coat pocket. I've got one too. When they come at me I'll put up a fight; you just slam that into the face of whoever's nearest to you.'

'Jesus, it's not much of a chance.'

'It's all we've got.'

After that, they could only wait. They hardly spoke; but they did cling together and strangely, Ellie felt some of the tension draining from him. He still jumped nervously when something moved in the darkness, and his body shook for minutes afterwards, but somehow the resolve seemed to be returning. It was as if he had been through so much that there could not be much more to fear.

But for Kelso, it wasn't that simple.

He had experienced – or he had *thought* he had experienced – something in the cellar the night before that explained many of the bizarre and often tragic accidents in his life. The reason for his bad luck. It was true: he *was* a Jonah. But if he tried to explain to Ellie, would she think him insane? She was scared enough without adding to her fears. The thought of being locked up in the dark with a madman just might send her over the edge. And was he mad? Or had the drug merely brought on a false revelation.

He pushed the memory away. Something like that could not exist. It had to be the drug playing tricks on his mind. Yet the effects of the drug, itself, had been counteracted. He knew that with the overdose he had been given, he should have been out of his mind for at least twenty-four hours. Could the shock of what he had seen have diminished the LSD reaction?

And now he knew that something terrible was going to happen. The tension he had felt building over the past few days was about to break, was about to erupt with cataclysmic force. Some inner instinct told him. He felt desperately vulnerable, yet strangely determined. It was as if his life had been heading towards this point, the culmination of every insane event that had occurred throughout his lifespan. Perhaps the LSD had freed his consciousness so that he was able to perceive the unseen 'force' that had plagued him for so long. Perhaps his mind's release had allowed the manifestation. He was confused, afraid, but not ready to give in to it. Kelso knew he could not; not for his sake alone, but for Ellie's. He now understood that she was in the most danger.

They held each other tightly and waited.

Movement from above made them both jump.

They heard a door slam and then voices. Someone was shouting and there were footsteps over their heads.

'They're here,' Kelso whispered, and he almost sounded relieved. He rose from his position and clutched at one of the rungs on the ladder. Ellie also scrambled to her feet and nervously held on to his arm. They heard a grinding, scraping noise and realised the weight on the trap-door was being dragged away. Blinding white light poured down on them when the trap-door was pulled open.

Kelso and Ellie covered their eyes, the pain piercingly sharp.

'Well, well, they're all ready to come out.' It was Bannen's voice.

'Get them up.' Unmistakably Slauden's.

They backed away as a heavy bulk began to descend. A rough hand grabbed Kelso and dragged him towards the ladder. Still unable to see, he was powerless to resist; nor did he choose to at that particular moment.

'No games, Kelly, otherwise your girlfriend ends up with a

disfigured face.' Bannen seemed to enjoy the threat.

Kelso climbed and hands pulled at his shoulders as he emerged from the pit. He fell forward onto his knees on the concrete floor and a well-placed foot helped him to topple all the way over. He stayed down, still covering his eyes with one hand to allow them time to adjust. Although the area in which they stood was lit by standard lighting, torches were being used to shine into the opening in the floor. Ellie emerged looking dazed and frightened; behind came Bannen and Kelso saw with grim satisfaction that part of his face was covered with a white gauze dressing; the fire-brand that Kelso had used against him the night before had obviously caused him considerable suffering.

'On your feet.' He felt a toecap prod him in the ribs and looked up to see Henson standing over him. Kelso pushed himself up and stood before the group of men. Bannen knocked him back against the wall.

The light was not as painful by now and he was able to look around. There were four men standing before him: Slauden, Henson, Bannen and one of the men who had dragged him through the underground passage the previous day; Ellie was on her knees beside Henson. There was something odd happening which had nothing to do with what Kelso could see; then he realised it was the sound he was hearing. A storm was in progress outside and the wind seemed to be smashing itself at the old building, almost threatening to tear away the weaker parts. He noticed that the group of men were well protected by waterproof clothing.

'Well, Kelly, have you considered your position?' Slauden stepped forward so that he was within reach of Kelso.

Kelso mumbled something, but could not be heard over the howling of the wind. Bannen backhanded him, knocking the detective to one knee. 'Speak up!' he snarled. 'Sir Anthony can't hear you!'

'That's enough, Bannen!' Slauden snapped.

'I owe him for this.' Bannen touched the bandages on his face and glared at his employer in defiance.

'Stand aside and allow me to question him in my own way.'

Reluctantly, Bannen moved away; but he still kept Kelso within easy reach.

231

'Now, Kelly, I'll ask you once again: Are you willing to co-operate? All this is so unnecessary, you know.' Slauden was almost anxious, as though he really did not want to inflict more punishment.

Kelso used the wall to push himself upright and nodded his head as if in acquiescence. Slauden moved in further to catch the murmured words.

Kelso struck out, but the little man was shrewder and more nimble than the detective could have guessed. His punch went wild and before he could reach into his pocket for the half-brick he carried, Bannen had slammed his shoulder hard into Kelso's face.

Ellie had more luck: she rose and struck the nearest man to her with the rough piece of masonry. The man screeched as bone in the bridge of his nose splintered; he fell to his knees on the edge of the open pit and Ellie tried to kick him into it. Henson grabbed her and slapped her face twice, knocking her into a corner of the concreted area.

Meanwhile, Kelso had doubled over as Bannen brought a knee up into his stomach. He seized Kelso's collar, pulling him upright, ready to bring his fist down hard into the exposed face.

Slauden held Bannen's arm. The look of undisguised pleasure swiftly vanished from the latter's bandaged face.

'No!' Slauden ordered. 'Julian, use the drug! This time inject both of them!' He bent towards Kelso. 'Did you hear that, Kelly? This time your girlfriend, too, will receive a dangerous amount of LSD! Enough to kill her! But not you! Just enough to send you into a nightmare world again! Only this time, you'll have the dead body of your girlfriend to keep you company.'

Henson opened the black case he had with him and picked up the already-filled syringe. He strode towards Ellie, avoiding the kneeling man who groaned on the floor, his hands red from his bloodied face. Ellie began to scream and kick out when she saw the approaching needle.

'Give him a hand, Bannen!' Slauden ordered and the grin of pleasure returned to Bannen's face.

Kelso was aware of what was happening, but was powerless to do anything; he clutched his stomach, trying to draw in breath. 'No . . . please, don't,' he managed to say, but his words were missed over the sounds of the gale outside.

232

Bannen grabbed at Ellie, who screamed even louder. He yanked her away from the corner and tore her jacket from one shoulder, ripping the blouse beneath it to expose the bare flesh of her arm. Henson's fingers curled around her arm and he raised the needle.

Kelso tried to stagger forward, but Slauden shoved him hard so that he fell against the adjacent wall. He looked up in despair as the glinting needle pricked Ellie's skin.

The rumbling sound brought all movement to a halt. Each man looked up and then glanced around at the walls. The building, itself, seemed to tremble and dust swilled around in the air.

'What is it?' Henson shouted.

Slauden looked towards the entrance and his face suddenly went ashen. Without a word, he ran for the stairwell.

The rumbling noise had grown to a rushing thunder. Then the heavy entrance door burst open as floodwater sped through the mill, tearing through crumbling walls, tumbling stacks of feedstuff and pouring into every opening. Churning water gushed in and smacked against the concrete, swirling around the walls and forming its own whirlpool as it drained into the pit. The man kneeling next to the opening was swept down and his scream could not be heard over the terrible noise. Kelso saw Henson drop the syringe, then lose his footing. The powerful current carried him towards the black hole in the centre of the floor and his face was a mask of sheer terror as he tried to prevent himself from being sucked down.

It was no use; he disappeared into the vortex, a thrashing, helpless figure.

Bannen was still holding onto Ellie in shock, his legs braced and back pressed firmly against the wall behind. He let her go and she fell forward, her body carried with the flow. The water was still only knee-deep, but its force was tremendous. Kelso cried out when he saw that she also was being swept towards the pit.

The trap-door, still resting against its hinges, juddered wildly as the torrent swept around it. Fortunately for Ellie, the water carried her behind the hatch and she grabbed at it. She clung there, gasping for breath, legs trailing in the rushing flow.

Sea-water gushed over Kelso's head, stinging his eyes,

threatening to dislodge him from his position against the wall. He knew he would have no chance of resisting the current when the level was higher. He forced himself upright, using the wall for support, then began to fight his way around the chamber towards the stairwell, going against the current, hands spread out on the rough concrete before him. He had to reach Ellie before her grip was torn loose for, once she let go, she would be carried into the deluge pouring through the entrance and knocked back into the pit.

He reached the door, the wall on that side protecting him from the worst of the onslaught. He gasped in deep breaths, knowing he would have to cross the open doorway to get close to the girl. The level was already waist-high.

Kelso lunged, hands outstretched, grasping for the metal struts of the iron stairway. The force from behind was incredible and, for a moment, he thought he wouldn't make it. A giant hand seemed to push his back, but his own hand curled around an upright. His body swung round, legs pulled by the current. His other hand scrabbled for another grip and then he was hauling himself up, his feet finding precarious support on the concrete floor. He could hardly breathe as the water beat against him, but he inched himself along the steep-climbing staircase, maintaining his grip as he went. Soon, Ellie's struggling body was just a few feet away.

'Ellie!' he screamed. 'Let go! I'll grab you!'

Whether or not she heard, or the current simply tore her loose, he had no way of knowing but, as she sped by, he grabbed a flailing arm. He was nearly jerked away from his own hold on the stair-rail as her body swept around, the cascading water from the doorway forcing her towards the centre. Kelso lost his footing, but he grimly held on to both the girl and the metal upright. Slowly he pulled her towards him. A desperate heave brought her up against his chest and one of her arms went around his neck.

'Grab a stair-rail!' he managed to gasp, and she obeyed his order, reaching behind him. The release from her dragging weight was instant and he turned in the water, grabbing her waist and helping her to press up against the staircase. Once she was secure, he let his own body stretch out again. By kicking against the fierce flow, his feet came within striking distance of the unsettled trap-door. He thrashed out and one foot came in contact with the wooden hatch. He fought against the current once more and this time the contact was more solid.

The trap-door toppled forward, for a moment the swirling water preventing it from slamming completely shut. Then the weight of water pouring across its upper surface forced it down until the opening was closed completely.

The chamber immediately began to fill even faster, although water still poured through cracks in the trap-door.

Below, Henson screamed as total darkness enveloped him and water rushed into his lungs. His only hope had been the area of blurred light through which the torrent cascaded. He was turned, over and over, buffeted against the walls, the pillars. Something heavy struck him and he did not know it was the already dead body of the man who had fallen into the pit before him. Water poured through other openings in the cellar, creating a mêlée of vicious currents, and small bristling creatures struggled with him in the darkness. Several bit his flailing limbs in their own panic, but he never felt the pain. The rising water pushed him towards the ceiling and soon his battered body could no longer continue the struggle. It twisted and turned without any resistance, a lifeless carcass entombed in a dark, airless world.

Above, Bannen knew his only hope was to reach the stairs. The chamber was filling rapidly – it was already at chest height – and there was no telling at what level it would stop. There was no danger of being sucked into the cellar below now that the trap-door had been closed, but water still spewed through the entrance.

He had found some metal piping protruding from the wall behind him and he clung to it gratefully, but was aware that it offered only brief respite before the floodwater rose higher. The heavy chest which they had used to weight down the pit's trap-door suddenly came into view, a few inches of its top showing above the water line. He plunged for it and tried to haul himself up onto its surface. He was only partially successful, for the crate began to roll over with his weight. Nevertheless, it carried him near enough to the stairwell for him to reach out and grab at the closest thing within reach. Which was Kelso.

Kelso's body was swung round as Bannen clung to his

shoulders. He tried to wrench himself free, but the other man hung on desperately. Only when Bannen could grab hold of a stair-rail was the pressure released. Another hand snatched up at the metal bannister and Bannen wrenched himself several feet out of the water. One foot found a step between the uprights and he felt more secure. And confident enough to deal with Kelso.

He swung a fist hard into Kelso's side, causing the detective to cry out and almost let go of the stair-rail. Ellie saw what was happening and tried to reach around Kelso and flail the other man with a clenched fist. Bannen ignored her efforts and brought his knuckles hard against the side of Kelso's head.

The detective slid back into the raging waters. Ellie caught him beneath one shoulder and managed to hold him there until he had grabbed hold again.

Then Kelso's head went underwater as the other man pressed down. Ellie went for Bannen's eyes, pulling herself up with one hand, lunging for the man's face with pointed fingers. Temporarily blinded and shaking his head against the pain, Bannen let go of Kelso and pushed Ellie's hand away as she stabbed and clawed at him.

Kelso emerged once more, coughing and spluttering swallowed sea-water. He yanked his opponent from his perch and both men went plunging back into the water.

For several terrifying seconds, Ellie could only see splashing limbs as the two men battled with each other; then she lost sight of them completely as they disappeared beneath the foaming surface.

She clung to the stairs, gasping in air and sobbing at the same time. Her hair was flat around her face, her eyes dark with the remains of running make-up; her water-sodden clothes dragged heavily at her weary body. She searched the bubbling waters, then turned away, pressing her face against the rails she clung to. She turned again in time to see two heads bob to the surface. They vanished, but quickly returned again.

'Jim!' Ellie screamed, stretching away from the staircase and reaching out with one hand.

A body swept by and, as it rolled over, she saw it was the other man. Something bumped into her from behind and Kelso was holding onto her, clinging to her waist to prevent himself from being swept around the chamber once more. Ellie pulled herself back towards the staircase, the effort tremendous, the current and Kelso's weight almost too much for her. The weight suddenly left her and then it was she who was being helped.

They clutched at the staircase, feeling their bodies rise with the still flowing water, and tried to draw in breath.

Finally, Kelso pushed at her arm, urging her to climb over the rail. With his help, she was able to do so and he dragged himself up after her.

They lay against the stairs, the lower half of Kelso's legs still in water, too exhausted to move, chests heaving. The roaring noise continued to fill their ears as the flood poured around and through the old mill, causing the very foundations to tremble.

It was only when the water reached Kelso's waist that he shook Ellie's hip. 'We've got to go up!' he shouted over the noise. 'The water's still rising!'

'How high will it reach?' she shouted back.

He shook his head. 'God knows! But we'll be safer up there!' He hauled himself from the water and pulled her to her feet. 'Come on! We can rest at the top!'

They began to climb.

And did not notice the hand that emerged from the churning water below to grab at a stair-rail.

NINETEEN

THEY HAD only reached the second bend in the stairs when the lights below began to flicker. They looked at each other anxiously, their features barely visible in the already dim light.

The lights flickered twice more then went out.

'Christ!' Kelso muttered.

Ellie held on to his arm, but kept a grip on the handrail with her other hand. The gushing water below echoed hollowly around the stairwell and, over that, they could hear the sound of the building, itself, creaking under the strain. Somewhere in the distance, something unable to resist the force of the swollen river, distintegrated with a dull crash.

'Can't we stay just here, Jim?' Even at that level, Ellie had to raise her voice over the noise. The howling wind outside added to the roar.

'No, it's not safe enough! The stairs could collapse under the pressure from below! We'll be safest at the top of the building, Ellie!'

They lurched onwards, feeling their way in the dark, shivering with the cold, and finally found themselves on a small landing.

The sound of the wind was much stronger and moonlight, poor though it was, managed to filter through gaping holes in the sloping roof. The landing opened out into a vast room and they could see round shapes, the tops of the grain silos. Railings on one side, protection for workers inspecting the open bins, disappeared into the gloom ahead and, to their right, they could just make out stout beams rising to the ceiling, long cobwebs, hanging from cross-sections, tossed and twisted by currents of air which had found their way into the building. The outlines of two windows at the far end of the huge room barely stood out among the surrounding blackness.

Kelso took Ellie's hand and led her forward; she hung back, reluctant to enter. There was an eerie atmosphere about the place, something foreboding. It was like entering a huge cave wherein lived something corrupt, something ugly. The putrid smell seemed to corroborate her fears.

A dark shape moved among the shadows.

Kelso and Ellie stopped and rain that had found entry through gaps in the roofing formed puddles around their feet. The shape came closer and Kelso stood in front of the girl.

Sudden light dazzled them and they crouched back against the glare.

'Where are the others, Kelly?' It was Slauden's voice. He held the flashlight before him, its beam wide and powerful, lighting up much of the grain room and the stairwell behind the two figures.

'They're dead, Slauden!' Kelso replied, his voice raised, unsteady. 'They drowned!'

The light wavered momentarily and Kelso tried to move forward.

'Stay there!' Slauden warned. 'I've a gun in my hand. It's small, but effective.'

'What's the point, Slauden? You're finished. There's nothing left for you!'

'Don't be ridiculous! I've lost one key figure – the other two didn't matter!'

'But your laboratory. It's underground – this flood will have destroycd it!'

'Flood doors will have protected it. It will still function!'

Kelso tried to move closer, keeping his body between Ellie and the girl. 'Look, Slauden, I had nothing to do with Trewick. I'm with the Drugs Squad. We've been watching you for some time. If anything happens to me or the girl they'll know where to come looking.'

'That's a rather stupid lie! If that were the case my estate would have been swarming with police when you both

240

disappeared. Perhaps you could have gone missing for one day, but not the girl the day after. I've had someone watching your caravan for the past two days – before and after she returned – and nobody has been in the least bit curious over your absence.'

Kelso tried to see beyond the flashlight. Did Slauden really carry a gun? It was impossible to tell. 'You can't kill us!' he shouted, unconvinced himself.

'I have no choice! It's too late for you both. You refused to co-operate, so you must pay the penalty. I daresay there will be many missing persons when this flood has abated – God knows what damage it's caused! You'll just be among the bodies never recovered!'

Kelso had to take a chance. Slauden was the type who let others do his dirty work for him – would he be able to soil his own hands? 'Back away, Ellie!' he ordered the girl. 'Back up towards the stairs!'

Slauden did not react. Perhaps he wanted them down there in the floodwater.

They were nearly out on the landing, moving slowly, shielding their eyes from the glaring light, when movement made Ellie turn to look behind. She screamed when she saw the figure waiting for them.

Kelso whirled around to find Bannen standing there, his oil-skins discarded, his drenched clothes hanging loosely around him. The bandage on his face had been torn away, and the skin was puckered and red where he had been burned. Bannen knocked the girl aside with a sweeping blow and came at Kelso, an expression of furious hatred distorting his scarred features even more.

Kelso went back with the impact, Bannen's charging rush sending both men crashing against the rail guarding the open grain bins. Bannen screeched his rage while his hands squeezed Kelso's throat. The detective felt his head was about to explode. He tried to pull away, but it was no use – Bannen was too strong. He brought his knee up hard into the other man's groin and the grip immediately relaxed. Kelso pulled himself clear and struck out with a clenched fist. Bannen hardly seemed to feel the blow. He lunged at the detective again and this time the momentum carried both men over the guardrail into the grain silo just below.

Kelso's open mouth became clogged with fine grain and he retched uncontrollably. Bannen twisted his body so that he was on top of the spluttering man's back. He grabbed Kelso's head and pushed it deep into the grain.

Ellie stumbled towards the guardrail and watched in helpless dread as Kelso's face disappeared. His hands scrabbled frantically as he tried to reach behind and dislodge the heavier man. Ellie moaned aloud, but she could only stretch a hand out towards the struggling men, her body too exhausted, too drained to move further. Her legs began to give way and she collapsed against the rail, sobbing and moaning, unable to help Kelso.

The wind reached a new crescendo and tiles from the roof above fell inwards with a rush. Rain poured through the huge rent, and the wind entered with fresh force, tearing around the chamber, ripping cobwebs from the rafters, rippling the surfaces in each bin. The grain rose up and flew around the two men like a yellow blizzard. Kelso's struggles were becoming weaker; his hands clenched and grain was squeezed through his quivering fingers.

And from the shadows, through the swirling dust and grain, through the drifting cobwebs caught in the screeching wind, through the torrents of rain that had found access into the building, something began to emerge.

They sensed it was there before it came into the beam of light.

Ellie had seen Bannen's round, staring eyes, his blistered lips turned down in a strange, contorted grimace, and had followed his gaze. A dark hunched shape stood just beyond the stream of light.

Slauden felt his body go cold. There was a sensation at the back of his neck, a clammy prickling that made him shiver spasmodically. He was aware of a crackling around his head, a sound felt rather than heard, and he knew that every hair on his body had stiffened, become brittle. His stomach muscles had locked tight as he experienced the extremes of fear. He forced his hand to turn the torchlight towards the scuffling shape, but the movement was slow, almost as if some part of him did not want to see what was there.

Ellie followed the beam of light, her face drained of blood, her body beginning to sink completely to the floor. A hand gripped the guardrail, but it did not have the strength to support her weight. Her fingers opened and the arm fell limply to her side.

The light moved across a stout, wooden beam and then touched something just beyond.

None of them could utter a sound, for the shock was too intense.

Ellie felt hot fluid jet from between her legs.

Slauden felt a whiteness sweep through him, a whiteness that blanked out his mind and threatened to send him into unconsciousness.

Bannen's throat rasped as his mouth opened and closed and he tried to scream.

The hunched figure moved and the light shone fully on it.

Its skin was scaly, dried and cracked in some places, ravaged and torn in others. In parts the flesh was completely open and tiny things scuttled among the red meat and sinew. It was almost bent double, one withered, claw-like hand with fingernails dangling a few inches from the floor; the other arm had no hand, just a knotted bunching of bone and flesh at the elbow, a mangled stump that looked raw and gangrenous. Both legs were twisted and deformed, one foot no more than stubby flat shape with no toes, no shaping of an ankle; the knee-joint of the other leg was bulbous, the thigh above, thin and wasted. Shadow covered the groin area because of its hunched stance, but dark hair reached down between its legs from waist-level, curling over its thighs like tiny legs of spiders. The skin across its shoulders was puckered and scarred, and huge lumps like angry boils covered the flesh. Its spine arched upwards from its back, the bone uncovered at several points, the skin around it moulded in as though it had grown that way.

Its head, which sat low on its shoulders, seeming almost to protrude from its chest, was covered with strands of wispy hair, long so that it hung around its face, but sparse so that the mottled scalp could be clearly seen.

Its face was the most hideous part.

Much of it was missing.

Black veins were exposed, but no skin or flesh grew around them; they hung against the bones of its jaw and cheek.

Brown stumps of teeth were visible, the gums they were

imbedded in yellow and glistening. A drooling substance dripped from its half-formed chin.

Holes punctured its other cheek as though small creatures had gorged their way through, and occasionally something wet and shiny jutted from the larger of the openings; it was its tongue, lolling around the cavity of its mouth, pressing through like a worm in the earth seeking moisture from above, for they could see its movement behind the stumps of teeth.

The nose came directly from what there was of the upper lip and this, too, was no more than a stump. There were no nostrils.

Its forehead was large and curving, descending in a broad triangle towards the misshapen nose; the skin appeared to be flaky, powdery, barely attached to the bone beneath. The one ear they could see was just a curled piece of gristle.

There were no eyebrows, no lashes. Its eyes projected from red-rimmed sockets like dull black marbles, for they had no irises and almost no whites.

A fetid smell of corruption emanated from the creature as it shuffled forward. It seemed to be watching the two men in the grain bin.

Bannen released Kelso, who thankfully drew his head from the grain, coughing and gasping for air. Bannen backed away, his feet kicking against the loose particles. He was at the centre of the huge circle when the grain moved inwards and he began to sink.

Somewhere deep below, the floodwaters had forced open the silo chutes so that the grain from the bins poured through separate funnels on to the motionless conveyor-belt.

Kelso felt the movement and immediately realised what was happening. He grabbed for the metal rim nearby. Bannen was in a less fortunate position. He cried out for help as his legs were sucked down. Grain immediately avalanched inwards around him.

'Help me!' he screamed. 'Please, please help me!'

His arms scrabbled outwards as though he were trying to swim, but it just seemed to hasten his descent. One hand touched Kelso's outstretched foot and his fingers closed around it in desperation. Kelso felt the tugging and slid backwards; he clung to the edge of the silo and tried to pull himself back up.

Bannen's grasp slipped from Kelso's foot and with a despairing scream he sank further into the quicksand of grain. Soon his shoulders were covered and his hands beat at the air to ward off the falling particles.

Kelso managed to pull himself onto the container's lip and he looked back in time to see Bannen's head sinking beneath the grain, his screams suddenly choked off, two grasping hands remaining, slowly going down, clutching at the air, until they, too, had disappeared.

Kelso grabbed the guardrail and hung there, too shocked to move. Even as he watched, the shifting of the grain slowed, its centre filling again until the surface merely dipped towards the middle.

'Oh, God, no,' Kelso groaned. Bannen's body had become wedged in the funnel end of the container, the tons of grain bearing down on him prevented from flowing out. The seawater had not drowned him, but the grain had.

Kelso slid over the railing and fell in a heap beside the prostrate body of Ellie. He looked at her and was barely able to raise a hand to touch her cheek.

'Ellie . . . ' he said.

He looked curiously at her staring, terrified eyes and then turned to see what had caused the transfixation. His body went rigid. His eyes widened. Revulsion swept through him.

Then the shock passed and there was something more in his expression. The deformed monster was silently watching him and, for a moment, the terrible cacophony of wrenching wind and rushing water seemed to abate; it could have been only in their minds, the horror of the sight before them closing out all other aspects from their consciousness. Ellie managed to force her gaze away and looked towards Kelso. Consternation mixed with her fear; was it pity on his face?

'Jim?' Her voice shook. 'What . . . is it?'

He did not seem to hear.

'Jim!' Ellie tugged at his arm.

Kelso slowly turned his head towards her, but there was no recognition.

'Jim!' Ellie screeched, and her hands beat weakly at his chest.

His expression changed, the cloudiness left his eyes, and he knew her once more.

She pulled closer to him and her hand clutched his coat collar. 'What is it? Please tell me, Jim!'

His mouth opened, but she wasn't sure of his words. 'Tell me!' Ellie urged, for somehow she knew there was a link between this creature and Kelso.

Kelso spoke quietly, his words slow and forced, and this time she heard, but could not believe.

'It's . . . my . . . twin,' he said.

The roaring returned. The wind blew at their hair, tugged at their clothes. Rain splattered against their skin with renewed vigour. Ellie stared at Kelso, oblivious to everything else. Then she turned her head towards the creature.

Its black, malformed eyes were watching her.

It tried to stand erect, but could not. The twisted, misshapen body lurched forward and spittle flowed from its hideous mouth. It came forward towards the two figures lying against the guardrail, one side of its mutilated body reflecting bright light from the torchbeam, the other side in deep shadow. Its eyes never left the girl.

Ellie looked pleadingly at Kelso, but he had withdrawn into himself, his eyes wide and staring, but his face expressionless. She shook him once more and called out his name, but there was no response. Ellie drew away from him, her head shaking in a gesture of disbelief, tears of panic, bewilderment, adding to the dampness of her face. She crawled away, wanting to find some dark recess to curl up in, to escape from the approaching monstrosity, to hide away from the malignancy that was part of Kelso.

She dragged herself along the rough floorboards and could not take her eyes from the lurching thing. It was near Kelso now, but still advancing on her. She felt her strength failing, her muscles becoming weak as though an immense pressure was bearing down on her. She lay there on her side, trying to make herself move, trying to make herself scream to release the hysteria that locked her body rigid. She could only raise a trembling hand to shut out the sight of the mutant.

The sharp blasts that rang out caused her body to jerk violently and her hand dropped reflexively to her mouth. Fresh nausea swept through her as the creature turned towards the source of light, for more of its body was exposed to the glare.

Ellie's stomach heaved when she saw the two long, distended breasts, their flesh cross-thatched with dark veins and sores. The nipples were red and pointed, almost like tiny fingers protruding from the softer mounds.

Ellie finally screamed and vomit poured from her when something thudded into the creature's face, tearing away the protuberance that was its nose. But the deformed figure hardly flinched and no blood flowed from the wound. It made no sound as it moved towards the torchlight.

The gunshots had shaken Kelso from his cataleptic state; his first thoughts were for Ellie and he wildly looked around for her. Another shot rang out and the bullet smashed into the stump of the creature's arm. Pieces of bone shattered outwards and a thick tendril of flesh swung freely, but the hump-backed figure did not seem to feel any pain. It continued to shuffle forward.

Suddenly, the torch was dropped and the light vanished. As Kelso tried to see into the black void, he heard scuffling sounds, someone running, moaning noises that resembled the whimperings of a trapped animal. He made himself move, crawling in the direction of the girl.

She heard him coming and tried to get away. His hand had closed around her outstretched leg before she had the chance.

'Ellie, it's me.'

She hesitated, then he was holding her, pulling her face close to his own, and she knew she had been mistaken; the creature was no part of him. She wiped the sickness from her lips and tried to speak, but it was still too soon – no words would come.

Someone screamed, a demented howl that joined the wind, and they knew it was Slauden. Shapes in the darkness slowly became visible, but only a gunflash and its simultaneous roar helped them locate the fleeing figure. He was near the end of the long room, his back against the wall. They had briefly seen the hunch-backed shape silhouetted in the swift burst of light; it was only a few yards away from Slauden.

Now Slauden had moved towards the far window and they could see him against the lighter patch in the general darkness, beating against the panes, trying to force a way out. Glass shattered, but it was a futile effort; the window-frames were never meant to be opened. He turned to face the thing that was reaching out for him with one withered hand and one mutilated stump. He screamed. And screamed. And screamed.

The explosive collapse of the wall behind and the floor beneath him saved Slauden from the nightmare, but its sanctuary was death.

Kelso and Ellie cowered away from the sudden fiery brightness and their heads reeled with the roar. The floor heaved upwards and they clung to each other, sure that the floorboards would break up and they would fall through.

The wall at the far end fell away, the old bricks torn apart by the explosion that had come from below. Large sections of the floor at that end disappeared too and, through the dust and smoke, Kelso saw the far grain bin begin to topple, the grinding, tearing sound just another element of the madness sweeping through the feed mill. It vanished into the night like the sinking funnel of a lost ship.

Small fires had started in the rafters and beams of the old building, but the pounding rain did not allow them to spread. The storm rushed in, for now there was nothing at all to hinder it, and they were blinded by its force.

Kelso stirred himself; he shouted at Ellie, but the explosion had momentarily deafened both of them. He began to drag her limp body towards the stairwell. He tried to stand and pull her to her feet, but the effort was too much; he sank to his knees and cradled her in his arms.

Ellie's fingers dug into his wrists and he winced at the sharp pain. Then he saw why she had squeezed him.

Through the swirling smoke and the pelting rain, through the shadows that were now disturbed by the weak flickering of dying flames, came the bent, black shape of the creature that Kelso had called 'twin'.

Ellie staggered to her feet and tried to run, for the mutant wanted her. There was no reasoning behind Ellie's fear, only instinctive knowledge. Her legs were too tired, her spirit too drained, for her to get far. She fell against a heavy rising beam and lay there, fingernails digging deep into the rotting wood, sobs wracking her beaten body. She felt, rather than saw, the misshapen shadow loom over her, and her senses began to spin. It was hopeless; the creature wanted her dead because she had become part of Kelso's life. Ellie understood, but did not know how she understood.

The voice was faint in her ears, for the deafness had not yet fully cleared. It sounded like Kelso. She forced her head around so that she could see.

He was on his knees between her and the monstrosity, one hand on the floor to keep his exhausted body upright, another hand raised against the creature.

Kelso looked at the sister who had never left him, who had been there all his life, seen only as something lurking in shadows, or sometimes in the periphery of his vision. An ugly, deformed sister, who had not lived after birth, who had been abandoned with him by a mother they had never known. But the sister had refused to succumb completely to death; her spirit had wanted to live, to experience life just as her brother would. She had clung to his life, living off him as a parasite lives off its host. Her spirit, her soul, had grown, just as his earthly body had grown, for she fed on his psyche, and had developed with him. Always there, always watching, the manifestation of her spirit always strongest on the anniversary of their birth. Who was their mother? What woman would so cruelly reject her offspring? And what manner of creature could spawn such an abomination?

He gazed up into the dull black eyes and his own filled with tears. Thoughts that were not of his consciousness were pushing into his mind. Their mother was unimportant: she had paid for perverted copulation and the abandonment of those whom she should have cherished, yet whom she considered to be the physical marks of her own shame. She was dead but her torment went on.

And through the alien thoughts, Kelso knew this miscreation despised him, envied him of the life that had been denied to her, his sister. And yet she loved him, also. The twisted seed of hate had grown as they themselves had grown, but her torment of him had been tempered always by that stronger instinct of kindred love. She protected him because he was her life-force; without him there was nothing but dark eternity for her. She loved him and despised his loves. No one would share him with her. Not even the couple who had reared him as their own. No friends. No women. No one.

Kelso's tears stopped. He stared at the creature in disbelief. 'No!' he screamed. 'Oh, God, no . . . !'

He struck out at the figure before him, but his fist touched nothing.

'Leave me alone!' he cried. 'Stop haunting me! For God's sake ... please ... please ... leave ... my ... life ... please ... !'

He bent forward, his face buried in his hands, body swaying backwards and forwards.

Ellie hardly understood what was taking place; she reached out for him, but was afraid to move closer – the creature was too near. She could only watch, emotion wrenching at her, pity and a burning love for this man who knelt before the strange gargoyle, fighting against the terrible dread she felt inside.

She watched, the dread deepening until it clawed at her throat, as the hunched figure touched Kelso's head with its withered hand.

And then it was gone, fading into the shadows like an apparition.

Kelso had raised his head, was looking around, searching. Searching for something that was no longer. When he turned back to Ellie, she knew the burden had been lifted, for she could sense the new hope in him, could feel it emanating from his exhausted body and flowing towards her.

For one brief moment, she felt a sickening apprehension, the dread returning like a swift debilitating disease. Her mind spun and she thought she would collapse. But it quickly passed. She held her arms out towards him.

TWENTY

THEY SAT huddled in the back of the boat as it sped them, and others, towards the safety of higher ground. The rain was just a thin drizzle and the wind no more than a chill breeze. The daylight was still grey, wintry, but it held no threat.

Kelso pulled the oil-skin further down over their heads and smiled at Ellie. 'It's all over,' he told her.

She smiled, but did not reply. She gazed into the distance towards the low-lying hills where warmth and comfort waited.

The helicopters had come at dawn, one appearing at the open end of the mill, coming into view like a giant dragonfly projected onto a huge grey screen. The dust and grain its whirling blades disturbed blinded them at first, even though they were far back inside the building, perched at the top of the metal stairwell, the only structure in the mill that they still considered safe. Kelso had stumbled forward, waving his arms and shouting, and the pilot had given him the thumbs-up sign in acknowledgement. Later, when the boat had arrived to collect them, they learned that the RAF had been particularly curious to study the damage done by old World War Two mines that had been uncovered from tombs of silt and raised to the surface once more by the floodwaters. Apparently the feed mill had not been the only building in the area damaged by the old defence weapons.

Ellie shivered and Kelso slipped a hand around her waist, pulling her closer. He was tired, his eyelids heavy, his limbs aching dully. And he was dirty, his chin unshaved, his hair matted and full of dust. But he felt a lightness inside, the feeling of just having

251

overcome a long, wearing illness. He was exhausted, but he felt alive, exhilarated.

'She's gone, Ellie,' he said again, for he had tried to explain everything to her before they had fallen into an exhausted but troubled slumber 'She listened to me. Maybe somewhere inside her she knew it was wrong to cling to my life. Maybe she really loved me enough to let me go.' The sound of the boat's engine drowned his words from the others around them.

'Or maybe the power she had just burned out.' Kelso shook his head. 'I don't know,' he said simply. 'The LSD made me regress, made me see what what had been happening all these years. It unlocked my mind, Ellie, and I think that was also the key to her manifestation. It unleashed some psychic power in me that she used. Oh, God, how she used it.'

He thought of the explosion. He thought of Bannen's horrific death. And Slauden's. *He thought of the flood itself.*

Kelso wiped a tired hand over the stubble of his chin. He needed a smoke, but felt disinclined to ask for one from the dispirited people in the boat. Their homes and lives had been wrecked by the flood; they had their own wounds to lick.

'She came to me that first night in the cellar. I didn't know if it was for real or just part of the nightmare. Even now I'm wondering if it wasn't all some mad hallucination.' He laughed quietly. 'But you were there too; you saw what happened.'

She nodded and her hand closed over the top of his.

'I feel free, Ellie,' he said. 'I can start again. No more bad luck – no more than anyone else gets, at least. No more Jonah, Ellie. Just me, on my own. Unless you want to be part of my life. I'm kind of counting on you.'

She squeezed his hand and smiled, then turned away, releasing his hand to pull the slipping oil-skin back over her shoulder.

Kelso stared at her as she continued to gaze into the distance. His face had drained white again. Had he imagined it? Was the drug still playing tricks with his mind?

For one brief instant as he had looked into her eyes, they had been totally black. No whites, no irises. Just a dull, reflective black. But before she had turned away again, they had become a clear blue, the pupils large but normal. He shook his head: it had to be his imagination. He was too tired and too much had happened. Jesus, he was going to sleep for a week after this.

A slight stinging sensation made him glance down towards his hand. He froze. Parts of the skin were pressed inwards: five tiny but deep indents. Indents that looked as if they had been made by a clawed hand.

He looked up at Ellie, but her face was turned away from him. She seemed to be scanning the distant hills as though discovering a new land.

THE SHINING
by Stephen King

Danny was only five years old but in the words of old
Mr Halloran he was a 'shiner', aglow with psychic
voltage. When his father became caretaker of the
Overlook Hotel his visions grew frighteningly out of
control.

For as winter closed in and a blizzard cut them off
completely, the hotel seemed to develop a life of its own.
It was meant to be empty, but who was the lady in
Room 217, and who were the masked guests going up
and down in the elevator? And why did the hedges
shaped like animals seem so alive?

Somwhere, somehow, there was an evil force in the
hotel — and that too had begun to shine.

NEW ENGLISH LIBRARY

NEL BESTSELLERS

T 51277	'THE NUMBER OF THE BEAST'	Robert Heinlein	£2.25
T 51382	FAIR WARNING	Simpson & Burger	£1.75
T 50246	TOP OF THE HILL	Irwin Shaw	£1.95
T 46443	FALSE FLAGS	Noel Hynd	£1.25
T 49272	THE CELLAR	Richard Laymen	£1.25
T 45692	THE BLACK HOLE	Alan Dean Foster	95p
T 49817	MEMORIES OF ANOTHER DAY	Harold Robbins	£1.95
T 53231	THE DARK	James Herbert	£1.50
T 45528	THE STAND	Stephen King	£1.75
T 50203	IN THE TEETH OF THE EVIDENCE	Dorothy L. Sayers	£1.25
T 50777	STRANGER IN A STRANGE LAND	Robert Heinlein	£1.75
T 50807	79 PARK AVENUE	Harold Robbins	£1.75
T 51722	DUNE	Frank Herbert	£1.75
T 50149	THE INHERITORS	Harold Robbins	£1.75
T 49620	RICH MAN, POOR MAN	Irwin Shaw	£1.60
T 46710	EDGE 36: TOWN ON TRIAL	George G. Gilman	£1.00
T 51552	DEVIL'S GUARD	Robert Elford	£1.50
T 53296	THE RATS	James Herbert	£1.50
T 50874	CARRIE	Stephen King	£1.50
T 43245	THE FOG	James Herbert	£1.50
T 52575	THE MIXED BLESSING	Helen Van Slyke	£1.75
T 38629	THIN AIR	Simpson & Burger	95p
T 38602	THE APOCALYPSE	Jeffrey Konvitz	95p
T 46796	NOVEMBER MAN	Bill Granger	£1.25

NEL P.O. BOX 11, FALMOUTH TR10 9EN, CORNWALL

Postage charge:

U.K. Customers. Please allow 40p for the first book, 18p for the second book, 13p for each additional book ordered, to a maximum charge of £1.49, in addition to cover price.

B.F.P.O. & Eire. Please allow 40p for the first book, 18p for the second book, 13p per copy for the next 7 books, thereafter 7p per book, in addition to cover price.

Overseas Customers. Please allow 60p for the first book plus 18p per copy for each additional book, in addition to cover price.

Please send cheque or postal order (no currency).

Name ....

Address ....

....

Title ....

While every effort is made to keep prices steady, it is sometimes necessary to increase prices at short notice. New English Library reserve the right to show on covers and charge new retail prices which may differ from those advertised in the text or elsewhere.(6)